Returning of the Way

A ROMANTASY BY STEVE TARRY

This book is a work of fiction, and therefore names, characters, businesses, places, events, locales, and incidents are either the products of the author's imagination, or have been composited or fictionalized. Any resemblance to actual persons living or dead or events present or past is purely coincidental.

Copyright © 2024 Steve Tarry

ALL RIGHTS RESERVED. No part of this book may be reproduced or transmitted in any form or by any means, electronic or mechanical, including photocopying, recording, or by any information storage and retrieval system, without the written permission of the author. Request permission from Publisher: icehousepress.com

ICE HOUSE PRESS ® & Logo
are trademarks

Paperback: ISBN 978-1-962057-00-4

1st Paperback Edition 2024

Printed in the USA
Ice House Press • Seattle

Returning of the Way

"Some are born great, some achieve greatness, and others have greatness thrust upon them." What happens when gods decide?

1

Young Lord Endrew knew what the lords and ladies of Wollaire said of him. He had heard himself described as the embodiment of all knightly virtues, strong in the use of arms, well mannered, and brave beyond doubt in tourneys. Yes, he supposed he had decent manners, but he questioned the rest as he sat astride his horse and surveyed the battlefield, swallowing hard so as not to lose the contents of his knightly stomach.

The battle had raged on since midday as both sides jockeyed for advantageous positions on the broad valley floor. In lulls when no one assaulted the crest of the slope that guarded the valley's exit, Endrew's men shouted encouragement to the soldiers of Chaussey province who fought below alongside other men of Wollaire who sought to drive the Glender invaders back to their own land. But now was no such lull. An arm of the enemy force drove up the hill, hoping to sweep Endrew and his soldiers from the vital spot they held.

A war was quite unlike a tournament after all, young Lord Endrew thought. The screams of men and horses sounded alike, as did the clang of sword against shield. The sweep of flags and pennants across the land appeared the same, as did the blood of the wounded. The blasts of magic that erupted here and there on the valley floor crackled like those the wizards set off for the entertainment of tournament crowds. Even death looked familiar to Endrew for, now and then men died in tourneys, of their own enthusiasm or someone else's. What differed now was not the nature of the carnage, but the scope.

"Our men hold well this ridge," shouted an officer, pulling his horse to a sudden halt on Endrew's right. The mount wore lather as thick as the scalloped padding that hung from its sides, and its eyes rolled back in equine terror.

"That they do, Bentlan," said Endrew. "Look. Even now the Glender soldiers again fall back."

A cheer rose from the archers and pike men that lined the ridge, and some few swordsmen rose to follow the retreating enemy.

Endrew swallowed once more and cleared his throat to steady his voice then roared out a call of, "Hold, there."

His call rang with the steel edge of command and the errant fighters stopped where they stood, held by the voice that would one day rule their province. "Back to your places," he said. "We are commanded to keep this ridge secure, that and only that."

"But, Lord Endrew," said a soldier, "we have them on the run, their backs to us."

"They are but a fraction of the Glender force. Nothing matters but this ridge. We have our orders and must obey them."

"But, sire–"

"I say you have your orders, as I have mine."

"But the other provinces will gain all the glory," protested the soldier.

"This man speaks for many," said Bentlan, his horse stamping nervously beside Endrew's.

"And I speak for your lord, my father," said Endrew. "We hold this ridge in his name and the king's. As long as both men live, we shall do as they have said."

The officer bowed his head slightly. "As you say, my Lord Endrew."

The young knight turned to look back over the field, trying to spot his father's banner with the blue and gold dragon emblem. His gaze took in the mass of swirling color that filled the valley's meadows, then spied the flag of Chaussey province atop a distant knoll.

"Do you see him?" asked Bentlan.

"There," answered Endrew, pointing.

"I do not ... ah, yes, I see it now. By the skies above, I swear you have the eyes of a falcon, to spot that pennant among such a host."

"I have my father's eyes," said Endrew with a slight smile. "Did you ever see him shoot a bow? Properly motivated, that is?"

The officer allowed a hearty chuckle to escape. "You mean when a wager stood in the balance? Aye, that I have, young master. Your father is the gamblingest man who ever drew a bow string."

"None who know him should argue that point," said Endrew. "Now, you had best inspect the lines to be certain–"

A blare of distant trumpets echoed across the field, and Endrew turned to see what action they hailed.

Glender troops drew together from both flanks, forming a solid mass of armored might, then surged ahead as a unit. The invaders, their two-crowned banners waving above them, charged forward like the blow of a smith's hammer. A company of men from Pollay fell beneath the wave's force, yet still it rolled on.

"The Glender swine must be mad," said

Bentlan. "They risk their flanks and rear."

"No," said Endrew, "look."

At another trumpet call, the army of Glender shifted form and changed direction, cutting off a band of defending soldiers and mowing them down. The invaders drove onward like a wedge, and nothing could stop them.

"See," shouted Endrew. "They mean to take a position on that side of the vale."

"There are springs there," said Bentlan.

"Yes, and trees for firewood and the building of palisades. If they reach–"

Endrew's voice trailed off into a silently held breath. Below him, he saw the blue and gold dragon banner of Duke Endron of Chaussey directly in the path of the Glender charge. Men from other provinces scattered before the packed might that bore down upon them, but still the banner of Chaussey held firm.

The front edge of the Glender force reached the flag's position, hesitated for the slightest moment, then rolled inexorably on as the blue and gold pennant disappeared from sight. Endrew fought the urge to scream his anger and terror across the field. He fought the burning desire to leave his post and rush to his father's aid. He fought back the moisture that threatened to overwhelm his suddenly world-worn eyes.

Bentlan looked at Endrew in solemn silence for a moment. "My duke," he began at last, addressing him by that title for the first time.

Endrew's hand leapt up to still the man, then he paused before replying. "Do not call me that," he said in a voice that barely topped a whisper. "Not yet. Not until we know,"

Bentlan pulled back the visor from his helmet, revealing his dark eyes and the thin, white scar on his left cheekbone. "But may we not now advance? May we not ride down and gain some measure of revenge?"

"No. We must guard this place, for only by this route can our army quit the valley if need be."

"But—"

"Take five riders," said the young knight, "and go down there. Find my father. Discover the truth, that we may all know for certain." The officer whirled and rode away to do as he was instructed.

Endrew patted the neck of his mount to steady it as the other horses and riders picked their way down the body-littered slope. He looked out over the field, following the course his men took toward the distant, now vacant knoll. From across the valley, the sound of trumpets once more rang clear, and the Glender troops fanned out to secure their easily won position.

In answer, horns blared from his own side of the field and a cry went up from the men. "The king," they cried as they spotted the axe and crown banner of Wollaire. "King Giarley himself rides out to smite the foe."

"Why?" Endrew asked himself aloud. Why should the king risk so much when the Glender army stood in so secure a spot?

Men from units broken by the Glender charge still milled about the field, and they scattered as the king's band surged forward. *He hopes to rally the army,* Endrew thought in answer to his own questions, but he could see the rashness of King Giarley's action. Few troops followed, and in moments the royal banner reached the enemy line.

The flag of the Kingdom of Wollaire waved high for several moments, then Glender troops surrounded it. A cry of anger went up from Endrew's men, but he stilled it with a shout. "Now you must pay for the king's trust, my friends. Behold."

The soldiers of Chaussey looked once more at the field and saw the truth of what Endrew said. No sooner had the king's banner been pulled down, than the massed armies of Wollaire fell into rout. Band after band surged up the slope and past their position seeking the safety of the hills, until finally men fought their way step by step, warding off blows from Glender pursuers as they walked. Endrew again formed his men into ranks across the narrow defile, allowed the last straggling remains of the king's army past, then dug in.

His archers sent volley after volley into the massed enemy, but still they came. The pike men planted their poles to form a barrier of sharp, horse-halting steel. All along the formation, swordsmen shed equal measures of sweat and blood to defend their homeland.

Endrew rode along the line, shouting encouragement to his troops. He seemed ignorant of the arrows that whistled past his head, and the shouts and screams around him went unheard. A blast of magic fire from an enemy mage erupted nearby and the tips of his fingers unconsciously tingled with sympathetic power. His stomach forgotten, he drove his sword into the bodies of any men of Glender who breached the ridge crest within his sight. His father had chosen this position well. It had allowed his small force to cover the army's retreat. Yes, his father had—

He thought of his father with every swing of his great sword. Every man of Glender who fell before him might have been the one. His eyes clouded as he planted his feet in the stirrups for leverage and slashed at an invader. The man fell like others before him, but always another stepped up to take his place.

Something caught at his horse's feet and the great mount shied to the left. The weight of Endrew's armor carried him off balance and he fell hard to the ground. He rolled to avoid the slashing blow of a great war axe, then planted his foot in the enemy's midsection, forcing the man back for a moment. He rose, slipped another blow with his shield, then dropped the soldier with an uppercut his father had taught him. His father—

His eyes clouded even more, and he waded into the thick of battle, not caring whether he lived or died. He screamed his loss with every swing of his sword, and his anger added power to each blow until no man of Glender stood before him. Nearly blind with tears, he sagged to the ground, hearing first nothing but his own heavy breathing, then the sound of his men's cheers as the enemy fled back to the valley floor below.

He became aware of hands helping him rise from his knees. Someone lifted the helm from his head and wiped a trickle of blood away from his left eye. He reached up to touch the spot, then found himself looking into the face of a peasant archer.

"Are you badly harmed, young lord?"

He found himself unable to reply. Instead, he shook his head, causing his tawny hair, wet with perspiration, to spill down over his shoulders.

"You did well, young sir," said the man, ducking his head lest he appear too familiar.

"Indeed," offered another. "You allowed our entire army to pass in safety."

"Right," said the first. "Our knights and soldiers can live to fight another day."

"Shall we follow the army now, young lord?" asked the second.

Endrew rubbed the sleeve of his tunic across his eyes to clear them, then he looked again into the soldiers' faces. Their features were wrinkled and old, testimony to the hardship of a peasant's life. These men, not all that much older than himself, looked more like the age of his father.

His father—

He swallowed twice, then spoke. "Yes. We follow the army and camp with them tonight."

He commanded scouts to keep watch on the Glenders, lest the invaders surprise them from behind, then formed his troops into a proper marching order. The men of Chaussey province trudged off into the afternoon gloom of the forest, following the obvious trail left by the horde of soldiers in flight.

A peasant, cap in hand, brought Endrew's horse to him. The young knight patted the animal's neck, then ran his hands up and down the great beast's legs. The horse seemed unhurt, except for a slight cut from the billhook that caused the mount to fall, and Endrew allowed himself the faintest smile as he cooed, "There, there," to calm the huge charger.

He climbed into the saddle, then turned when he heard his name called. Bentlan rode slowly toward him, holding the broken staff which bore the tattered dragon banner of their province. Behind the officer rode another man, leading a third horse with a large bundle draped across the animal's back.

Bentlan looked down for a moment, then stared straight into Endrew's eyes and addressed him again as, "My duke."

The heir to Chaussey province took the proffered banner and nodded slowly in quiet recognition of this news. "Bring him along," he said. "My father deserves burial at home, with his ancestors."

"As you wish," said Bentlan, with a salute. The two men and their heavy burden fell in behind the procession as Endrew spurred his mount toward the unit's head. The whispered news sped forward even more swiftly than he rode, and all along the line heads bobbed in sympathy and respect as he passed. He held the torn, mud-spattered dragon pennant aloft but kept his gaze straight ahead.

The army camped that night on high ground above the river Denn, and the men of Chaussey province built their fires a little apart from the rest. Endrew sat alone beside the blanket-wrapped bundle, thinking how his life had changed in one day. He was now Duke Endrew, Lord of Chaussey, with all the responsibility that brought. He stared fixedly into the dancing flames that gave him small comfort against the growing chill.

The groups of men who huddled around nearby fires spoke in whispers so as not to disturb their new duke, but soldiers of Chaussey who sought the warmth of more distant blazes waved their hands near the flames and wondered aloud about the future.

"How do you suppose he will be?" asked one, giving his head a quick jerk in Endrew's direction.

"Him? Oh, just fine," said another. "You mark my words."

"You seem certain," said a third man, shifting his weight on his haunches so the scales of his armor rubbed together in metallic protest. "He feared to pursue the Glenders when we had them on the run."

"He held to his post," said the second. "All would have been lost if we let the army's path of escape fall."

"Some would call it cowardice."

"Not within my hearing," said the second.

The third shook his head. "But, what do you really know of him?"

"Well, his father was right fair," said the man who spoke first. "Would any man deny it?"

"No," said the second, "he was as good a master as a man may serve."

"But who says the lad is like the father?" asked the third.

"I do," said a fourth man, kneeling on the far side of the flames from the other three. "Greatly like him, or his better, perhaps."

"His better?" said the second man, rising with his hand on the hilt of his sword. "No better man ever drew the breath of life than Duke Endron of Chaussey. Any fool who says so must answer to me."

The man across the flames rose, his features etched in sharp contrast by the fire at his feet. "Be still, and listen. I speak no ill of Endron, only that the son is indeed the shadow of his father's casting. Did you see him stand and fight today?"

"He was near to me," said the first man. "His bravery kept the line from buckling."

"Aye, a fair man of war, our young Duke Endrew," said the soldier across the fire, "but more than that. He came to our village four springs past. Little more than a lad he was, sixteen or thereabouts, but already grown so well." The man paused to shake his head at the memory.

"And?"

"He judged three disputes so wisely that the village marveled at his fairness, even those the suits went against."

The soldier who had been offended let go of his sword. "That is odd in one of so few years"

"But there is more. Our mill had burned and

young Endrew brought with him materials and workmen the duke had sent for its rebuilding."

"That is no more than proper," offered one of the others. "A village without grain cannot feed itself or pay its taxes."

"Of course, but wait, the lad stripped off his fine tunic and joined the laborers in moving the heaviest stones. He sang their songs and sweated for two days alongside them."

"No."

"I saw it with these eyes. Moved a stone half the size of a horse, he did."

"Half the size of–"

"Near to half," insisted the man. "No, our young duke will be more than just fine, he will. You mark me, we stand in the presence of greatness."

The other three nodded and silently resumed their places at the flames. At other fires, similar tales were told and the soldiers of Chaussey slowly reached the same conclusion. The old duke was dead; long live the new.

At another, larger fire in the central, most protected part of the main army's camp, lords and ministers argued over particular pieces of mutton and the proper thing to do next.

"Nine dukes dead, by my tally," muttered one lord, barely pausing to swallow.

"Ten," growled another, his hoarse voice rumbling as he spoke. "Lendell of Shompette just died."

"And King Giarley himself captured," moaned yet a third.

Duke Piren of Baretton, the lord who spoke first, tossed a bone into the fire. "A foolish thing to do, charging the Glenders like that."

"He expected us to follow," said a man in a tunic that barely clung to him, so badly was it slashed.

"Not damn likely," said Lord Piren. "Who would be that stupid?"

Duke Robear of Tushan, the lord in the tattered tunic, shook his head. "Some of us were."

"And you see the good it did," said a minister in flowing robes threaded with gold that reflected the fire's light.

"The Glenders will likely cut his throat," guessed Showann of Alpenne, the lord with the hoarse voice. "Serves the idiot right."

"Impossible," said Foshay, the gold-robed minister of negotiation. "No, I fear we shall all be made to pay most dearly for the return of our king."

"Ransom?"

"Of course," said the minister. "And the amount will be greater than can be found in all of Wollaire."

Duke Showann of Alpenne snatched a piece of meat from the plate of the man who sat next to him. "Let them keep him, then."

"Impossible," shouted another.

"If we do nothing, the peasants will rise up against us at the thought of the king imprisoned in a foreign land," said a third.

The hoarse-voiced lord growled inarticulately as he pulled a bit of meat from the bone he held.

Duke Robear, his fingers tugging at the torn edges of his tunic, took a step forward. "But if they hold our king, we will be powerless to drive the invaders from our land. The Glender swine will use the threat of his death to hold us back."

Another lord stood and glared at the others in disgust, as if they failed to grasp something obvious. "Are you all without your senses? There will be no more war this year," he said. "Can you not feel it in the air? Can you not see your own breath before you? Already leaves cover the ground and soon the snows will blanket them."

"Duke Jonale speaks truly," said Foshay. The golden robed minister looked into the others' faces and spoke with an air of certainty. "The Glenders will build a garrison in that valley and leave enough men to hold it. The rest will sail across the waters that separate their land from ours, and they will take our king with them."

"Then we have all winter to arrange his release?" asked Duke Piren.

"Certainly," said the minister. "And that is work for such men as me, not for the like of you."

Duke Showann looked up and wiped the grease from his face with the back of one hand. "If the gods still lived," he said hoarsely, "I should thank them that there is at least something for such men as you to be useful at."

The minister of negotiation sneered. "There is, my lord, and you had best be grateful for it."

"Oh, I am," he growled his answer. "I live with no other thought."

"There," said Foshay, raising his hands to the others assembled. "You see how men of diplomacy are able to forge peace?"

No one spoke, but the lord with the torn tunic spat, then tossed his chunk of mutton into the fire. The meat hissed and sizzled as a shower of sparks swirled upward into the night sky.

2

Winter arrived sooner than anyone guessed, and the army of Wollaire awoke to find the world covered by a light dusting of snow. The next few days saw no contact with the enemy, and finally scouts reported that the majority of the invaders had marched to the sea and set sail for their homes. As predicted, work had begun on a fortress to solidify the Glender claim to occupied lands for at least another year. The dukes and ministers conferred briefly and empowered Foshay to contact Glender through proper diplomatic channels regarding the ransom of their captured king. That being done, the host disbursed to their respective provinces.

The journey to Chaussey took just over three weeks as Duke Endrew and his men plodded along roads deep with mud and frustration. They passed through a drab landscape of skeletal trees and poor hamlets where hollow-eyed peasants peeked from doorways to watch them trudge by. The weather alternated between sleet and a general greyness, with the occasional snow flurry thrown in for variety. The soldiers grumbled, but Endrew said nothing. The weather suited his mood.

Eventually, they reached Chaussey province and men dropped out of line here and there to journey to their own villages. The size of the procession gradually diminished, until one day Endrew led scarcely more than a few hundred men around a familiar bend in the trail. The troop halted for a moment as the walled town and stone towers of Chaussey keep loomed into view, standing alone on a broad, alluvial plain.

"Home at last, sire," said Bentlan, wiping the rain from his eyes.

"Home, indeed," answered Endrew. "Come." He urged his horse forward and the others followed. Endrew looked at his lands with new eyes and he studied every detail of the nearly barren countryside around him. Fruit lay rotten at the feet of leafless trees in sparse orchards. Grapes and berries, hung black and useless on vines. The fields were half filled with hay that had gone unharvested, now wet and molding where it stood.

"Minstrels sing of the grand adventure of war, Bentlan," said the young duke.

"That they do," agreed the officer.

Endrew looked to both sides of the path, thinking of the hard winter ahead for his people. "They fail to sing of who will bring in the crops while the men are off and fighting."

"Our people will have done what they can. Surely the women and the–"

"Of course," said Endrew. "They will have done their best." He looked to where a small boy tended three bony cows, prodding them along with a switch. "Still, why should they have to endure this?"

"The Glenders, sire," said Bentlan. "They invaded our lands."

Endrew nodded. "So they did, and all because their King Alrick's great-grandfather sent his eldest daughter to wed the Duke of Pollay province long before any of us was born. Now Alrick uses that ancient marriage to lay claim to Pollay for himself."

"It cannot be allowed, sire. The people of Wollaire would never serve a Glender lord."

"Does it really make such a difference?" asked Endrew. "Do the people really care who they serve? What will the women who weep tonight as new widows say? Would the people we are about to starve with our war declare that it was worth it?"

Bentlan looked at his young master. "The people of Chaussey would say so, sire. These people have known you since you were born. They loved your father with all their hearts, and they will take you to their bosoms as well. I cannot speak for the people of other provinces, but I can say this with certainty: the people of Chaussey would go to their graves as one before they let another usurp your place."

Endrew rode in silence for several moments, then said, "Thank you for your words, Bentlan. I fear the loss of my father has colored my view of things."

"As well it might, my duke. Your father was a great ruler of the province."

"And a wonderful father to me. I doubt many men of rank are as able at both."

"Surely not. But, hold, sire, we approach the gate. What are your orders for the men?"

"My orders?" Endrew thought a moment. "Quarter those of your standing troop in their barracks and send the rest to their homes. These fellows deserve whatever small comfort we can give them."

"Shall I have the chamberlain arrange an official welcome?"

"No, but send him to me. I shall have him make plans for my father's interment. That is all the ceremony I wish at this time."

Endrew absently returned the salute of the guard who held himself at attention by the heavy wooden gates that stood wide open where the road entered the town. The man eyed the procession in confusion until he spotted the bundle with the tattered remains of the banner of Chaussey tied to it. Then his spirits seemed to sag as suddenly as his shoulders.

The chamberlain made the required arrangements, and the townspeople assembled the following evening to see the duke to his rest. The crowd began to gather in the town square at dusk, torches in their hands to push back the damp night air. Then Endrew appeared from within the keep, walking before a carriage that bore the body of his father. Without looking to either side, he strode through town and out the gate, passing between rows of townspeople whose torchlights reflected damply in his pale blue eyes.

The people of Chaussey fell in behind the carriage and the procession wound its way through fields and pastures until it reached a low, round hill that stood oddly alone on flat land. Endrew gestured, and several soldiers stepped forward to roll away the huge stone that sealed the entrance to the cairn. They stepped back, then the mage of Chaussey moved forward to speak a word of power that lit the passages within. Endrew stooped and entered the chamber.

His body almost pulsing with the energy from the magic light, he walked between the stone-lined walls to the place where the passageway split, then turned to the left as he had so many times before. In a niche off the hallway, he spotted the familiar bundle he'd left here at the age of ten when his mother fell to a fever. Beside it lay the smaller bundles of his two brothers, both dead before they could walk. The one had been his special joy, always laughing and cooing before the illness took him. The other, closer to his own age, he could barely remember. They were all here now, except his sister, and she lay in the tomb of her husband's family in Marnay province.

He turned back to the soldiers who bore the litter carrying his father, then nodded his head in permission The four men set the bundle down, then placed it beside the others as gently as they could. They stepped back and the chamberlain glided forward to set evergreen boughs beside the body and scatter sweet herbs and the dried petals of flowers over the bundles.

The man stood and lowered the ceremonial hood from his head. "Is there anything you would say?" he asked Endrew.

The young duke nodded, then knelt beside what remained of his family. "I am sorry I could not bring your sword to you from the field of battle, father. I wanted to, but it seemed more necessary to ward your men safely away once the army had passed."

"Your father would have understood," said the chamberlain, caressing the young duke with his words but holding his hands respectfully at his sides.

"All the same," said Endrew, "it would not do for him to lie here for all time unarmed." He reached to his waist and unbuckled the belt that hung there. "Here, father, take mine. You gave it to me for my first tournament, and now I give it back to you. May it serve you as well as it has me."

"But, my duke," protested the chamberlain. "Your sword—"

"I can get another. He cannot." With that he rose and ushered them all from the cairn. As the group turned and left, Endrew reached inside his tunic and pulled forth the tattered dragon banner, its gold highlights gleaming with the glow of magic light against its blue background. "This is also yours," he said, stooping to place it on his father's chest. Then he stood again and left the chamber.

He drew in a deep breath of fresh night air as he stepped from the passage, aware that all eyes were focused on him. He nodded to the mage who caused the light to vanish, then to the soldiers who once again rolled the stone back into place.

"My father is now no more than memory," he said to the people of Chaussey. "Let that memory live on in all your hearts that he should likewise live forever."

"It shall be done," said every voice in unison.

Endrew raised his hands and gestured toward the walled town, then took his proper place, this time at the rear of the procession, as the people returned to their homes. For a moment he stopped and turned back to face the cairn, barely visible in the darkness. He wanted them to live, he wanted them all to be with him. He felt the least tingling in the tips of his fingers, then he turned and marched back to the keep.

Endrew spent the night in private thought, staring into the dancing flames that filled the fireplace of the main suite of what were now his private chambers. Toward dawn, the keep began to stir with quiet sounds of movement and he rose from his chair to seek the stewards. "Send men to every village in the province," he instructed them, "to tally all available food."

"All food, my duke?" asked one.

"All," he repeated. "Every grain of wheat, every chicken, every pig. Only by knowing what the province has in total and distributing it as it is needed this winter will our people survive."

"A wise plan, sire," said a steward, "but some few will grumble."

"Let them," answered Endrew. "At least they will be alive to do so. Now, go."

There was much to do and it was work for which he had little training, but Endrew knew it was work that must be done and that he must be the one to do it. With a little luck, and careful planning, the people of Chaussey province might all see spring.

Careful planning of another sort was the key feature of a meeting in the port town of Kauley on the first day of the new year, halfway between the shortest day and the vernal equinox. Two men sat in a sparsely furnished room of the guard tower and plotted the land's future.

"This is a bit like condemning one's countrymen," grumbled Duke Showann of Alpenne, his hoarse voice made even rougher than normal by the cold that clogged his nose and throat.

"Nonsense," said Foshay, the minister of negotiation. "The Glenders have asked a sum greater than we can raise. We have countered by asking them to release the king on partial payment and the pledge of twenty nobles to stand in his place until the balance may be secured. It is business, nothing more."

Showann took a bite from a chicken leg, tossed the bone away, and wiped the grease from his chin and the moisture from his nose in one motion. "They will rot in a foreign prison before such another sum can be raised."

"All the more reason for us to choose with care," said the minister. "Now, what say you to Duke Robear of Tushan province?"

"As faithful to the king as any man who lives," answered Showann.

"I thought the same," said Foshay. "Let us add his name to the list."

Showann grunted his ascent.

The minister sat silent for a moment. "What say you to Jonale of Quitole?"

"The same."

"Then let us send him also," said the minister. "And Piren of Baretton?"

"A man of no opinions at all, neutral in all things except to his own benefit."

Foshay raised an eyebrow. "We should have thought to invite him here. Oh, well, let us add his name also."

"Why?"

"Such men can be dangerous."

"He is like us," growled Showann, "but less ambitious."

"That is his misfortune," said the minister. "Let him spend some time in Glender that his presence in this world will serve some good end,"

"How many is that?" asked Showann with a sniff and another backhanded swipe at his nose.

"Nineteen. We have need of but one more."

"You have given the name of every noble in the realm."

"Not the new ones who succeeded to their titles after the battle of the vale," said Foshay.

"Boys," grumbled Showann.

"But boys of title," said the minister. "That is all that is required."

Showann sneezed, took a deep breath, spat on the floor, then sighed. "Oh, I suppose. Read the names."

"Rolenn of Shompette—"

"—is only ten years old," completed Showann. "Not even the idiot Glenders would count such a sliver as a whole man, noble birth or not."

"What say you to Dalene of Zaks?" The minister paused to smile. "His lands lie next to yours."

"The boy is no more than twelve and a fool in the bargain. No, his lands will be mine within a year anyway. Read on."

"Hmmm, this one bears thought. Endrew of Chaussey."

"A troublemaker," snorted the duke. "The boy is too much like his father. He is too clever, I think, for his own good ... or ours."

"And not such a boy, either, I fear. He is twenty, is he not?"

"Something like that," muttered Showann. He stopped to sneeze loudly. "Whatever his age, he now commands a rich province."

"With a large population faithful to his family for many years. Such wealth and loyalty could breed ambition. Such ambition is dangerous."

Showann wiped his nose, then waved his hand at Foshay in irritation. "Be done with it, then. Add his name to the list."

"As you say," said the minister with a smile.

"Besides, the Glenders will be more impressed with a full grown hostage."

"Of course."

Showann allowed himself a half-sniffled laugh. "Damn fool will probably consider the whole thing an honor, standing in for the king and all that."

"The boy does seem to be a man of principle and duty."

"Then send him, by all means. We simply cannot have such people walking about loose. It is not safe for the rest of us."

"Very well," said Foshay as he rose. "That concludes our business."

"Good," said the duke, hauling himself to his feet. "I am glad we reached peace, you and I."

"There is no reason we should not be friends," allowed the minister.

Showann sniffed, rubbed his nose, then wiped his hand on his tunic. "Good, good. Now, if you have no objection, I shall retire to the bedchamber you have so thoughtfully provided."

"Do so with my blessing and the king's."

"The king's?" asked Showann. "Oh, yes. The bed is one of his, eh?"

"But he shall not be using it for a time," said Foshay, half closing his eyes and nodding his head.

"Likely not," said Showann, laughing as he turned to leave the room. "Likely not."

Foshay listened as the duke sniffed and snorted his way down the stairs. As a distant door banged shut, the minister smiled and turned to a portal behind him. He passed along a short, dark hallway, then entered a dim room in which the glow of a single candle revealed three men. One wore a gown similar to Foshay's, only trimmed in blue instead of gold. The two other men wore plain traveling clothes of brown, the drabness of their garments in stark contrast to the careful tailoring. They sat on stools on either side of a small table, bare except for writing implements.

"I am sorry to have kept you," said Foshay, "but I had need for advice in generating the list you requested."

"And do you now have it?" asked one of the men in brown, his voice carrying the unmistakable accent of Glender.

"I do. It is good that we are able to come so easily to a conclusion, you and I."

"We are ministers of negotiation," said the first man of Glender. "It is what we do."

"True enough, Caelwin, my friend, but do you not feel that it is somehow more than that?"

"Of course it is," said the other man in brown. "By prolonging hostilities between our lands we have been able to stifle the open trade that would occur."

"To our great and mutual profit," said Foshay, with a thin smile. "As we ministers of negotiation fan the embers of conflict, you ministers of commerce reap the rewards of the high tariffs that ensue."

"It is good that the waters divide our lands," said the Glender minister of trade. "Otherwise these royal fools might talk to each other and end our profits."

Caelwin leaned forward. "That is why your king must be ransomed quickly. I believe our King Alrick suspects nothing of our plotting. Are you sure the same is true for yours?"

"King Giarley is not a man gifted with intellect," offered Pyer, the Wollaire minister of trade.

Foshay nodded. "Any man stupid enough to charge the massed army of his enemy with no more that his personal guard is not a man to fear."

"Good," said Caelwin Cyniod, as the Glender minister of trade smiled beside him. "We are fortunate that subtlety is beyond them both."

"That we are," said Foshay.

"And now, the list," reminded Caelwin.

"Ah, yes," said Foshay. "Allow me a minute to make a copy of it for myself."

The Glender minister of trade rose and Foshay sat at the table, then drew the candle a bit closer. One after the other, he wrote the names of the nobles who would journey to confinement in Glender that their king might walk free.

Then toward the end of the list, he paused. "I have one change I should like to make with your permission."

"Certainly," said Caelwin.

Foshay carefully drew the quill's tip across the name of Duke Piren of Baretton. In its place, he listed Duke Showann of Alpenne, then smiled as he copied the name onto the second paper.

"You seem pleased by something," observed Caelwin.

"If one is going to do a thing," said Foshay, "one ought to do it correctly. Business such as this leaves no room for error or omission."

Then he again bent over the paper and went on to finish the list.

3

Only twenty days of the new year had passed, when the sun brought some small warmth instead of mere light. Endrew thought he detected more than the merest hint of spring in the air as he urged his horse into a canter and rode toward Chaussey keep with a smile. The province was not saved yet, but the promise of salvation lay only slightly beyond the sun's promise of a new growing season.

His visits to the outlying villages had taken more and more of his time as winter dragged along, but he felt them necessary. As the stewards had predicted, many people objected to providing food for those they didn't know. Endrew had needed to personally convince every soul in his province that all could survive only by acting as a unit against the common enemy, hunger. If one village had fruit to spare, he arranged for it to go where another enjoyed more than minimal grain. Similar exchanges were made with all sorts of foodstuffs and his men were busy acting as carters. People eventually saw their efforts returned, and grumbling quickly ended.

Poaching ceased to be a crime and new rules encouraged people to hunt. Endrew even passed laws requiring that sufficient breeding stock of all domestic animals be maintained, regardless of immediate need, and made the keeping of such numbers the responsibility of an entire village. Penalties for failure to maintain minimal stock were to be meted out to all within a community. People, naturally, began to take an intense interest in what each other killed and ate.

Now he rode home from another visit, feeling some small amount of accomplishment, and he looked again at the trees, vines, and fields that surrounded the walled city. He could almost imagine life returning to each plant, and pictured the buds and blossoms that would soon appear. Distant hills caught at clouds that would rather have rushed by and he thought of the snow that would be falling from them, snow that would provide his people with river water for the driest days of summer to come.

He waved a hand to the guard at the town gate, then pulled at his horse's reins as the man called, "Hold, Duke Endrew."

"Yes?" he asked, pulling the horse around to face the man.

"There are strangers here, from the capital," said the guard. "King's men. Six of them."

"Here?" asked Endrew.

"At the keep," said the soldier. "Captain Bentlan has quartered the men and the officers await an audience with you."

"News of King Giarley, perhaps," said Endrew, and he whirled the horse and rode as swiftly as the street and its occupants allowed. The horse's hooves struck the stone paving with hollow clopping sounds that bounced off the sides of shops and houses. People bowed and lowered their heads to Endrew as he passed, but though he smiled and nodded, his thoughts were less with them than usual in his desire to meet the visitors.

Grooms took his horse and he strode up the

ramp to the keep's entry off the inner bailey. The chamberlain met him at the door, his hands flapping nervously around his face, and words pouring out faster than could possibly make sense. Two stewards and a scullery maid fluttered behind the man, similarly agitated.

"Calm yourself," urged Endrew.

"But they want something," insisted the chamberlain. "I know they do. They have the look of people who have come to take." The others nodded vigorously in agreement.

"Nonsense," said Endrew, walking away. "It may be news of our king."

"Perhaps, but mark my words," said the chamberlain as he followed Endrew along the passage to the great hall, "when all other business is done, you will find they have come to take something."

"If they have and it benefits the king, then we shall give it to them if it is ours to give." Endrew shooed away the entourage of servants, pushed open the doors to the huge chamber, and saw two armored officers of the king's own guard standing beneath the central chandelier, its candles unlit for the moment. "Ah, welcome, visitors. I am Endrew of Chaussey."

One of the officers stepped forward and brought his heels together, causing the spurs he wore to clink and the floor's reed covering to rustle. "We have a message for you from Foshay, minister of negotiation, sire. We are instructed to give it to you and wait for your reply." The man held out a pouch which Endrew took, broke the wax seal, and opened.

He unfolded the piece of parchment within and held it so the light coming through the room's high windows caught it best. He read the words, rapidly at first, then slower as he progressed so that the details of what was being asked might be better absorbed. At last he lowered the document and looked at the two officers.

"Have you been told the essence of this message?" he asked them.

"We have," said the officer who had handed him the pouch.

"And are you also sent to 'escort' me to Kauley in case I should be reluctant to go?"

"Minister Foshay has expressed his faith in your willingness to serve the king."

Endrew nodded. "The minister has judged correctly. Tell Foshay on your return to the capital that I stand ready to do my part for King Giarley and he may find me in Kauley in ten days, as requested, or as near to that time as I am able."

"He told us you were a man of honor who would recognize his duty. That is why so few of us were sent to you," said the officer who had not spoken before.

"Yes," smiled the first. "Some dukes received much larger delegations, in anticipation of certain differences of opinion."

"Such is not the case here," said Endrew. "Now, as regards Chaussey's portion of the payment. I have nearly the amount specified within the treasury. The rest will be secured from the people before I journey to Kauley."

"Very good, sire," said both officers.

"Give my regards to all the ministers and tell them that I wish only for the speedy return of our king."

"We shall," said the one who had spoken first.

"You may spend the night within the comfort and safety of my town. Ask for Captain Bentlan."

The two men then left the room and Endrew

paused a moment to reflect on the nature of duty and obligation. Then he walked to the hall, called for the chamberlain and stewards so they might make plans for all that must be so quickly accomplished.

The people of Chaussey province muttered about taxation in the midst of already trying times, fearful that their hard-earned funds might never find their way to Glender and the king's release. In each village, though, heralds read Duke Endrew's proclamation and his pledge that he would personally accompany the ransom to its goal. Much wailing met the news that Endrew would be held in Glender, but the people vowed to make the most of the coming growing season and buy their young lord from captivity.

With the Chaussey share of the king's ransom thus secured, Endrew trusted the safety of his province to a council of landed knights and rode toward the coast. They left later than he would have preferred and their progress was slow, encumbered as they were by the treasure wagon and supplies for the troop of soldiers who guarded it. They were already four days later than Endrew had promised when they topped a rise in the trail and saw a sweeping bay, its sandy beach packed hard and flat by the waves that pounded in from the sea.

Dune grass bent flat as tiny grains of sand flew by, pushed onward by the wind that blew in off the ever-roaring waves. Endrew looked out across the breakers to the horizon that lay hidden beneath dense, grey clouds that squatted just above the water line and masked his goal. He tugged at his cowl, and pulled his cape tighter around him.

"It is a cold wind that stands between Glender and Wollaire," he said.

"You would be warmer in armor," offered

Bentlan.

"It is not permitted," he said simply. Then he turned again to stare out at the cloud-masked horizon.

"They say Glender may be spotted across the sea on a clear day," said Bentlan.

"You give voice to my thoughts," said Endrew. "I wondered if we might see it."

"I am in no hurry to lay eyes on that wicked land, nor should you be, my lord."

"What must be done, must be begun," said Endrew. "Come."

He led the procession forward along a path that skirted the shore, and by late afternoon they climbed a grade and in topping it saw their goal. The port town of Kauley sat in a cove, protected by a sand spit that nearly filled the harbor's entrance. Ships dotted a pier, with smaller boats pulled up along the protected inner beach. Smoke blew from chimneys and holes in roofs, pushed ever inland by the constant salt wind. Above all rose the small, round watch tower that passed for the town's fortification.

"Raise the banner of Chaussey," said Endrew. "Let us make for that large building that flies the king's flag. Foshay waits there, no doubt." With that, he led the procession down into the town, causing little more than the most minimal notice on the part of the residents.

"These people seem used to strangers," said Bentlan.

"We are late in arriving," said Endrew. "No doubt many others have come before us."

"All the same, these people should bow before a man of your rank."

"Persons of rank are only a novelty when there are few of them around," said Endrew. "These poor folk have been swimming in dukes lately."

"Duke Endrew of Chaussey?" called a voice from the street.

Endrew turned toward the sound and spotted a soldier standing before the large building that bore the king's banner. He pulled his horse to a halt in front of the man and said, "I am he."

"Minister Foshay waits within. Is this your portion of the ransom?" he asked, pointing at the wagon.

"It is."

"Leave it. My men will take it to the ship."

"I think not, soldier," said Endrew. "I have promised the people of my province that I would personally see this money on its way to Glender. If you tell me which ship, my men and I shall be happy to deliver these funds and submit them to whatever tally is required."

"Minister Foshay said–"

"With all respect to the minister," said Endrew, "he acts on behalf of the king and has no authority over business in the provinces. Until such time as this money becomes part of Wollaire's ransom of King Giarley, it still belongs to Chaussey. What is Chaussey's, is mine, and I do not part with so great a sum lightly. Now, I ask you again, which is the ship?"

The soldier lowered his jaw and looked puzzled, but said nothing. Instead, he pointed toward the wharf and said, "The one they call Racer's Pride."

"Thank you," said Endrew. "Tell the minister that I shall join him when this errand is finished."

"Yes, my lord."

The young duke led the way down the street toward the dock, leaving the soldier standing slack-jawed behind. "I only met minister Foshay once," Endrew whispered to Bentlan without turning his head. "I cannot say I was particularly impressed."

Bentlan tried to control a chuckle. "No doubt he expected a boy who could be easily commanded."

"And as benefits our king, that is what I shall be. But there is no sense in letting the fellow believe I am easily led in all things. Years from now I may be called upon to protect the interests of our province. I want the minister to remember this moment."

"You place your thoughts far in the future, my lord."

"A distant future is the only one I have," said Endrew. "The immediate future appears well spoken for." He pulled his horse to a halt and swung down to the planked surface of the wharf.

Bentlan did likewise, then halted Endrew with a quiet, "My lord, your people think to buy you back with one good harvest, but it may take years for all Wollaire to raise a sum great enough to bring you and the other dukes to freedom. How will you manage?"

"As I must; from day to day, in the knowledge that my province waits for me. Come, let us find which is the Racer's Pride."

He said it loud enough for nearby workers to hear, and one of them turned. "Racer's Pride?" asked the man. "That be she over there." He indicated a dark vessel just ahead at the wharf, with men busily engaged in mending sails, splicing lines, and arranging cargo.

"And the master?"

"Auell, the cranky old one there in the bow," said the worker, pointing to a portly man with grey hair streaming around his face in the wind.

"Come, Bentlan," said Endrew, motioning for the others to stay by the wagons. The two men walked to where the ship waited and Endrew called out,

"Master Auell of the Racer's Pride?"

"Go away," snapped back the older man. "I am busy and my vessel is engaged."

"You are speaking to Duke Endrew of Chaussey province," said Bentlan. "Show some manners before my lord."

"It is no matter," said Endrew.

"Hrmph, sorry," allowed the shipmaster, though his voice and manner contradicted his statement. "I thought you were a merchant looking for transport. Damn pests, they have been."

"Pests?" asked Endrew.

Auell took a long stride off the ship's rail and lit on the dock beside them. "Every vessel in the harbor is occupied in this exchange business, and at no fee, I might add. My ship holds a fortune and I go without the slightest reward."

"A country must have its king," said Endrew.

"Hrmph," muttered Auell again. "I wonder. Well, never mind that. Chaussey, eh?"

"Yes."

"You came a long way, then. And what do you have for me to carry?"

"Several casks of coin and these large boxes of plate and bejewelled items," said Endrew, pointing back toward the wagon.

Auell raised an eyebrow. "You dukes," he said with a snort. "You recite lists like that as I might call out a lading of vegetables. Well, let me get the lads to working on it. Have your men bring the wagon down here."

Bentlan waved the soldiers forward as the shipmaster instructed, and Auell had a company of sailors ferry the goods from the wagon, across a narrow gangplank, and onto the Racer's Pride. He shouted instructions to his men with every step, then loudly directed them to rearrange the cargo on deck. Endrew studied the shipmaster's orders to the crew and tried to divine the system which underlay them. If such a system existed, though, he failed to uncover it.

At last he asked, "Do you not intend to take inventory on my portion of the ransom?"

"I am not the one who needs to be satisfied, lad," said Auell. "The one you have to please is the Glender king." With that, he spat into the water between the ship and the dock. "Besides," continued the shipmaster, turning back to look Endrew in the eye, "I doubt you brought more than your share, eh?"

Endrew smiled. "You are wise in the ways of men."

"I figure if every duke does the same, the total will be so close to what was agreed upon that you would be hard pressed to get drunk on the difference."

"Will I be sailing with you?" asked Endrew.

"That you will," said Auell. "The ministers decided to keep you folk and your money together as long as possible. Peace of mind, I suppose."

"And who will be coming with us?"

"Oh, hang me, what is, the fellow's name? It is ... uh ... 'Rob' something."

"Robear of Tushan?"

"The very man. His goods are mixed with yours even now."

"Robear is a great duke and a good man. My father always spoke well of him."

The shipmaster nodded. "Seemed pleasant enough, anyway. I hope the third is as easy to get along with as you two."

"Who is the third to be?"

"Sorry, young fellow, not a clue. I suspect that

minister will have saved someone special to complete the batch. Nothing else has gone right lately." Again he spat into the water.

"Am I to stay aboard your vessel now?"

"Are you daft? You would only be in the way. No, take yourself up to that inn that flies the king's banner. The lords are staying there, waiting for the last stragglers to come into town."

"Thank you," said Endrew, turning to walk away.

"A most insolent fellow," muttered Bentlan. "I should like to teach him manners on your behalf."

"He is a plain man, accustomed to running his ship as he chooses and unused to any rank higher than his own," said Endrew. "I think I shall enjoy his company." He stole a look over his shoulder at the cloud-swagged horizon where Glender still hid. "I wish I might have it for even longer," he added.

The soldiers backed the wagon off the dock, then turned and followed Endrew and Bentlan up the dirt and gravel street that led to the inn. The guard who had greeted them before still stood at the entrance.

"Where may my men stay until the transfer is complete?" asked Endrew.

"There is no need for them to stay," said the soldier.

"Perhaps not, yet stay they will until I say otherwise. Now, I ask you again, where may they go to be out of this wind?"

The soldier looked perplexed. "Our men are quartered in that large stable at the end of the street. Perhaps I should check with minister Foshay."

"Perhaps you should," answered Endrew, and the man turned and went inside.

Bentlan smiled. "My lord duke, you are going

to acquire a reputation for being difficult."

"With certain people, that is not such a bad thing to have."

"My lord, Duke Endrew, welcome to Kauley," came a smooth voice from behind in flat, calm tones that bespoke years of practice.

Endrew turned and looked at the gold-robed man who stood before him. "Thank you for your welcome, lord minister. I am sorry to have come later than the appointed date."

"Think nothing of it," said Foshay, waving the apology off with a flick of his wrist. "We still await three of your fellow lords before the exchange can be completed."

"Even so, my regrets."

"I understand you have already placed Chaussey's share of the ransom on board the ship that will carry you to Glender?"

"We have. Now I wish to quarter my men."

"Certainly. They may, of course, share accommodations with the king's own guard. I believe you were told of the stable's location."

He gestured up the street to where the soldier had previously pointed, but all conversation stopped at the sight of a group of wagons rolling into town. Seated beside the driver of the lead team sat Duke Showann of Alpenne bound with chains at the wrists and ankles. Behind the procession rode more than fifty of the king's guards.

Endrew turned, shocked that a duke should be so treated. "Foshay, what is the meaning of this?"

"I am sorry, Duke Endrew. Not all of your noble brethren go to make this sacrifice as willingly as you."

Showann half stood in the wagon as it rumbled

past. "Foshay, you betrayed me, you traitorous bastard," he roared in a voice more gravel-laden than the surface of the road. "If the gods yet lived I would pray to them to smite you where you stand."

"Pay him no mind," said Foshay.

"Endrew, you young idiot," roared Showann as the driver pulled the duke back into his seat, "can you not see this is a plot to be rid of us?"

Endrew turned and looked at Foshay. He did his best to look unruffled by his fellow duke's outburst, but he had a difficult time hiding the fact that Showann's thought had more than crossed his mind.

Foshay lowered his voice and spoke confidentially. "Duke Showann of Alpenne lacks your love for king and country, I fear. A selfish concern for his own safety blunts the sense of obligation that should come with nobility."

"Lord minister, the king has seen fit to grant you administrative office, and I will not question that decision. But as you were not born to a title, you ought not speculate on the obligations that come with one. Besides, I saw Duke Showann at the battle of the vale. He is not a coward; his banner flew close to the front all day.

"Indeed it did," answered the minister, "but men brave in battle often quake at the thought of confinement. It is not so unusual."

"I suppose. I must confess, the thought of imprisonment troubles me as well."

"It will not be imprisonment," said Foshay, expansively. "No dungeon cell will hold you, nor any other of the dukes. Is that what troubled you?'

"But I thought—"

"My lord duke," said the minister, "I have arranged for you to be quartered more as a guest than a prisoner. The only concession you make to captivity is that you will not be allowed to return to Wollaire until the balance of the ransom is paid."

"I see."

"Once Showann understands this, his agitation will cease also. Now, come inside and spend some time with your fellows while we wait for the last of your number to arrive."

"Very well," said Endrew. "Bentlan," he said, turning to where the officer still stood, "quarter your men and stand by until I have departed for Glender."

"It is not necessary," said Foshay.

"But my lord has requested it," said Bentlan, "and it shall be done." With that he turned, remounted his horse, and led the Chaussey guard up the street.

"Your people are most loyal," said Foshay, evenly.

"They trusted my father. I am glad they are learning to trust me."

Endrew turned and entered, stepping into a dim, smoke-filled room with a low ceiling and a central fire pit, over which a side of beef turned on a spit. Shields decorated the walls and long trestle tables filled the floor with stools along one side so servants could tend to the waiting men from the other. A low murmur of subdued conversation almost stopped for a moment as those within paused to identify the newcomer.

"Duke Endrew," came a shout from the right. "Come join us here."

Endrew walked in the direction of the call, then spotted a familiar face through the room's dingy haze. "Duke Robear," he said with a bow, "I understand we are to share passage to Glender."

"It shall be my pleasure to travel with an honest and honorable man," said Robear. "I see you have already had your measure of the other sort."

Endrew looked to where the duke indicated and saw the minister of negotiation engaged in conversation with another administrator. "You mean Foshay?"

"None other," said Robear. "The man has the ogle of a serpent."

Endrew paused. His father always said it was better to listen and learn the truth than to speak from mere suspicion. "I hardly know what to think of him."

Another man's voice broke in, "What to think? Why, it seems obvious. Look around you."

"Forgive me," said Robear, "have you met Duke Jonale of Quitole province?"

"I fear not," said Endrew.

"Yes, you have," said Jonale, "but you were too young to remember the occasion. Your father brought you to my court when you were eight or thereabouts."

Endrew bowed his head. "I am sorry, sir. I had forgotten. Yes, I remember the trip to Quitole; it is a lovely land."

Jonale snorted into his ale. "I hope I live to see it again."

"Come," said Robear, "sit with us and tell us of your adventures in getting here."

"There is nothing to tell," said Endrew, walking around the table and sitting on a stool between the two men. "I was delayed only by the raising of the last portion of the ransom money."

"They starve our people, then pick the bones for scraps," said Jonale.

"It is true the people have little enough," said Endrew, "but the growing season is nearly on us. They will get by."

"Each duke here tells the same story," said Robear. "Every province in the kingdom was brought to the edge of poverty by this ransom. Only the sky above knows when the other half may be gained."

Jonale looked about the room, his lips pursed in disgust. "Yet no one speaks above a whisper of protest."

"One man does," said Endrew. "Showann of Alpenne arrived in chains while I was in the street. He shouted at Foshay, calling him traitor and accusing him of conspiring behind Showann's back."

"Exactly what I feared," said Jonale. "If you were ambitious and wished to weaken the nobility, which twenty dukes would you prefer to be rid of?"

"No one would dare such a thing," said Endrew. "There would be an outcry–"

"None would give action to such a scheme openly," said Jonale. "But I would put nothing past Foshay, especially if he thought he could dispose of the dukes who hold the greatest power in such a way that not a person in the land would question the method."

"It makes sense," said Robear, scratching his beard.

"Your pardon, but it does not," said Endrew. "If Foshay– or anyone for that matter– wished to be rid of powerful dukes, why should they wish to include me? Surely my age–"

"Your age, my boy," said Jonale, "is one of the things that makes you most dangerous. Why, every man here saw you hold the pass that allowed our escape from the vale. We all heard how you forsook your steed and waded into the Glender scum on foot, trading sword blows with the enemy until they fled before you. You are known to be as valiant as the most experienced warrior among us."

"Your courage is beyond question," said Robear. "In addition you are known to be well schooled by your late father in all the courtly graces and you have title to one of the richest provinces in all Wollaire." The older man paused to smile warmly. "Besides, you have a commanding presence and are handsome as a cad. Why, if my daughters were not already wed—"

"But my age—"

"Is exactly the point," continued Robear. "Endrew, look at us. Look around you. The others in this room are twenty, thirty, even close to forty years older than you. If the second half of this ransom takes as long to raise as I fear it might, many of us will not be coming home."

Jonale leaned close and put a hand gently on Endrew's shoulder. "My boy, you may return as the most powerful noble in all the land, just by having outlived the rest of us in captivity."

Robear nodded. "Your power could grow to equal that of the king, himself."

Jonale tightened his grip on Endrew's shoulder. "I doubt the king is clever enough to be fearful of that kind of power. But that one," he said, glancing at where Foshay still stood, "I fear that one will stop at nothing to protect the interest of the man he serves."

"Or his own," interrupted Robear, "whether the threat is real or not."

"I have no desire for such power."

"But power you shall have," said Robear. "And people like Foshay will always view it with jealousy."

They talked on into the evening, concerned for the twin futures of Wollaire and themselves. Servants brought full measures of wine and ale to the tables, then finally placed platters of roast beef, stewed vegetables, and steaming bread before the dukes.

"One last meal, perhaps," muttered Jonale.

"But a good one," said Robear, pulling a loaf of bread into pieces.

Endrew shook his head. "My people have lived on the edge of starvation all winter. No table in Chaussey, including my own, has seen such a feast."

"Well, they are not likely to ship the scraps from this one to your servants," said Jonale. "No sense fussing over it."

"Our lord of Quitole is correct," said Robear. "You will need the strength of this meal for the trials ahead. Your failing to eat will not help your people."

"I suppose," said Endrew, "but still, it offends me to see such abundance when my people are in want."

"Let it offend you, then," said Robear, "and hold the memory for such time as you are able to do something about it. In the meantime, eat."

Endrew looked down at the platter before him, then quietly filled it. He ate without a word, silently vowing to make someone pay for every measure of guilt he felt in doing so.

As the dukes neared the meal's end, the door burst open with a rush of cold sea wind and the last two of their number hurried inside, shaking drops of rain from their cloaks and stomping their feet on the floor. Foshay rushed to greet the men, bowing with great ceremony. He talked with the two for a moment, then he turned to the room and loudly announced, "Your party is now complete and your mission of mercy can begin. You lords begin your noble and sacrificial journey on the morrow at first light."

Jonale belched into his cup. "If I had known we

would be bouncing across the waters so soon, I might have partaken less heartily of this meal."

The sun had not yet risen when servants wakened Endrew with a knock on the door. He dressed himself and gathered the scant belongings he had been told he would be allowed to take with him, then stepped into the hallway and walked downstairs to the main room below. A few lords sat at the tables, some eating steaming cereal, and all muttering about cruel fates that must be endured.

Endrew stepped into the street and saw the first hint of dawn in the east. He looked at the now cloudless horizon and saw an irregularity on the distant line, silhouetted by the rising sun.

"Glender," said a familiar voice from behind.

Endrew started and turned, his hand reaching by habit for the phantom hilt of a sword he was not allowed to carry. "Bentlan, you startled me."

"Sorry, my lord."

"It is nothing. My thoughts were over the water, that is all."

"There is no surprise in that. Are you well?"

"As well as might be expected. Did they feed you and the men?"

"They did not dare otherwise. We made ourselves at home among the king's guard."

"Good. It will not be long now."

"I know. The guards were alerted to be ready in case any one of you should change his mind. They seem particularly concerned on that issue."

"All the lords are mistrustful, but none is likely to jeopardize the king's release."

"Except Showann of Alpenne," said Bentlan, "He was taken directly to the ship so as not to color the ideas of the other dukes."

Endrew nodded slowly. "That explains why we

did not see him inside last night."

"You shall see enough of him soon," said Bentlan. "Guess which vessel is to carry our unhappy duke?"

Endrew could feel Bentlan smiling in the dark. "Shipmaster Auell said they would likely saddle him with a difficult passenger. I fear he does not know the full measure of his accuracy."

"He has had the man on board all night," reminded Bentlan. "I suspect he knows by now."

"Where are the men?" asked Endrew.

"Down the street nearer to the wharf," answered the officer. "They would not allow the troop too near the inn, fearing insurrection, I suppose."

"Let us go to the ship, then," said Endrew.

The two men walked down the street that sloped toward the harbor, Bentlan glancing to the sides as they went and Endrew staring fixedly on the ever lightening horizon. Distant Glender became clearer now in the growing light, a dark mass of low hills that sat too far away to reveal secret details.

"Here are the men, sire," said Bentlan. "We are allowed no closer to the ships."

"Then I shall say goodbye here."

"Your orders, sire?"

"My orders are to wait here until you see the king land safely, then return to Chaussey and help the council keep the province safe until I return."

"And if the king does not."

"He shall. If not, return to the council. I have given them instructions."

It was now light enough to see Bentlan's lips curl in a cruel smile. "I hope that Foshay is the first one I am to kill."

"Do not dwell on such thoughts. Think instead

on the days when I am back and the fields of our river valley are green with abundance."

"The people will not forget you, my duke."

"Nor I, they. Tell the council my thoughts are with them. Goodbye, Bentlan, until we are able to meet again."

Endrew turned and walked to the wharf where the Racer's Pride waited. Sailors scurried about the deck, now crowded with the goods of three dukes, and tossed lines aloft to a man who threaded them through blocks.

"Well, that makes two," said Auell as Endrew crossed the plank and stepped onto the vessel's deck. "Where is your friend, Robear?"

"The other dukes should be along shortly. I understand Duke Showann is our third."

A frown crossed Auell's lined and craggy face. "You will find him bound and gagged in the stern castle there."

"Bound and gagged?"

"I was told to keep him tied until we were at sea."

"But gagged?"

"That was my idea," said the shipmaster. "Damn fool kept jawing at me until I could stand it no more."

"I should like to see him."

"I suspect you would, but I think not for the time being. You would want to untie him– take the gag from his mouth, no doubt– and I would suffer at the hands of that blasted minister. No, you shall have your fill of him once we are at sea. Ah, and here is Duke Robear."

Endrew turned to watch the third of their party step on board, then Auell shoved the two men gently to the bow.

"Stay here until we are well out of the harbor," he said. "You will only be in the way if you move about."

The two men did as they were told, and watched quietly as the last dukes settled in on their ships. Foshay passed from vessel to vessel, thanking the nobles for their patriotic sacrifice and wishing them speedy return from exile. Then the masters of the various ships called to their crews to cast off lines, and one by one the boats pushed away from the dock, swept toward the harbor's mouth by great oars. The Racer's Pride, third ship from the lead, ghosted silently across the still waters and past the flaming beacon that marked the entrance to the port of Kauley.

Endrew placed a hand on the ship's rail when he felt the first swell lift the vessel, and his body lurched back and forth until he caught the rhythm of the waves and settled into it. He looked at Robear and saw him gripping the opposite rail with both hands.

"There," called Auell. "The last one is out of the harbor. Raise the sails, lads."

"Can I help?" shouted Endrew.

"Yes," said the shipmaster. "Stay out of the way, where I put you."

"How can you sail in such little wind?"

The shipmaster looked aloft, then scanned the sea in all directions. "Oh, there will be wind enough when we pass the shadow of that headland. A breeze from the south should come up."

"How can we sail east when the wind is from the south?"

"By the skies above, man, do you know so little?" roared the captain. "Why else would ships have keels if not to keep them on course?"

"But the wind—"

"Be quiet and listen," said Auell, pointing to the triangular sail the men were raising. "You may learn something. That is a lateen rig, it lets us point close to the wind instead of always running before it. The men who sail northern waters insist on square rigs, but they fail to point worth an ounce of spit. No, a lateen is the only thing for a vessel of this size; simple, easy, and reasonably safe."

"Only reasonably safe?"

"See that lower boom?" asked Auell, pointing to the spar of wood that held the bottom of the sail firm. "Mind when we change course," he warned. "If that boom sweeps across and you stand in the way, your head will pay the price if you fail to see it coming."

The sail filled with a loud slap, and Auell called for the men to draw in on the lines until the vessel heeled slightly. He called a heading to the helmsman, then turned back to the dukes. "You gentleman may make yourselves comfortable now. Can even talk to that other fellow, if you have a mind, though I cannot imagine why you should wish to." With that he turned and walked away.

"An insolent rascal," said Robear, still clinging firmly to the starboard rail, "yet you bear his insults well."

"I suppose I do not hear them as insults," said Endrew.

"No?"

The young duke shook his head. "Did you not hear what he said? 'Be quiet and listen; you may learn something'?"

"I did," said Robear. "Most ill mannered."

"My father used to say the same thing to me all the time. I found at last that it was good advice."

4

The two dukes freed Showann of Alpenne from the cabin and listened to twenty solid, scorching minutes of his theories about treason and treachery, particularly as concerned Foshay. They heard the minister characterized as a "snake at the breast" and a "back stabbing son of a plague-ridden whore." Robear and Endrew listened to the man's raving but made little sense of it, for Showann neglected to mention his own involvement in choosing the other hostages and his tirade made scant sense with that fact missing.

Finally, the three of them settled into the voyage, each in his own way. Showann and Robear clung firmly to the lee rail, the former out of fear of the sea and the latter in payment of the previous night's meal. Endrew, on the other hand, moved about the ship's deck, talking to the crew when Auell would allow it and learning what he could of boats and sailing.

"How long will the voyage to Glender last?'

"We should fetch the coast by early afternoon, at this pace," answered the helmsman. "If the wind picks up, we could gain a bit."

"Get away from there," Auell shouted at Endrew, "and stop bothering the men."

Endrew did as he was told, but minutes later

found him beside a sailor on the main deck, giving the line the man held a trial tug. "And what happens if 1 pull in on this?" he asked.

"You hold the main sheet," said the sailor. "Let it out, and we catch no wind. Pull in and we heel until the sail no longer presents enough of itself to the wind to move forward. No, the thing to do is trim the sail so the wind glides over it."

"And that pulls us forward?"

"Aye."

"Get away from there," shouted Auell. "Are you trying to take over my ship? How are we to deliver you to Glender if you keep bothering my men?"

Endrew again backed away. He drifted to the bow where the forward lookout stood and marked their place in the line of vessels. The lookout offered little in the way of conversation, so shortly he stood beside the helmsman again, this time giving the tiller a try.

"Point us to that mark on the right of Glender," advised the helmsman.

Endrew adjusted the ship's course the least amount into the wind. The sail luffed slightly and the man on deck trimmed the line, but the momentary sound of the canvas alerted the shipmaster who came running to the steerage deck.

"By the skies above, how many times do you need to hear me say a thing to heed it?"

"I mean no harm, sir," said Endrew. "My curiosity–"

"Your curiosity will have us on the rocks of Domnall Ua Cnoba."

"Your man is right here to watch me."

The shipmaster looked silently at Endrew for a moment, then turned and glared at the sailor. "And mind that you do," he said gruffly, then he turned and hopped down to the main deck, cuffing the man who held the sheet. Endrew saw the captain point to where he stood at the tiller, then wave his hand at the sail. The sailor saluted, but their words were lost in the wind which had begun to whine in the rigging.

"Breeze is picking up," said the helmsman. "Hold the tiller firmly."

"I hope I have not caused you trouble with your captain."

"Oh, he is more noise than harm," said the helmsman. "Actually, I think he likes you."

"How can you tell?"

The sailor smiled. "He only shouted. If you had not found favor in his eyes, I think you would now be swimming to Glender."

"I must confess I do not fancy the trip at all, but that would make it even less attractive." Endrew leaned to see past the sail and be sure he kept the ship on course. "What did Auell mean, the rocks of— what did he call them?"

"Domnall Ua Cnoba," said the man. "The words are of a long forgotten tongue. It is a large island off the coast of Glender, a place of spirits, dark magics, and ancient evils."

"Do we pass near it?"

"You are steering for it now, though you cannot distinguish it at this distance. When the time comes, we shall duck between Domnall and the Glender shore. The waters are shoal near the island, but it is safe enough to pass if we keep our eyes sharp. By evening we should be at our landing site up the coast."

"And how far to King Alrick's capital?"

The helmsman shrugged. "A day, perhaps two. I cannot say with certain knowledge. We always exchange cargo at the port of Cinioch. I have never been inland."

A man at the forward lookout shouted, "Sail, ho," All sailors not engaged with running the ship rushed to the rails and leaned out to see what the lookout had spied. Endrew peered as best he could but the sail blocked his view.

"What is it?" he called to the helmsman who leaned out over the water.

"A ship of Glender," he answered, "bound for Wollaire. We shall pass port side to port. Here, let me take the helm so you can see."

Endrew allowed the other man to steer and he stepped to the rail as the helmsman had done. Sure enough, there ahead was a ship flying the two-crowned banner of Glender heading toward them and bound in the opposite direction. As the ship drew close to the first vessel in the Wollaire line, a second banner rose into the rigging. There below the two crowns flew the axe and crown of Wollaire.

"It is the ship carrying King Giarley," shouted Endrew, excited with the thought that this trip had purpose, after all. "Robear, Showann," he called down to the main deck. "It is our king being returned. The Glenders have kept their word."

The two dukes looked out across the water to where the foreign ship surged by. No change of expression passed across either face, but Endrew could not let the moment go without waving his hands overhead and calling as loudly as he was able, "Long life to King Giarley." No signal of any sort returned, and the Glender vessel soon passed astern, moving down the line of ships on its way to the port town of Kauley.

"I doubt they could hear you," said the helmsman.

"The king would know we wished him well," said Endrew, "even if he could not catch the words."

The helmsman stood quietly for several minutes, then asked, "Do you wish the tiller again?"

"It is a great honor," said Endrew.

The sailor again relinquished the helm and Endrew could feel the man staring at him from behind.

"You are a strange young man, Duke Endrew," said the sailor at last.

"Why do you say that?"

"You go to captivity in a far different manner than I would."

"When a thing is done for a good purpose, what matters the difficulty of the doing?"

"Many men say such things," said the helmsman. "I never before met anyone who seemed to mean it."

"I do mean it," said Endrew.

"I know. That is the interesting part of it."

Endrew stood at the tiller for an hour or more, then passed the steerage of the ship back to the helmsman. They talked of their childhoods, Endrew's in the great river valley and the sailor's in a fishing village near Kauley. They spoke of pranks and adventures, of quarrels with siblings, and lessons well learned on the seat of their trousers. Each man felt grateful for the other's company and neither found the other's rank the least hindrance to their talk.

Another sailor came to relieve them at the helm at last, and the two men stepped down to the main deck where Auell stood with his hands on his hips and a great scowl on his face.

"Well, you kept us from capsizing for a while, at least."

"Let him take the main sheet," said the sailor.

"By the voyage's end we shall make a proper sailor of him, sure."

"He is not a sailor, he is a duke," reminded the captain. "You, take forward lookout," he said to the seaman. "And you, Duke Endrew, see if your noble friends hanging over the rail there want anything to eat."

"I doubt they do," said Endrew, "but what do you have to offer them?"

"A kettle of chowder is simmering below. They may not be hungry but a bit of warmth would not hurt them."

"The wind off the water is bitterly cold," said Endrew. "I shall see if they find the sound of chowder as warming as I do."

He asked. They didn't.

Endrew took a cup of the chowder and sat alone with his back against the ship's starboard rail, thinking a thousand thoughts on as many topics. The thick soup soon cooled enough to swallow, and he felt its warmth heat his core. When the chowder was gone, he rose and returned the cup below deck. He found the ship's motion disconcerting in the enclosed space, though, and went back up on deck to watch wisps of spray spread across the water and the occasional seabird swoop down in search of fish.

Time swept by with the waves, and soon Auell stood by his side. "Glender is clearer to the eye now, eh?"

"Very much so. Is that Domnall Ua Cnoba there?" he asked, indicating a rocky shore where wind-bent evergreens crept toward the sky in twisted parodies of trees. Waves crashed on black stone stacks in great, white billows of foam. Inland from the shore, a great peak of naked rock climbed toward the clouds.

Fingers of fog clung to the island, masking the clarity of other features.

"Aye. We pass between the main shore of Glender and it. An evil place," said Auell and he spat in the direction of the island, but the wind blew his spittle back toward them.

"How is it evil?" asked Endrew.

"The legends say that long ago, when the gods still lived, Glender and Wollaire were connected and one. Domnall Ua Cnoba was a mountain top where the gods were worshiped by the people of both lands before the ground sank and the sea filled this channel. Only spirits of the old ones live there now."

"It does not look especially evil."

Auell stomped his foot on the deck. "By the sky above, boy, did you learn nothing from what I said?"

"Yes, I did," said Endrew. "I learned one should never spit into the wind."

Auell looked blankly at the duke for a moment, then burst into laughter. "I have an even better lesson for you, then," he said. "Always pee to the lee."

"Yes," said Endrew. "I can see that would be good advice."

The Racer's Pride followed the lead ships between Glender and Domnall Ua Cnoba, tacking back and forth in the narrow channel as the wind swirled around the island of rumored evils. Finally, the procession emerged from the shadow of the island and the ships made their way along the coast. At last, they rounded a point of land and turned toward the north.

"Watch your head now," warned a sailor as he passed by.

"Why?" asked Endrew.

"Look," said the man. "See how the wind is from the stern now? The sail is full out to one side and we run before the wind."

"I do not see the danger."

The sailor shook his head. "There likely is none, but if all hands are not attentive, the sail could jibe."

"Jibe?"

"The wind can catch the canvas, making it move rapidly from one side of the ship to the other without warning. Even a large wave can turn the vessel enough to cause a jibe."

"I shall be alert."

Endrew walked to where Robear and Showann now stood at the starboard rail. "You moved, I see."

"That blasted sail was right over our heads where we sat before," said Robear.

"It was set out thus because we now run before the wind."

Showann snorted. "Oh, give the lad a few hours with a boat's crew and he fancies himself a sailor."

"Come now," said Robear, "he meant no harm."

"No," said the gravel-voiced duke, "I suppose not." Robear looked ahead. "How long, do you think, before we shall land?"

"Hours yet," said Endrew. "The sailors said—"

"Look out," came a panic-filled voice from the stern.

Endrew did not pause to look, but grabbed Duke Robear and pulled him to the deck. The sail snapped loudly overhead and its wooden boom caught Showann in the chest, sending him flying out over the rail. Endrew reached for the man's feet but just missed. Without thinking, he rose and leapt over the side. A cry of, "Man overboard," was the last thing he heard before his head went beneath the waves with a splash.

He came to the surface and wiped the stinging

salt from his eyes, then spun to find Showann. At first he saw nothing, as he bobbed up and down on the waves, then a patch of purple showed him where the duke's cape floated on the sea.

Endrew struck out for the cape, kicking hard and stroking hand over hand. The sea was more difficult to swim in than his river at home, and the waves seemed to want to push him back. In seconds, though, he reached the cape and pulled Showann's face above the surface. He put an arm around the duke's chest and turned in the water to see where the Racer's Pride had gone.

At first he saw nothing of the ship, then the bob of a wave revealed the vessel tacking back toward him. He waved his free hand, then turned his attention back to the unconscious duke. "Live," he shouted over the splashing and the spray. "I will not see King Alrick's twenty jeopardized by your neglect."

He placed both hands around the duke's waist and squeezed. Showann coughed and sputtered, with water pouring from his mouth. "Live," shouted Endrew, and he squeezed again with like results.

Showann began to struggle, turning in Endrew's grasp as if to climb on the younger man to escape the water. He put one hand on Endrew's head and drove his rescuer beneath the waves.

Endrew fought the man's weight and bobbed above the surface to snatch a breath. "Stop it," he called. "You will drown us bo–"

Showann pushed the boy under again. The cold sting of salt water burned Endrew's eyes and he fought to free himself of the struggling man's grasp. Then Showann rose free of the sea, as a bird leaves the land in flight. Endrew kicked hard and his head broke the surface to see hands reaching down to him from the ship. With what he judged to be his last strength, he reached up and felt himself pulled on board.

"That was either the bravest thing I ever saw," said Auell, "or the stupidest. Do you know how long a man is likely to last in water that cold?"

Endrew shivered, coughed water from the back of his throat, then looked at the shipmaster. "Of a truth, I do not."

"Well, not long, I assure you."

Sailors helped Endrew to his feet. "Did you bring a change of clothes with you?' asked Auell.

"Yes."

"Well, I suggest you get into them. Those wet ones will freeze you solid in this wind."

"Thank you," said Endrew. "I shall heed your advice."

"There, you can use your head after all," said the shipmaster, but he clapped Endrew firmly on the shoulder as the young duke walked away.

For the rest of the trip, Endrew was content to bundle himself in a cloak and lean against the stern castle, trying to get some degree of warmth back into his fingers. They reached the port of Cinioch before dusk and the ships tied up, one beside the other, at a dock reserved for them. Endrew gathered his belongings and stepped to the rail, awaiting the plank that would let them go ashore.

"Well, young sir," said Auell, "I cannot say the passage was uneventful."

"I am glad to have kept it from being so," said Endrew, as Robear and Showann came up beside him.

"You three watch yourselves," said Auell. "These Glenders have always been fair with me, but you may find it different. You kings and lords have been making war with each other over one damn fool thing or another for a long time."

"It is not your place to judge the business of your betters," said Showann.

"And I shall avoid doing so, if I ever meet any," the shipmaster snapped back. Then he turned his gaze on Endrew alone. "You be especially careful, my boy."

"Me, why?"

"Because you have more to fear than the others. The remainder of the twenty have only the Glenders to threaten them."

"And Endrew?" asked Robear.

"Endrew has to keep an eye on his friends, as well. Why, he saved the life of this one and has not received so much as a thank you or a fare thee well."

"It is not necessary," said Endrew.

"I would have done the same," said Showann.

"Oh, would you now?" asked the shipmaster. "Yes, I think I shall carve that on the vessel's stern. 'I would have done the same'."

Endrew offered his hand to the captain. "Thank you for our passage and all your advice."

"You mind it now," said Auell, gripping the lad's hand firmly.

"I will." With that, Endrew stepped up to the gangplank and led the other two ashore.

They looked about the wharf and saw other small knots of nobles standing similarly ill at ease. A glance to the landward end of the dock revealed a troop of Glender soldiers. In front of them stood a man in rich robes of gold and blue who beckoned the dukes toward him.

"He wears the colors of Chaussey province," Endrew whispered to Robear.

"Put no great trust in that coincidence," answered the duke. "He is a Glender."

"Of course," Endrew whispered back.

The dukes drew together in front of the man,

waiting to find what happened next.

"My name Caelwin Cyniod, Glender minister of negotiation," said the man in robes. "I trust your passage was smooth?" None of the dukes answered, so the minister continued. "Good. I expect you wonder what is to occur next. You dine tonight in the main hall of this town's inn. You will stay tonight in rooms provided by the inn and guarded by these soldiers. Tomorrow at first light we will ride to the castle of King Alrick Nectu in the capital of Talorcan where the king wishes to meet each of you and receive your ransom, I suggest you put thoughts of escape out of your heads. It will not be allowed and it would violate the terms of this exchange."

Endrew raised his voice. "We harbor no such thoughts. Each of us is here for one reason alone, that our good King Giarley should walk free."

"Fah," said Showann, half under his breath, but Robear stilled him with an elbow to the ribs.

Endrew walked slightly forward of center in the pack as the dukes followed the minister, escorted to the inn by half of the troops. Each of the Wollaire lords looked into the strangely silent faces of the people of Cinioch who lined the street on both sides to glare their fear and hatred at the strangers.

"This crowd looks capable of violence toward us," grumbled Showann, his hoarse voice coming to Endrew's ears from behind. "Why is not the whole troop to ward us safely to the inn?"

"Because they stay to guard the treasure, you damn fool," came an answer from Duke Robear. "Now, be quiet. Let us conduct ourselves as gentlemen and lords before these foreigners."

Jonale of Quitole nudged Endrew in the ribs and said in a hush, "Note the size of the keep that wards this town." He gestured toward the stone structure that loomed over all Cinioch and its harbor. "It is much more formidable than the simple tower of Kauley."

"Cinioch is a bigger town," offered Endrew.

"But that is not what I meant," said Jonale. "We met, ate, and slept in Kauley's inn because the king's tower was not large enough to accommodate all of us in comfort. Surely a keep the size of this one could hold twenty prisoners such as we."

"Foshay said we were to be treated more as guests than captives," said Endrew. "Perhaps this is the Glender way of reinforcing that notion."

"Perhaps," allowed Jonale, though he sounded unconvinced.

"Regardless," said Endrew, "here is the inn."

Minister Caelwin Cyniod ushered the dukes into the main dining hall of the inn and urged them to be seated. Goblets of wine waited at each place and the lords tasted them, though most found the wine unlike that they were used to at home and therefore unpalatable. In due time, servants appeared with steaming trays of food, which they laded onto the guests' plates. The meal relied heavily on fish and mollusks, seasoned with combinations of spices not familiar in Wollaire, and despite the hunger most of the dukes felt, they pushed the food unenthusiastically around their plates like small children.

Caelwin Cyniod looked up from where he ate and noted his guests' reluctance. "I see your appetites suffered from your voyage," he said, loud enough to be heard over the dukes' grumbling.

A moment's awkward silence greeted the query, then Endrew who was seated nearby broke it with, "Our apologies, my lord. Some of us were made ill by the sea and many of us are unused to the

Glender manner of cooking. More likely though, all of us are new at confinement of any sort and have left our appetites in now distant homes. I am sure you understand."

The minister nodded. "Yes, I can imagine how you must feel– so far from home and for such an uncertain period of time."

"I am sure, my lord," continued Endrew, with the slightest polite, formal bow of his head, "that the time you refer to will give us ample opportunity to adjust our tastes in food to yours."

Minister Caelwin Cyniod looked at Endrew for a moment, appraising the young lord. "And what is your name, my duke?"

"Sir, I am Duke Endrew of Chaussey province."

The minister nodded, as if making a mental note of the name. "This is the second time I have addressed this group, to hear only you answer. Do you speak for your fellow dukes?"

A derisive snort came from the area where Showann of Alpenne sat. Endrew said, "I would not presume, my lord. I speak only for myself."

"Yet you, at least, have the manners to do so when all your fellows sit silently in their fear and loathing of all things Glender."

"And why should we not loath Glender?" Showann shouted. "We are at war with you."

The minister sat back and allowed himself a thin smile. "Correction, my lord. Our countries are at war, but for you the war is over, I think."

"Oh? And why is that?" asked Jonale of Quitole.

"You have pledged your lives and emptied your treasuries that your king could walk free. You expect your people to work, in turn, for your own freedom.

But winter will soon be fully past and we shall once more sail to Wollaire to press our king's claim on Pollay province. Do you think your peasants will be able to return you to your lands when they will be working every moment to support an army in the field?"

Caelwin Cyniod glanced slowly from one face to the next, pausing to let the idea sink in.

"Our king will not leave us here," said Robear. "He will borrow the money if he must, but he will find a way to free us."

"For your sakes, I hope so," said Cyniod. "However, it is not something upon which I should be tempted to wager large sums. Oh, I am sorry, that was ill mannered of me. You no longer possess large sums, all your wealth having gone to the freeing of your king. Well, my apologies," he went on, picking up a shell and absently pulling the meat from within, "it was only a figure of speech." He popped the morsel into his mouth, then sat back, smiling as he chewed.

5

In the morning, the dukes were again herded into the inn's main room, fed a breakfast of foods no more familiar than those of the night before, then led into the street. Each man clutched his few belongings close to him and watched wagons laden with the combined wealth of Wollaire lurch by, climbing the stone-paved street that led up from the harbor, past the keep, and into the interior of Glender. A troop of mounted soldiers led the caravan, with another behind. Men at arms on foot flanked the wagons, their spear tips dancing above them and catching the morning light as the soldiers marched.

When the treasure wagons had passed, a pair of empty carts pulled up in front of the inn and paused. Caelwin Cyniod appeared on horseback, and called, "Come now, my lords, do not delay. Into the wagons with you; King Alrick awaits."

Endrew climbed into the lead wagon and took a seat behind the driver on one of the benches that lined the sides.

"An insult," grumbled Showann of Alpenne, his hoarse voice rumbling in complaint. "They treat us as cargo instead of dukes. We should be allowed to ride."

"They want us to recognize our place," said Robear, as the last lords settled into the wagons.

"Hrmph," growled Showann, "our place is at

home in Wollaire."

"I fear not for the present," said Endrew.

"Onward," the minister shouted to the drivers, and the carts lurched into motion. A third troop of cavalry fell in behind the hostage dukes, and the captive twenty glumly watched as the road rose up away from the harbor and soon left the city behind.

They traveled across a countryside not dissimilar to their own, and many of the dukes quarreled about which of their provinces the land of Glender was most like. Great forests lifted their canopies of branches above the trail in places, and small villages stood in clearings where peasants waited patiently for spring.

Endrew took special notice of the tiny hamlets, and noted that the fields and animals of these communities had the same half starved quality as his own. Whatever could be said of Glender's claim to Pollay, and regardless of who had won the battle of the vale, it appeared that the war was equally unkind to the common people of both sides.

The caravan stopped to rest now and then, and the dukes were allowed to step down and briefly stretch their legs. A portion of their escort always stayed in the saddle though, and every duke saw that Caelwin Cyniod had no intention of being accountable for a hostage lost during the journey.

The wagons bumped along the rutted mud path that served as a road, then toward late afternoon as the sun dropped below the line of hills that filled the western horizon, the minister rode up beside the carts and pointed ahead. "Observe, my lords," he said, "we near Talorcan, King Alrick's capital."

The dukes took hold of the cart rails and leaned out to see. Slowly, as the trees which blocked much of their view passed, a broad expanse of gradually sloping valley opened up before them. A tree-lined river wound swiftly along, and the road sloped down a bit to meet it. The city of Talorcan hugged the river's far bank, spilling out of its walls with peasant huts clinging to the stone and forming a small village on the near side of the stream. Just across an arched stone bridge stood a citadel with walls ten feet higher than those of the city. Within a portion of the citadel, the towers of Talorcan keep climbed seventy feet or more into the air, with Alrick's two-crowned banner flying from the highest point.

The wagons rolled on through fields and orchards until they reached the village that guarded the bridge's approach. The caravan passed down a row of squalid shacks, then followed a bend in the road that brought them past a guard tower and onto the bridge deck.

Endrew glanced down into the river and watched the current bubble its way over water-smoothed rocks, thinking how much more swiftly this river flowed than his own. Then he looked up as they passed between a pair of huge, solid towers that flanked an enclosed space lit by torches and then went through a gate set into a second, even larger pair of towers. He looked up at the huge portcullis as they passed beneath it, and for a moment he imagined himself storming this gate, open to the rain of arrows that would fall from the three walls above.

They emerged in an open courtyard beyond, and once again the wagons' wheels rumbled over stone paving. On the caravan's right stood the huge keep, dark and ominous against the sky in the fading light. Lamps burned high above on the ramparts and painfully narrow shafts of light appeared here and there through arrow slits and Glender windows.

"A mighty fortress," said Endrew as the wagon passed through another gate which led to the inner bailey.

"Built by a wicked people to defend them from the rightful retribution of their foes," said Jonale of Quitole.

"Indeed," said Showann of Alpenne, agreeing with someone for the first time that day.

"How can one be sure of motive?" said Robear of Tushan. "Is it so unlike our own capital?"

"Our capital is strong to resist invasion," said Showann.

"And is it not possible we see that same thought duplicated here?" asked Robear.

"Absolutely not," said Showann.

"Not even possible?" pressed Robear.

"Of course it is," said Endrew, as the carts lurched to a halt.

"It is treason to even suggest such a thing," insisted the lord of Alpenne, his hoarse voice raising in anger. I am not surprised to hear such things from a boy of Endrew's years, but you, lord Robear, you surprise me."

Robear rose as if to defend his honor with action, but Endrew jumped to his feet and stood between the two men. "My father always said one cannot know the thoughts of another man until he sees the world from where that man stood. None of us is Glender–"

"If the gods yet lived," said Showann, "I should thank them for that, at least."

"None of us is Glender, and we cannot know their minds," continued Endrew. "Duke Robear has spoken a thought which may contain the truth, however much we might prefer not to accept it."

"Is there some problem, my lords?" asked

minister Caelwin Cyniod, pulling his horse to a halt alongside the wagon.

"No, my lord minister," said Endrew. "We were merely discussing the ... relative strengths of our two capitals and their defenses."

Lamps suspended from the courtyard walls lit the minister's face and revealed the lifting of one eyebrow. "Really?" he said. "You take a rather more heated interest in architecture and fortification than I might have guessed. Come, my lord dukes, alight and follow me."

The lords of Wollaire climbed stiffly to the ground and stretched as Caelwin Cyniod handed his horse over to a groom. Then they followed the minister and a group of soldiers, trailed and flanked by more of the same.

They climbed a ramp and entered the keep through a gate tower on the second story, then passed along a wide hallway until they reached a spiral set of stairs. Cyniod led the way, followed by four of the guards. The rest of the soldiers stood aside and watched as the dukes one by one climbed the stairs. They emerged in an antechamber with passages leading off in two directions and a pair of large carved doors with metal bands ahead. More guards stood at either side of the entrance, with others blocking the passageways.

"You are about to enter the great hall of Talorcan keep," said Caelwin. "I need not remind you to watch your manners; you will be meeting King Alrick Nectu within, and he is the lord who holds your fate in his hands."

"May he rot," muttered a duke.

The minister exercised selective deafness and let the remark pass. "Oh, and another thing," he said,

"I should hope that your appetites have returned. The king prides himself on the caliber of his kitchen staff. He should find your failure to enjoy the meal the gravest insult."

"I am so hungry," said Showann, "that even this Glender slop sounds good to me now."

Caelwin Cyniod allowed himself an indulgent smile. "There," he said, "that is the proper spirit, and elegantly phrased, too." With that, he turned and nodded to the guards who stood by the huge, wooden doors. Two men leaned heavily on the portals, which creaked open to reveal the chamber within.

The bright sounds of instruments met their ears and a brilliant wash of light poured from the room to assault their eyes. Great chandeliers, blazing with candles, hung from the ceiling and brightly colored banners dangled from the beams that spanned the room from side to side. A fireplace large enough to hold one of the carts they'd ridden in sat on one side of the room, roaring with a blaze of leg-thick logs. On the room's sides sat rows of tables and at the far end rose a platform that held a third table, facing the others. Behind each table sat a row of stools, except that at the center of the platform, three high-backed chairs stood above the rest of the furniture, the center one being highest of them all.

The minister split the group in half and sent ten dukes to each side of the room. Servants guided them to their seats at the opposite end of the room from the raised platform, and each lord of Wollaire stood awkwardly for a moment.

"I thought you said we were to meet the king," said Showann.

"We are alone in this room," said Robear, gesturing at the vast number of empty seats.

"Please be seated, my lords," urged the

minister. "You have come here directly from your arrival in the courtyard. The royal house of Glender and its guests will join you shortly."

The dukes of Wollaire sat, and Caelwin Cyniod nodded to the guards who spread out and flanked the walls. Then he bowed to the lords and left the way he'd come in.

"Again, they insult us," complained Showann. "They bring us to this place and make us wait for their arrival."

"What else would you expect from the Glender?" asked Jonale.

"None but this," answered another duke.

Endrew leaned close to Robear who sat on his left. "We have a roaring fire at our backs and pleasant music to hear. If we must wait, I can think of many worse places."

"Our fellow dukes," said Robear, "would find insult in anything."

"Perhaps that will pass in time," said Endrew.

"Time," mused Robear. "I have been thinking on what the Glender minister said last night. Time is the one thing we appear to have an abundance of."

Endrew nodded. "I also found much truth in what he said. If the Glenders press their claims in Pollay, our people will be hard put to survive and fund an army, much less buy our freedom."

"An army," continued Robear, "leaderless except for the weakest dukes."

"And our king," reminded Endrew.

"Ah, yes, our king. The same man who got himself captured at the vale." Robear shook his head. "With such a man in charge, the Glenders may soon find themselves feeding all Wollaire, once even the lowest peasant joins us here as hostage. Perhaps that is how we shall ultimately triumph."

Endrew opened his mouth to reply, but at that moment the doors of the room burst open and a crowd of elegantly clad men and women entered the room. The smiles disappeared from their faces as they eyed the dukes, and the dukes glared back in silent hostility. The party of Glender lords and ladies walked quietly behind the men of Wollaire and took seats close to the raised platform, being careful to leave several stools empty between themselves and the foreigners.

A crowd of servants then emerged from a side room, placing silver platters and goblets before every seat. Others followed behind, pouring the same odd wine the dukes had balked at the night before in Cinioch.

Then the minister returned with several other Glenders, and they made their way to the raised platform, taking seats on either side of the three high-backed chairs. After a few minutes pause while the occupants of the room glowered at one another in silent enmity, the musicians stopped playing. Endrew glanced up at them and saw each man put down his other instrument and take up a long trumpet. One of them nodded, and together they blew a loud fanfare that brought the men and women of Glender to their feet.

Caelwin Cyniod stared down at the dukes of Wollaire and said, "Stand, my lords, for King Alrick."

Slowly the twenty rose to their feet, then a barrel-chested man of nearly fifty entered the room, garbed in royal fabric of crimson that shone with the candles' light. On his broad chest were embroidered the two crowns of Glender and atop his head, a single band of gold echoed the design. Behind him walked a couple, the young woman's hand on her escort's arm.

His face was like the king's, only more youthful, but with a harder set to his eyes. Her face was cast downward, as if she dared not look at the newcomers in their midst.

The king made his way to the platform, where he took the center of the three chairs. The young man led the woman to the king's left then took the chair on the right. The king looked out over the assembly and raised his hands to indicate all should be seated. A loud scurry of stools being pulled across the plank floor greeted the gesture, followed by a moment's hurried conversation.

"Well," said King Alrick loud enough to still the murmuring, "perhaps our minister of negotiation would do the honors."

"Of course," said Caelwin Cyniod, rising to his feet. "My lords of Wollaire I am pleased to present King Alrick Nectu, lord of all Glender. This is his son, Prince Gartnait, the man who led our troops to victory in Pollay last autumn."

This announcement was met with urgent mutterings by many of the dukes, but the minister continued. "And this is Princess Briduen. My lords, my lady, may I present the dukes of Wollaire."

"Twenty dukes who have come to stand in their king's stead," said King Alrick, shaking his head. "Twenty is a great many; who speaks for them?"

Caelwin pointed. "The young one, your majesty, lord Endrew of Chaussey."

6

Every head in the room, including those of his fellow dukes, turned toward Endrew. The young lord froze with his cup to his lips, looking at the assembly over the gilded rim, the unswallowed wine still held in his mouth and suddenly without taste. Slowly, self consciously, he let the wine run down his throat, then placed the cup back on the table and stood.

"Your majesty, my lord minister, I fear there has been an error. These good dukes of Wollaire have chosen no leader, least of all me."

"What?" said Alrick, turning to his advisor.

The minister of negotiation again raised a critical eyebrow. "My good Duke Endrew," he said "I serve my king, protect this land, and make my living by the precision of language. Does the accent of Glender so mar our common tongue that it grows unintelligible to you? I did not say you were their leader; I said you spoke for them. There is a difference."

"Well, yes, I see that there is, but the one often implies the other."

"Has it not been you who has answered for the group when I have spoken to it?" asked Caelwin Cyniod.

"Well, yes, but–"

"There you have it, King Alrick. Address all

your questions to Duke Endrew."

"Oh, tut tut," said the Glender king, waving Caelwin Cyniod to silence, "there is no need to badger the poor lad. Plainly, the role of leader is one he prefers not be thrust upon him."

"Nor have I done so," corrected Caelwin.

The Glender king shook his head in irritation, causing his bewhiskered jowls to flap. "Leader, spokesman, what difference does it make? I have warned you not to play at words with me."

"Begging your pardon, your highness," said Endrew. "The word matters little. I seek neither role."

"But there is none among us upon whom the burden would better sit," said Duke Robear, rising by the young duke's side. "Endrew is brave, honest, and fair. He comes from an old and long honorable family and rules a great province in northern Wollaire."

"I agree," said Jonale of Quitole, getting to his feet behind the table on the opposite side of the room. "Endrew is reluctant to assume this role because of his years, but there is no finer knight among us than this young lord, regardless of age."

Endrew looked helplessly from one duke to the next. "My lords—"

"It would seem, my boy," said King Alrick, "that your fellows have more confidence in you than you have in yourself."

"Not all of us," said a duke at the opposite table, though Showann of Alpenne sat strangely silent.

"This is hardly the time or the circumstance for such a decision to be made," said Endrew. "We ought not discuss such matters in front of—" He stopped and bowed slightly to the monarch. "Well, begging your pardon, sire, but you are the enemy."

King Alrick stuck out his lower lip and turned

the comment away with the flap of a hand. "Think nothing of it, my boy. You are absolutely correct. If Prince Gartnait here or any of my other lords of battle were captive in your land, I should hope they would have the sense not to settle such matters in front of you."

Endrew bowed again. "Thank you, sire."

The king waved away Endrew's gratitude as if it were a swarm of biting insects. "Think nothing of it," he said. "Now, be seated, young lord, and you other dukes, too. We are here to enjoy a great feast of welcome prepared by my wonderful kitchen."

"Welcome, hmmph," snorted a duke to Endrew's right, half under his breath.

"Indeed," said Endrew to Robear, as he sat. "I am confused. Are we not prisoners, or did Foshay speak the truth?"

"Ask him," urged the Duke of Tushan.

"He will then think me leader."

Robear grunted in frustration. "You have acted as leader in word and deed; you shall soon be so in name. Nothing you say now will alter this."

Endrew sighed and rose once more to his feet. "Your majesty, I beg a word."

The monarch paused in his solicitations of approval for the coming meal from the lords and ladies of Glender. "What is it, young Duke Endrew?"

"Highness, many of us are anxious to know our fate here. We are hostages, prisoners of war, and yet you speak of feasts of welcome."

King Alrick knitted his brow and the crown dropped a notch on his forehead. "Yes, of course, you probably expected to be clapped in irons and all that. Well, perhaps 'welcome' is not exactly the best word to choose."

Prince Gartnait reached out and put a hand on

his father's arm, then looked at the dukes of Wollaire and spoke for the first time. His voice rang with a sharp, metallic edge. "My father, the king, has decided that you shall be quartered together here, in a large room on the ground floor of the keep. You will of course be guarded, but neither shall you be confined to our dungeon cells nor shall you be chained. Does this satisfy your curiosity?"

"Well, yes it—"

"Good," said the prince, "because there are many of us, especially those who fought and suffered on your cursed soil, who would as soon see otherwise."

"Why, you impudent pup," said Showann, rising to his feet.

"Showann," cautioned Endrew.

"I would see all of you hobbled, were it up to me," said Gartnait, half rising and pointing a finger at the Duke of Alpenne.

"Oh, we shall have no more of this talk now," said the king. "Sit, sit. We will discuss the matter at length later. Ah, look, here they are with the food now," he said, beaming broadly as troops of servants entered the room with great trays of steaming dishes. The people of Glender broke into applause.

"I must confess to being hungry," said Robear, quietly, "despite the food's taste."

Endrew sat and inhaled deeply. "It smells good to me."

"That is because you are from the north," said Robear. "We of south and central Wollaire have more refined palates."

Endrew looked up and saw his companion was teasing him. "Yes, I suppose you do," he admitted. "I saw how the delicacy of your palate was assaulted by the voyage, and that was with familiar dishes."

"I yield," said the older man, "to your point." The two men attended to their meals for several moments, then Robear again spoke. "I hope you realize that I meant what I said before."

Endrew looked at the duke. "I know. Thank you for your confidence, but I–"

"Hear me out. You are the ideal one of us to act as spokesman."

"But why?"

"Not every man here is as much a friend to the king as you."

"You are," said Endrew. "And Jonale, and–"

"Yes, yes, many of us are completely loyal, but others are not. Those who are of my age have lived long enough to see great rivalries arise with our neighbors. If I sought the role of leader, there are some who could keep it from happening. The same is true of Jonale and many more. But you, my young friend, are new to all this. You have not yet had the time to make enemies of your own."

"Surely Showann–"

"You saved the man's life yesterday. Showann will grumble, but he will not openly oppose you. At least not for a time. You saw how he grew quiet when you requested it."

"But eventually he–"

"Oh, yes, sooner or later he will forget that trifle and act as benefits himself, but for the time being you are free to claim what is yours for the taking." Robear saw the youth hesitate. "You must," he said, as quietly but firmly as he seemed able.

Endrew nodded. "I suppose you are right," he said. "I must do this for my king."

Robear smiled and raised his cup to his lips. "Your father would be proud of you." He drank the wine, then said, "This is not so terribly bad, once you get used to it, is it?"

The people of Wollaire and Glender managed to get through the meal without any major international incidents occurring though Endrew imagined it would be difficult to further strain the relations of kingdoms already at war.

Finally, King Alrick pushed his chair back and patted his stomach. At that signal, the lords and ladies of Glender all rose to their feet. Endrew and Robear stood, and slowly the balance of the dukes joined them.

"Well, it has been a lovely evening," said the king. "Good night." The people of Glender echoed the king's wishes as the monarch rose and walked out of the room followed by his son and daughter.

"But, your majesty," said Endrew, taking half a step to the side. His words were evidently lost in the Glenders' calls of, "Good night," though, and the king never hesitated as he strode out of the room. Only Prince Gartnait paused to recognize the young duke had spoken, and that took the form of an icy glare.

"Gentlemen of Wollaire," called Caelwin Cyniod, when the monarch was out of sight. "Please be seated while the people of Glender leave the room. Then we shall see you to your quarters."

The dukes somewhat reluctantly sat, and the lords and ladies exited, still staring all the while at the foreigners as if they were odd beasts on exhibit in a menagerie. Finally, the minister gestured to the guards, and half of them went to the doors. "Follow these soldiers, please," said Cyniod. "They will take you below."

The hostages rose and followed the guards down the spiral stairs they had ascended earlier, then down another set directly below the first. They emerged at the bottom in what obviously served primarily as a storeroom. The space was lit only by two bowls of oil that burned with thick, black smoke rising from the wicks that floated in them. The light revealed a low chamber with piers of stacked and fitted stone supporting heavy oaken beams across the ceiling. Boxes and crates filled one side of the chamber as if they had been pressed together hastily to make room for the meager cots that sat in two lines of ten on the opposite wall.

The dukes of Wollaire stood motionless for a moment as they took in the bleak picture, then Cyniod spoke from behind them. "Make yourselves at home, my lords. Be sure to find a spot in which you will be comfortable. This may be your home for a while. Good night."

No one answered the minister, and they heard his footsteps echo up the stone stairs and away.

"Well," said Showann, "if this is not a dungeon, it will certainly do until a real one comes along."

"Wollaire pig," said a guard. "We have worse if you misbehave."

"We have no intention of causing you trouble," said Robear. "Come, my lords."

He led the dukes toward the cots and the guards retired upstairs, except for four who seated themselves by the stairway. Endrew chose a cot at one end of the far row, with Robear on one side of him and a wall on the other. Each of the dukes placed their meager bundles beneath their cots and most of them sat in silence, considering no doubt the contrasts between their own chambers in their respective provinces and this dank, new one.

"Well," said Jonale at last, "this is the first time we have had alone together since the inn at Kauley two nights past."

"Even then we were not actually alone," protested Showann. "That flick-tongued serpent Foshay watched us every minute."

"Then we must have much to discuss," said Robear.

"What say you all to this question of spokesman?"

"Is one truly needed?" asked Endrew.

"Definitely," said another lord. "King Alrick will not want to speak with all of us at once."

"Who says he shall wish to speak with us at all?" asked Showann.

"He will," said Jonale.

"Not if that son of his has a say in it," said another duke.

"Who objects to Endrew acting as spokesman?" asked Robear.

"Is it seemly," asked a duke, "for the youngest member of our number to take such a vital role?"

"Do you doubt he can perform well in this capacity?" asked Jonale.

"Not in the least," answered the duke. "I merely questioned whether the Glender king would be insulted by our choice."

"You saw the king tonight," said Robear. "He did not seem the least put out."

"Any other objections?" asked Jonale. He looked around the room, pausing to stare a moment into Showann's eyes. The duke of Alpenne hesitated, then looked down. No one spoke.

"Very well, then," said Jonale. "It is settled."

"I am honored by your confidence in me," said Endrew, bowing his head.

"See that you justify it," said Showann.

The dukes talked of a wide variety of other matters about which they could do nothing and debated their differing opinions as to the likely length of their captivity. Eventually, the day's journey caught up with them, and loud yawns began to echo off the clammy walls. When enough such noises accumulated, each lord lay back beneath his single blanket and slept.

They were awakened in the morning by a group of kitchen workers bringing in a kettle of porridge. The servants distributed bowls to each duke, and the lords of Wollaire made the best of an unpleasant meal. A similar kettle filled with stewed fish and vegetables was brought in at midday, and only the arrival of a third kettle told them when evening had come, for the room had no windows.

Endrew asked the guards when they would be taken up, but the soldiers only answered, "We have our orders."

Several days crawled by in this manner, and the passage of time was marked only by the coming and going of food and the common slop bucket. The guards always answered the dukes' protests with the same response. "We have our orders."

After a heated debate regarding how many days had passed, wherein two of the dukes had to be kept from trading blows, one of the lords began scratching marks on the wall. Endrew pressed their collective complaints on the guards, but still the answer remained the same. "We have our orders."

On what they generally believed to be the eighth day, most of the dukes lay back on their cots thinking unspoken thoughts that no doubt centered on the twin themes of tunnels and daylight. Such a combination seemed logical in every mind, though each would have thought the pairing unlikely a scant month before. Then the sound of footsteps on the spiral steps brought every lord to attention. The next meal was not due for some time.

A guard appeared at the foot of the stairway and said loudly, "I am to bring the young duke of Chaussey to King Alrick."

Endrew rose, and immediately every tongue roared a dozen requests to be taken to the king. Every hand grasped Endrew's as he walked toward the soldier.

He followed the man upstairs and found himself squinting in the brighter light that streaked in through the keep's narrow windows. The guard led Endrew to the floor above the banquet hall, took him down a passage with its walls painted a vivid scarlet, then pushed open a door and stood aside.

"Ah, there you are," came King Alrick's voice. The monarch sat in a chair before a roaring fireplace. "Come in, come in."

Endrew tugged at his cloak to straighten it and entered, aware of how disheveled he must look. "Your majesty, I must apologize for my appearance—"

"Appearance be hanged. These are difficult times for us all." He gestured to a second chair like his own. "Come join me here."

Endrew drew himself as straight as he was able and made not the slightest move toward the offered seat. "Majesty, I do not wish to seem impolite, but I must register the strongest protest."

The king's face clouded with confusion. "Protest? Well, why wait so long with your complaint? I have not seen you since the night you and your countrymen arrived."

"It is that of which I speak. You have held us prisoner in the storage room of this fortress. This moment is the first that any one of us has seen the light of day since that time."

"Impossible. I gave orders."

"Begging your pardon, highness, but should that be true, it would appear your orders have not been obeyed. I doubt you are frequently in the habit of being thus ignored."

"Certainly not," said the king, leaning forward in his chair. He turned and stared into the flames for several moments, then looked back at Endrew. "You must understand, young lord, that my war with your land is a matter of property and legal claim. I bear no personal animosity to you or any other man of Wollaire."

Endrew remained silent, though he supposed such a thing was possible.

"There are others, though," continued the king, nodding to himself as he spoke, "who fought on your soil and saw comrades fall in battle beside them. Their views of you and your people are colored by that experience."

Endrew found his words creeping out so softly that he feared the king might miss them. "I also know what it is to feel the loss of battle."

The king turned again to gaze into the flames. "Prince Gartnait has the impatience and intolerance of youth," he said, then he moved his head to look back at Endrew. "Most youth, anyway."

"If you say the order for our confinement was not yours, my lord, then I can but believe you."

The king nodded silently. "Good," he said at last. "The time you are to spend here may be substantial. We may as well arrange it in such a way that neither party shall suffer unduly by your presence. Now, come, sit beside me that we may hammer out the specifics of your party's movements."

"Thank you, highness," said Endrew as he sat. "We lords of Wollaire shall cooperate fully. You have my word on it."

Again the king nodded. "And I suspect your word is one that I may trust fully." He stared at Endrew for several moments, some secret thought hovering unspoken just behind his lips. "Your parents must have been very proud of you, young duke."

"I hope so," said Endrew, "though my mother died of a fever when I was but a boy of ten."

"My wife died much the same way six years ago. And your father?"

"He died in battle, defending his homeland against invaders."

The king paused. "In the vale?"

Endrew nodded.

"You mask your hatred for me well."

"I do not hate you, highness. I save such feelings for myself."

"Yourself?"

"I guarded our army's path of retreat, a position of some importance as it turned out but one designed for a young lord of unproven worth in battle. Had I but ridden at my father's side, I might have saved his life or at the very least died with him as your son's army drove over his position."

The king shook his head. "Nothing you could have done would have changed the outcome of that battle, and Wollaire will need such men as you in the years ahead. Someday, when this matter is resolved, there will be peace between our lands. You may not believe that now, but it is always thus when battle is done. I hope then to call you friend and ally."

Endrew bowed slightly. "As you will, highness."

"Polite," said King Alrick, "but without much

conviction. Well, I suppose there is no great surprise in that, under the circumstances. But, come, let us attend to this more immediate matter of getting your companions some fresh air."

"Perhaps from such small things may greater understandings be built."

7

The dukes of Wollaire voiced their gratitude for Endrew's negotiation of their relative freedom, but only in passing as they sped by him on the way to a guard-escorted trip to the fresh air of the keep's tallest battlement. If the young duke hadn't quickly stepped to one side, they might have carried him with them without his feet once touching the floor en route. Instead, Endrew let them pass, then shook his head and smiled at their haste before following them.

"My lords," he said, when they had finally all breathed in the clean scent of the evening breeze as the sun made its way down close to the Glender hills. "There are terms we must observe if we are to continue enjoying such latitude of movement."

"What matter the terms?" asked Jonale, still puffing from his rapid trip up so many stairs.

"Indeed," agreed Robear, "so long as we are allowed out of that cellar."

"But there are limitations," said Endrew. "We must follow King Alrick's directions to the letter or these privileges will be revoked."

"State them, then," said Showann.

"The rules he set for us are few and simple," said Endrew. "We are hereby freed of the chamber that has held us these many days. We shall still go there to sleep, but are not otherwise required to spend even the slightest moment there."

"Nor shall I do so," said a duke, and the others laughed at the enthusiasm of his vow.

"We are allowed free passage throughout the keep without escort, so long as we do not travel in large groups," continued Endrew. "We are barred in these wanderings only from such chambers as are guarded against our entry."

"The treasury," offered Robear.

"The king's bedchamber," said Jonale.

"Or that of the princess," added Showann, bringing another laugh from the dukes.

"May we leave the keep?" asked another duke.

"Yes," said Endrew, "but only with the escort of one king's guard for every duke. We may freely explore the city as we wish, but only within its walls. Even as we speak, the guards are all being notified that we are not to pass beyond any of the town gates."

"Alrick fears we will escape," said Jonale.

"And we shall," said Showann, "at the first opportunity."

"No," said Endrew, "we must attempt no such thing."

"But, Endrew," interrupted Robear, "surely we must try to find our way back to Wollaire to help lead our army against this foe."

The young duke looked at the older men and shook his head. "We cannot all escape, there is no way we could manage it."

"Not all, but if only one..."

"No," said Endrew. "If even one of us leaves, privileges will be curtailed for all that remain. The hardship for those left behind might be too great for some of us to bear."

"That is their problem," said Showann.

"It is everyone's problem," said Endrew. "There

will be no escape."

"But—"

"I gave King Alrick my word."

The Duke of Alpenne leaned toward Endrew and growled, "Your promise does not hold me."

"Enough," said Robear. "Let us hear no more of it. Endrew has done well and we should praise him for what he has accomplished rather than waste our time in wishing for more."

"I agree," said Jonale. "Our lord of Chaussey has brought us again into the open air. Is that not enough for now?"

The dukes nodded their agreement and finally Showann muttered, "For now."

"But, Endrew," said Robear of Tushan, "how did you manage such freedoms for us after so many days of imprisonment."

"I told you the lad was persuasive," said Jonale.

"Not in the least," said Endrew.

"Then how—"

"King Alrick was surprised to find we had been held in that cellar chamber all this time. He had not intended any such limitation on us."

"Pah," said Showann, "there sits the boldest lie of this day, and the sun is nearly down. Will another have time to challenge it?"

"I have spoken with him and I believe him," said Endrew.

"You are a boy," said Showann, "and easily led."

Endrew half opened his mouth in reply, then set his jaw and remained silent.

"If we were not held by the king's order," said Robear, "then whose?"

"I cannot be sure, but I think Prince Gartnait

may have been responsible."

"It makes sense," said Jonale. "Who else would have the power to command the guards?"

"He would not dare countermand his father's order," said Robear.

"Perhaps not," said Jonale, "but he might have subverted it. He could have told the commanders of the guards that the king had changed his mind. Who would have doubted him?"

"That is what I thought," said Endrew. "I do not believe King Alrick would have treated us so badly."

"He is a Glender," said Showann.

"But not a cruel one," said Endrew. "Regardless of his claims against Pollay province, he is not an evil man."

The lords of Wollaire stood in silent regard for long moments, then Robear said, "I urge you to caution, young friend. Such words of one's enemy might spell treason in many minds."

"Not 'might'," said Showann, "'do',"

"Is it treason to speak the truth?" asked Endrew. "Is it treason to say that one man may disagree with another without either of them being evil men? Is there any one of you who has not pressed some claim against a neighbor? A border here, a toll there? Why, some of you have forced our good King Giarley to mediate disputes before you came to blows."

"Such things happen between lords," said a duke.

"Of course," said Endrew, "but in any of these disputes, was there a one of you who adjudged himself an evil man?"

"Of course not," said Jonale.

"Thus no more need Alrick of Glender be an evil man," said Endrew, "though he be our enemy as sure as anything is certain."

Again the dukes stood in silence, then Jonale smiled and said, "I must admit it, Duke Endrew, you have a way of stating things. If this be treason, I have never heard treason stated so patriotically."

Showann snorted. "Or patriotism so treasonously."

"Either way," said Robear, "Endrew has shown great wisdom in dealing with the Glender king. He has explained his beliefs and statements and should be commended for his accomplishments and insights."

"I agree," said Jonale, "Come, let us return below and find something that resembles a decent meal."

"In Glender?" asked one of the dukes.

"Anything will be better than what they have brought to the cellar these past days," said Robear.

The lords made their way downstairs, but many of them found their way back to the battlement after eating. Unseen clouds blotted out the stars in parts of the sky, and the wind picked up as the evening wore on. One by one, the dukes reacted to the growing cold and returned below, until finally only Endrew remained on the roof walk, staring out into the blackness.

He stood for a long time, trying to see what lay beyond the pale light of the city's many lamps and torches that flickered below him in their feeble efforts to push back the night. The chill finally overcame him, but reluctant to go below, he pulled his cloak tighter and sat with his back against the stone wall, crouching down so as to be out of the wind. He closed his eyes to find complete blackness, then pictured his father's face. At that moment he was truly alone for the first time since arriving in Glender, and he found the sensation troubling.

The sound of footsteps made him snap his head in the direction of the noise, his ears mindful to every nuance of the tread. The steps halted at the top of the stairs, then slowly approached. Still, he said nothing and he held his breath as the steps again paused, this time no more than six or seven paces to his right.

Against the faint glow of the city's lights he saw the slight figure of a woman, her head hooded against the wind and her face for the most part obscured. At first she made neither sound nor movement, then she brought her hands to her chest and spoke in a tongue that Endrew did not know. Her words continued, soft but carefully articulated, for many minutes. Then, as quickly and quietly as she had come, the woman turned toward the stairs and went below, her steps echoing on the stones for long moments.

Endrew spent a great deal of time wondering about the woman over the next few days. Who had she been and what had the odd words she spoke meant? Gradually, though, his interests passed to other matters as he explored the city of Talorcan, wandering its markets without money and charting its twisting streets in his mind.

He saw King Alrick often, sometimes passing in the halls of the keep and occasionally spending a few minutes before the royal fireplace. Mostly they spent their time haggling over complaints and petitions from one or the other of the lords of Wollaire, but they always managed to include at least a few moments of mutual inquiry as to their respective healths and states of mind.

He saw Prince Gartnait nearly as often, but no word ever passed between them. Endrew always bowed to the prince, but the royal heir never returned anything more than an icy glare or the slightest curled lip.

Princess Briduen remained out of sight for the most part, though several times Endrew caught sight of the girl as she ducked back behind a door or into a chamber at his approach. He didn't know whether she hid out of shyness or a fear of foreigners. After a while, he ceased to care.

At last, the dukes of Wollaire noted a frenzy of movement among the soldiers of Glender that told them the day they had most dreaded now approached. The weather had warmed enough for the armies to again take the field, and Prince Gartnait pressed his troops hard to make them ready for the campaign. Finally, great caravans of wagons were assembled outside the city walls, and wave after wave of soldiers arrived to camp and wait. Finally, the prince judged they were ready, and one bright morning found him leading the host toward the port of Cinioch to once more journey across the sea and press Glender's claim on Pollay province.

King Alrick and Princess Briduen stood atop the battlement and waved as the great force made its way across the bridge and into the forest that blocked the road from sight. Endrew stood beside Robear and Jonale, the three of them watching the same procession with entirely different feelings and keeping their distance from the royal family.

"Well, there he goes then," said Alrick, as the two crowns of Glender that led the host disappeared from sight. "Are you coming?"

"I should like to watch a bit longer," answered the princess.

"As you wish," said the king. He turned to go below, and just for a moment his eyes met Endrew's. Each of them recognized in that glance the gap of unvoiced enmity that still remained between them, then Alrick looked away and went down the stairs.

Endrew looked back out over the long line of men and material traveling to his own land. As he had expected, his heart yearned to be a part of the procession, or at least to share in its travel and destination. He looked at the faces of his two companions and saw his own longing mirrored in their eyes.

He looked again to the army of Glender, then caught a movement from the corner of his eye. The princess had turned and was walking toward the stairs. Without realizing it, he found himself marking her progress, watching her go and listening to her steps. Then it came to him; she was the same woman who had stood atop the battlement in the dark night of their first freedom. His eyes and ears followed her as she descended the stairs, and he wondered again what the words were that she had spoken.

"Hrmph," said Jonale, from behind him, "young men are always the same."

"Indeed," agreed Robear. "Show a young duke a pretty face and watch him concentrate on nothing else."

Their words cut through Endrew's reverie, and he turned with an expression protesting his innocence. "No, I was merely watching her leave."

"He was watching her leave," said Robear, in an even voice.

"We noticed that," said Jonale. "There is no harm in a young man looking at a pretty girl."

"Even if she is a Glender, and the daughter of our greatest enemy, at that."

"Yes, I suppose you are right there," said Jonale. "In that regard there may be harm in our young friend here getting involved with a maid."

"It may be too late," said Robear, with a smile designed to show he was teasing, but the expression escaped Endrew's notice.

"I am not taken with her," he protested. "I merely marked her exit."

"As you said before," said Jonale.

"Did you not hear her footsteps?"

"No," said Robear, "I cannot say that they caught my attention."

"Nor mine," added Jonale. "Only yours."

"She means nothing to me," said Endrew. "We have never even spoken to each other. In all this time I have barely seen her face."

"But she is a fair child," said Robear.

"With lands and titles of her own," said Jonale.

"You are both mad," he protested. "Her nose is too sharp and her eyes are a trifle close together."

"He has never studied her face," Jonale said to Robear in mock seriousness.

"Though he appears to know it well."

Endrew lacked further words to argue, and he turned and strode toward the stairs.

"Oh, yes," came Jonale's voice from behind. "He has no chance at all now."

"Done," agreed Robear. "Absolutely."

During the next days, Endrew kept to himself to avoid the abuse of the other lords. Robear and Jonale found great pleasure in tweaking the younger man's every word and twisting every comment into some reference to Princess Briduen. Finally, Endrew had reached his limit, and when the two dukes passed him in a hallway with a polite inquiry of, "Any luck?" he boiled over.

"That will do," he snapped. "These comments are unfounded and most unseemly."

Robear clapped a hand on Endrew's shoulder, but the younger man pulled away.

"We mean you no ill," said Jonale. "We seek only diversion."

"Diversion is improper at this time," insisted Endrew. "The army of Glender must by now be again on Wollaire's soil."

"All the more reason," said Robear. "If we dwell too much on that over which we have no control, we shall all go mad."

Jonale nodded. "Levity may be the only thing to save us."

"I suppose," said Endrew, "but must it be at my expense?"

"You are more serious than we," said Jonale.

"You are more serious than anyone we know," added Robear. "Who better should we tease?"

"Showann has a glum view of the world," reminded Jonale.

"Yes, but he would likely answer with a murder rather than a harsh word," said Robear.

"There is that," said Jonale.

The sound of running steps caused the three men to stop their conversation. A trio of soldiers hurried down the corridor and past where the men of Wollaire stood without uttering a word. Moments later, a larger group of soldiers hurried past in the opposite direction, part of them going upstairs and part down.

"What do you suppose it is?" asked Robear.

A pair of guards ran toward them from behind and lowered their spears. "You three," commanded one of them, "down to the cellar with you, at once."

"What is it?" asked Endrew.

"Go," shouted the soldier, prodding them toward the stairs with his spear. "Go now, or die."

The three dukes did as they were ordered and descended to the cellar room where many of the dukes already waited. A large group of guards stood at the foot of the stairs, growing larger with each soldier who escorted a duke of Wollaire to this chamber.

"We have done nothing wrong. Why have you brought us here again?" one of the dukes called above the murmured questions and complaints of the others. No one answered his or any other inquiry.

Endrew craned his neck to look over the crowd of his countrymen and he counted heads. Seventeen, eighteen, nineteen– Only nineteen lords stood together, someone was missing. Who?

Before he could look again to identify each face, the loud voice of Caelwin Cyniod spoke from the foot of the stairs. "You lords of Wollaire have broken the terms of your freedom."

"We have not," insisted the dukes with one voice.

"I fear we have," said Endrew. "Only nineteen of us stand here."

The other lords began to count, but Endrew suddenly realized whose face was absent. "Showann of Alpenne," he said aloud.

"He took his escort soldier drinking last night, then lured him into an alley where he killed the man," said the minister. "We are not sure what happened next, but we suspect he may have taken the guard's uniform and fled, possibly by the river."

"Lord minister," said Endrew, "you must believe me when I say none of us knew of his plans."

"If ignorance is your best excuse," said Cyniod, "you had best pause a moment and think of another. At any rate, my lords, you shall have ample time to fabricate whatever tales you wish. You are once again confined to this chamber, at least until we find Duke Showann and return him here with you."

The men of Wollaire muttered their anger and disappointment as the minister turned and left. One by one they sat on their cots and fumed.

"Leave it to Showann to spoil things for all of us," said Robear.

"We should have tied him to these columns," said another lord.

"Or clapped him in their deepest cell," offered another.

"It is done and cannot now be altered," said Endrew. "What we must do next is work to rebuild the trust these Glenders had in the rest of us."

"Duke Endrew of Chaussey," came a loud voice from the stairs.

"Here."

"You are to come with us," said a soldier.

Endrew stepped toward the guards, but Robear rose in protest.

"Where are you taking him? What do you mean to do with him?"

"It is none of your concern."

"It certainly is," said Jonale. "Do you mean to punish him for the misdeeds of another?"

One by one the lords of Wollaire rose and shouted their objections in a noisy clamor. Endrew feared their anger and mistrust were so great they might rush the guards. There were enough of them that they might prevail for a moment, but the soldiers' spears would quickly cut the ranks of his friends in half.

"Be still, my lords," said Endrew, and the dukes slowly grew silent. "I am certain that King Alrick means me no harm." He turned to the soldiers. "You shall have no trouble with me or with any one of us," he said. Then he turned back to his fellows. "Look well to yourselves. I shall rejoin you shortly."

He fell in behind a pair of soldiers and four others followed him. The rest stood at the foot of the stairs, their spears lowered and pointing at the remaining dukes. He climbed up the spiral steps to the main floor, then one of the guards waved him out into the courtyard.

"Climb into the saddle," ordered King Alrick from atop his own horse.

Endrew looked puzzled. "What–"

"We mean to catch that damn fool before he suffers from his ill-thought deed," said the king. "Your presence may persuade him that we mean well."

Endrew put one foot in a stirrup and swung himself onto the horse's back. "Ill-thought deed?"

"There is no time to discuss it," said Alrick. "Come."

With that, he spurred his horse and rode out the gates of the citadel and the city wall. Endrew followed as closely as he could, with four mounted soldiers behind. He noted that the accompanying guards wore grim expressions and each of them was armed as if only he alone stood in the path of invasion. Even King Alrick wore a huge sword at his side. Endrew immediately saw that only he among this company rode forth unarmed.

8

The king tugged hard at his horse's reins just before reaching the bridge, and turned the mount along a trail that paralleled the city walls. Alrick rode through a collection of mud and stick huts, then followed the river to the north as it tumbled over rocks on its way to the sea. Endrew kicked his horse so as to stay close to the king and he heard the soldiers behind him doing the same.

Alrick drove the little band hard for as long as the horses were able, then he slowed the pace to allow the animals some rest. Endrew took this calmer moment to drink in the feeling of openness that made him want to shout with joy after so many weeks of confinement. Then a glance behind him showed the still-grim faces of the four guards. Their expressions sat in vivid contrast to the blossoms that made the trees glow with color and the exquisite blue of a perfect spring sky. Endrew urged his horse forward and hailed the king.

"Keep an eye out for your friend," ordered the monarch, when the younger man came alongside. "With luck he may yet be close to the city, waiting for us to pass so he may escape at his leisure."

"If I were the one in flight," said Endrew, "I should put as much space as possible between myself and the castle."

"And quickly, too, I warrant."

"Yes."

The king looked at Endrew and nodded, his features fixed in a grimace. "So would I."

"Highness," said Endrew, "what danger causes you and your men to seem so fixed with dread?"

"You do not know the lay of our land," said Alrick, "nor, I suspect, does your Duke Showann."

"No, I imagine not."

"Did it not strike you as odd that we brought you to our kingdom through the port of Cinioch, then by land across a range of wooded hills to my city of Talorcan? Why, do you suppose, would our people build our capital on a river and not use that river as a means of transport or at least build a more convenient port at its mouth?"

"I must confess, majesty, that the thought had not occurred to me."

"Nor, you may be certain, has it occurred to Showann. The truth is we cannot build a port at the mouth of this river."

"And why not?"

"The river flows swiftly by my capital, but the valley widens out downstream, and by the time the waters reach the great sea they barely creep through a swamp; a swamp so vast that it is itself a swirling sea of muck, weeds, and sucking death in bottomless deposits of mud. Small channels and sloughs drain the water from the land but not even one of them is deep or wide enough to allow passage or anchorage for a ship."

"And you think Showann will enter the swamp?"

"Almost inevitably. We know from our guards that no horse left the city gates last night. His next swiftest means of escape would be to hurl himself into the current with a goatskin or some such item for flotation. If he stays in the water, he will travel rapidly for a time, then find himself in the swamp before he recognizes what has happened."

"Will the current not slow before then? Perhaps he will abandon the river if he sees his progress coming to a halt"

"That is our best hope to reach him: that his desire to escape does not overbear his good senses"

Endrew thought on that remark in silence. He had known Showann of Alpenne only passing well before this enterprise began, but since then he had seen little evidence that the duke possessed a great deal of good sense even under the best of circumstances.

"You should have brought more men," said Endrew, "and sent out other search parties."

"The sight and sound of more men would only drive Showann further into hiding. Besides, they cannot be spared," said the king. "Most of my soldiers are abroad. The balance are needed to defend the castle if we are attacked."

"Who would attack you?"

The king shot a look of weary indulgence at the younger man, and Endrew instantly flushed with a sudden feeling of public stupidity. It had not occurred to any leader of Wollaire to cross the sea and besiege the Glender capital last year, but now that things were more desperate, anything was possible.

"I am sorry, your highness. It was a foolish question."

The king sighed. "Forget it, my boy. Wars seem far away when you are not in them. Besides, such undertakings as this one place burdens on us all. I am bound to forget something obvious at any moment, myself."

"Nevertheless, sire, please accept my apology."

"It is well offered," said the monarch, "and as well accepted."

The six men rode in silence throughout the balance of the afternoon. Then as the shadows began to lengthen on the ground, Endrew noticed the river's character change. Rocks no longer dotted its path and the current made no rippling bubbles as it passed objects in its way. The valley floor had indeed flattened out, and before much longer even the sound of the horse's hoofbeats were muffled by the increasingly soft and moist earth.

"Are we near the swamp?"

"Closer," answered the king, "though we shall not enter it tonight." He pulled at his reins and lowered himself to the ground. "This looks like as good a place to camp as any," he said to the soldiers, and they too climbed down out of the saddle.

"But, highness, we have an hour or more of light yet available."

"And that hour would put us firmly within the swamp's borders. It is not the most pleasant place to spend the night."

Endrew heard one of the soldiers mutter, "Or the safest," as he dropped to the ground.

The guards gathered wood and built a trio of small fires so all six men might draw close to the flames and be warm. They ate a spare meal as darkness came on, then the king tossed Endrew a pair of blankets and bid everyone retire for the evening against an early start at first light. One of the soldiers clambered to his feet and drew his sword. Then the guard began to slowly circle the campsite's fires.

"What do they fear?" asked Endrew as he lay

back.

"Eh?"

"Your men. Their hands never stray from their sword hilts. What do they fear?"

"Stories," came the king's voice from across the flames. "Likely nothing more than that."

Endrew remained silent, but he found no comfort in the king's words. He had seen such expressions on men's faces before. The fear in his own men's eyes as they overlooked the army of Glender had been much like this, but different somehow; the expressions of these men were even more wildly apprehensive. These four were the best soldiers Alrick had available, and something had them terrified. He took one last, careful look into the all-obscuring darkness and tried to sleep.

The young duke started when he felt something touch his shoulders and his hand shot to his waist where a sword should have hung. His fingers gripped nothing though, and he jerked his head around to see King Alrick's face hovering over his.

"Time to wake," said the monarch, barely visible in the pale light that comes just before dawn. "We must eat and be off as soon as possible."

"Showann has a great lead and would have rested little during the night," he said as he sat up. "Is it possible to catch him?"

The king stared into the wisps of mist that hovered over the sluggish waters ahead. "Possible," he said, "though I fear unlikely."

Endrew rose and walked to a clump of brush near the water's edge to relieve himself. He was just about to turn back when a faint splash caught his attention. He stepped through the brush to the riverbank and peered into the still dim flow. The water swirled in an eddy, but he saw nothing. He held his breath, listening, but no other sound reached his ears until the king shouted for him.

He walked back to where the others waited and took a few bites of the food they offered. He considered mentioning what he had heard– and failed to see– in the water, but thought better of it. It was undoubtedly only some small river creature, an otter or something of the like, and these men were nervous enough as it was. He saw nothing to be gained in making them more so.

They mounted their horses and rode onward. By midmorning the ground had grown even softer and great clumps of moss hung from the limbs overhead. By the time they stopped for a meal, their feet and the horses' hooves made squishing sounds when lifted from the ground and the trees were so laden with moss that they seemed to sag under the weight. Insects buzzed around their heads and the croaking of unseen frogs threatened to drown out every other sound. The river had divided many times by then, and the party kept to the west bank of what was now a sluggish backwater.

"This is a most dismal fen," said Endrew, stretching his back to ease the muscles tightened by the ride. He looked up, trying to spot the sun through the trees which spread their frowning branches overhead.

"It is said to be even worse in the center of the delta," said the king. "Have you no such place as this in Wollaire?"

"Not the like of this. At least, not that I know of."

"If you had it, you would know."

Endrew turned to watch the soldiers as they fanned out on foot, peering under shrubs and fallen logs and poking their swords into any place that might hide a man. "I despair at finding Showann," he said. "Your swamp is vast, and we are but six."

"We are all–"

A cry cut off the king's voice. Endrew snapped his head in the direction of the call but was too late to see anything except a swirl of water near the point where one of the men had stood on the bank. They all rushed to the spot, weapons drawn except for Endrew whose hand again fidgeted helplessly at his side.

"Did you see anything?" the king shouted at the soldiers.

"Nothing," said one man, and the other two shook their heads to indicate the same.

"I saw something," said Endrew.

"What?" asked Alrick.

"Not now, this morning. When I stood by the riverbank, I heard a splash and looked down to see the water swirling as this does now."

"The cadwegan," mumbled one of the soldiers. "Or worse."

"The what?"

"Nothing," said the king. "Pay it no mind." With that he turned and led the band back to where their horses waited.

"But the soldier," protested Endrew.

"He cannot be helped now," said Alrick. "The rest of you, keep your vision sharp."

The five mounted up and rode onward with two soldiers in the lead, followed by the king, Endrew, and finally the third soldier. This last man led the now extra horse.

"If there is danger, I should be armed," said Endrew as they rode.

"You have nothing to fear," the king said back over his shoulder. "Now save your breath, unless you feel like calling out to your countryman."

They rode onward for another hour or more. Endrew peered into the gloomy depths of the sodden forest on his left, trying to find Showann's familiar face in a thousand hiding places. He gave up after a time and turned to look out over the marshes that grew off into the distance beyond the nearest arm of the river, now that it had divided and redivided unknown times.

"It would only be by chance that we were even on the same side as he," Endrew called to the king.

"I agree," said Alrick.

"But we go on?"

"We do."

Endrew shook his head, then allowed himself a half smile. "I can see how you hold a kingdom together. You are as stubborn as–"

His words faded as he looked back to his left and saw a pair of riderless horses sauntering off at an angle to the procession. Endrew whirled and looked for the soldier who had been behind him. "Highness," he shouted.

Alrick and the guards who rode in the fore pulled their horses to a halt. "When?" asked the king.

Endrew shook his head. "I do not know. I heard nothing."

"Cadwegan," said a soldier. "It can be nothing else."

"In the trees, perhaps, this time," said the other guard.

"Impossible," said the first. "They are too big."

"I have a right to know of what these men speak," protested Endrew.

Then the ground before the band seemed to explode as a huge figure rose up from the reeds and brambles, roaring its fierce challenge. Its two great hands that hung at the end of improbably thin arms pulled the guards from their saddles. Its long and curving head ended in a giant maw that bristled with teeth the size of daggers. In the split second it hovered there, the king's horse bolted in terror, carrying the monarch into the forest depths.

Endrew's own horse reared and bucked, throwing him to the ground, then galloped off in a blind frenzy. He landed in a heap on the soft earth, then looked up to where the unimaginable figure loomed overhead, holding the still-screaming men in its hands as water coursed down the beast's pale, leathery body. Endrew spotted the sword dropped by one of the flailing guards and rushed to grab it. The cadwegan, if such it truly was, looked down with tiny eyes and marked his movement. In an instant it squeezed the life from the soldiers and tossed them aside.

Endrew backed away, holding the sword high as he retreated, hoping to find some firm footing to meet the charge he knew was coming. The creature moved on legs back-jointed like a bird's and seemed to half crouch with every step of its rolling, coiled gait. The beast seemed half folded into itself with its long, pipestem arms swinging from its sides and the sharp-clawed hands nearly touching the ground. Time after time it opened its gigantic mouth to roar another warning to the puny creature that refused to run.

Then the great beast lunged forward, perhaps hoping to catch Endrew with one swipe of a great hand, but Endrew saw the move coming and leapt back at the right moment, swinging the blade at the hand as it went by. He missed, but the creature took notice and paused. It roared again, showing every one of its teeth, then it rose to its full height, nearly three times Endrew's own.

"Come on, then," said the duke, "but be quick about it." If he must die, he thought, he preferred death to arrive in one swift rush.

The beast complied and surged forward, its lanky form moving in a near waddle but covering ground faster than its ambling gait implied. The great creature provided more targets and less vital spots than Endrew could have imagined possible. He ducked a swipe of a clawed hand and aimed at the creature's midsection. It roared in pain, but shot its head down and snapped its jaws together. Endrew rolled to one side and sprang to his feet. Now covered in mud, he circled as he and the cadwegan looked into each other's eyes.

The creature swiped at him again, with its left this time, and Endrew caught the hand with his blade as it went by. The gigantic thing screamed, then suddenly its other hand shot forward and caught the duke in a huge paw that engulfed his chest. Like lightning, he found himself lifted halfway to the sky in a grip that seemed to force all the air from his body. The huge beast roared in triumph and held Endrew aloft for a moment, then lowered him toward the waiting jaws.

Endrew looked at those rows of teeth and lifted the sword overhead, both of his hands on the hilt with the tip pointing straight downward. He would only have one chance, if that.

His feet nearly touched the dagger teeth when he drove the blade down with all the power in him. He feared he might miss by a fraction of an inch and see the sword glance off the creature's skull, but his aim proved true. The blade entered the great head, dead between its eyes, and Endrew fell to the ground as the cadwegan toppled over. Endrew clambered free of the creature's grip and watched as the beast twitched once, twice, then lay still.

He paused to breathe deeply, then realized how much it hurt to do so. His ribs had been broken in the creature's powerful grasp, cracked at the very least. He pressed at his chest with the heel of each hand, probing for the most tender spots, but found them too numerous to count. He warily stepped closer to the fallen form, gave it a kick to be sure, then put both hands on the hilt of the sword and pulled.

His ribs screamed at him, but he managed to draw the guard's blade from the cadwegan's skull. He backed away, the sword dragging across the damp earth, and stood panting in pain, exhaustion, and a growing sense of panic. He was alone, horseless, in a foreign swamp filled with creatures beyond the worst nightmare. For a moment his mind nearly snapped, then the roaring challenge of another cadwegan brought him to his senses.

He whirled to see a second creature approaching from across the shallow slough they had been following. Endrew raised the blade and backed up, easing his way toward the cover of the forest. The great beast stepped from the stream, water dripping from its body, and tossed aside the hindquarters of what looked like one of the party's horses, perhaps even his own. The creature eyed Endrew for a moment, then turned its attention to the still body of the lifeless monster that lay in an awkward heap beside the river.

Endrew continued gaining distance as he watched the great beast nudge its lifeless fellow, then toss its head as if sniffing the still air for some remaining sign of life. "A mate," Endrew muttered to himself, and he turned to use the creature's hesitation for his escape. The forest offered many paths, but he chose only one.

The king had ridden into the wood, clinging to his mount for all he was worth. Endrew was no tracker, but the fleeing horse had left a trail even he could follow. The crushed undergrowth showed the horse's straight-line flight of panic. Broken branches, snapped clean above head height and fallen yards ahead, told him what kind of ride the king had endured.

He followed the trail, always expecting one of the creatures to appear and snuff out his life at any moment. None came, though, and he walked for nearly half an hour, scrambling over downed logs and obstacles the fleeing horse must have flown over. Then, as he paused to listen again for the approach of imminent threat, he heard a hum from the recesses of the forest on his left.

Endrew raised the sword and froze, listening to the sound. The hum continued, and thoughts of giant insects momentarily flashed through his mind. On more careful hearing it sounded like the gathered voices of a chorus, though, and for a second he hesitated. He glanced ahead to where the horse's path continued, then once again to the side from whence the sound emanated.

He drew in another painful breath and walked toward the hum, stepping carefully so as not to alarm whoever or whatever lay ahead. The ground gave beneath his feet with every tread, but he eased forward, gradually becoming aware of a growing light. A clearing, perhaps, or did something glow with magic? He paused a moment, suddenly aware that his entire body tingled, and listened. Nothing but absolute silence now greeted his ears.

Endrew walked toward the light and felt the ground slope up ever so slightly. The soil seemed more solid beneath his feet with every step, as he cautiously eased his way through the forest. Then he froze at the sight that rose before him.

A circle of great stone spires grew out of the ground like the fingers of some huge hand. Each monolith loomed thicker than a man could reach around and half again Endrew's height. Within the circle of stones lay a clean carpet of perfect moss, twenty feet or more from side to side, unmarked even by a single leaf or fallen twig. In the center of the enclosure King Alrick lay on his back, whether dead or asleep, Endrew could not tell.

"Highness," he said, and he burst into the circle. He crouched beside the fallen monarch and studied him. His tunic was torn, nearly shredded by his wild ride through the forest, but his face and arms bore no marks. No, the king himself seemed unharmed; not even the slightest scratch marred his flesh. Endrew stared again at the tunic, then turned to look behind him, imagining the branches that must have beaten the king nearly senseless. How could this be? Something here lacked logic.

He reached out a hand to touch the king, and felt an almost palpable vibration from the supine form. Alrick's chest rose and fell in slow rhythm, but his heart beat strongly. Endrew glanced around at the circle of stones again, and wondered how the king had gotten here when the horse's runaway path had so plainly continued on.

He turned back to the king and nudged him gently. "Your majesty," he said, "wake." The monarch failed to respond, so he shook a bit more firmly. "Highness," he said again, a bit louder this time, "wake."

The king made no response, but from all around him Endrew was answered by the humming sound. He rose to his feet and spun, holding the sword out to meet enemies yet unseen. From the damp forest floor around this glade, thin tendrils of mist reached out, creeping toward him from among the trees. Like snakes they writhed and wriggled, trying first one path and then another. Endrew whirled from side to side, but in every direction he saw the same thing.

Thin, pale arms of fog crawled over one another, crossing and coalescing, but bearing ever closer to where he stood. And hovering over everything was the persistent, almost palpable hum. It was clearly the voices of individual men, he thought, but still no figure presented itself. Then from out of the forest gloom, robed and hooded forms seemed to float toward him, scarcely stirring the growing blanket of mist as they moved forward. Their faces lost in the dark folds of their garments, they approached from every side until they stood between the stones and enclosed the circle completely. Endrew kept the sword before him and forced his body into a ready position despite the pain in his ribs. He felt a shiver of fear, though perhaps it might have been the thick, air-crackling magic he sensed that made him tremble so.

Endrew whirled, first one way and then another, but always keeping one heel in contact with the king and watching to see if these men meant them harm. "Keep back," he almost shouted. "I wish nothing from you but to take this man away."

One of the figures lifted its hands to the hood of its robe and pulled the grey-green cloth back to reveal a face made all of leaves. Endrew started as he saw the forest mirrored in that visage. His own eyes wide, he stared and it was as if a branch of oak looked back, completely treelike except for the dark eyes between the leaves.

"What are you?" asked Endrew. "What do you want with us?"

The figure made no reply, but it waved its hands and the humming from the others raised a notch in volume. The robed figure then drew its hands to its chest in a half familiar gesture and the leaf encrusted face spoke a series of unfamiliar words. "Ainmuire menn boruma," it said. "Maelgar!"

At that last word, Endrew felt the air around him crackle with magic, and he sagged to his knees. He looked up into the face one last time, searching the forest colors for those bright and human eyes, then pitched forward onto the moss.

9

Endrew heard his name spoken, then felt a faint touch on his shoulder followed by a firmer grasp and shake. He blinked his eyes, then sat bolt upright, searching for the hooded figures. His hand again shot to where his sword should wait but he found no hilt. His quick glance spotted the blade he'd claimed from the cadwegan-slain soldier waiting on the ground a half dozen safe paces away, then he turned to look into the face of King Alrick.

"Well, my boy, I see you have chosen to join me after all," said the monarch. "I had thought perhaps you intended to sleep forever."

Endrew lifted his hand to his head in an attempt to stop the drumming throb within. "At this moment, that does not seem so poor a choice."

"Aches, does it? My head felt the same when I woke. Perhaps your pain will likewise quickly pass, as mine did."

"Did they do this to you also?"

The king shook his head in obvious confusion. "They? What they? Of whom do you speak, lad?"

"The men in robes. The man with the leaf face."

King Alrick paled and he paused a mite before replying. "I saw no such men."

"Yet you know of them. I can see it in your expression."

The king rose and pulled Endrew to his feet. "They are no more than legend."

"You said the same of the cadwegan."

Alrick nodded. "Yes, I suppose I did. Oh, by the by, I must tell you how glad I am to see you safe. How did you manage to escape the creature?"

"As your horse bolted, the cadwegan lifted your men from their own saddles. I picked up that sword when it fell from the hand of one of your soldiers."

"Without armor or shield, you fought a cadwegan and survived?"

"Yes, though I fear I cracked or broke–" His words faded as he lifted a hand to his chest and realized that the pain in his ribs had eased into a now distant memory. He drew in a deep breath and probed his torso with his fingertips, standing slack-jawed at the normalcy of the feeling.

"What is it?" asked the king. "What gives you pause? Are you injured?"

"No, but I surely was. The cadwegan caught and held me in its great hand. It nearly squeezed the breath of life from me before I plunged the sword into its skull. I felt as if my chest burned deeper with every step when I followed your trail."

"Why did you do that?" asked Alrick, appraising the younger man with his eyes. "My men were dead. You could have escaped, perhaps."

"I gave my oath that–"

The king interrupted with a skeptical snort that seemed to imply such statements were unworthy of other response. "Your oath."

"Means everything to me. You are free to believe me or disbelieve me, as you choose, but your failure to believe does not alter the truth of what I say. Besides, a second cadwegan approached from the water, pausing to sniff at the body of the one I killed.

I could not leave you alone at the mercy of such a creature."

"Many men would have."

"Yet I would not."

"Even though I am your enemy?"

Endrew looked the Glender king in the eye. "I do not see why that must necessarily be so. If the times and the affairs of nations were different, who knows how we might have regarded one another?"

Alrick studied his companion in silence for a moment. "You are a strange young man, Duke Endrew."

The boy smiled. "You are not the first to make that claim, highness. My father used to say the same thing on a regular basis."

"Your father," said the king. "Your father who died by my hand, after a fashion."

Endrew turned and stared off into the dark distance, letting his gaze stray from one oddly-leaning tree to the one beyond it until the forest was no more than a blur. The memory of the Glender army rolling over the knoll his father held, the sight of the banner of Chaussey being trampled by invader hooves and boots, the sound of his own anguish screaming within his helmet; these images were still as fresh in his mind as if he experienced them only moments before.

"Yes," he said at last. "By your hand."

"You must hate me."

Endrew turned his gaze back to the monarch. "No. Of a truth, highness, I do not."

"You hate my son then."

One corner of his mouth turned up slightly. "I fear Prince Gartnait has given me little cause to celebrate his life, either in my home land or here."

The king nodded and allowed himself a slight,

disappointed sigh. "I made the boy master of the king's troops, and he does seem determined to play the role to the hilt. Oh, well," he said, clapping his hands together, "enough of such matters, tell me what you found when you pursued me."

Endrew shrugged. "I found you."

"But tell me how. I was felled by a branch and remember nothing after striking the earth."

"I see." Endrew paused to gather his memories, looking around him at the unfamiliar spot they stood in. "I marked your progress through the forest for some time. Judging by the broken limbs that littered the ground, you must have taken quite a beating."

"Beating, my eye. I thought I might have fetched my shoulder out, lost an eye, or had my head snipped off by goblins." The king swung his left arm around, testing for any sign of pain. "Odd, I feel perfectly fine now. No thanks to that damn horse, you understand. He wouldn't stop for anything. Nearly killed me."

"Its flight may have saved you instead."

The king looked puzzled.

"The cadwegan," reminded Endrew. "You stood next in the beast's path."

"Oh, yes, I see what you mean. Well, all the same, the trip was still something less comfortable than an afternoon's romp outside the castle. Now, go on."

Endrew hesitated a moment before speaking. "At last I reached a point along your path where a peculiar sound caught my attention."

"A sound?"

"Like humming."

"Humming, you say?"

"Yes, like a group of voices united in a wordless, tuneless song. It sounded something like the chant of a mage when spellmaking, but different."

"How so?"

Endrew lifted his hands, circling the fingers slowly in front of him as if he sought to draw the unwilling words from the air before him. "I do not know how to describe it," he said at last, "but it differed. I turned from the path and started up a slight slope toward drier ground. The sound halted as I approached, then at last I saw a light ahead among the trees."

"A light?"

"It may have been no more than the sun through an open spot among the branches, but I thought I felt the presence of magic."

"You felt magic? Impossible. Only the mages themselves have such powers."

"Do not ask me how this can be, for I have no idea myself, but I have always been able to detect the workings of a spell."

"That is most odd in one outside the ranks of mage."

Endrew nodded in agreement, then continued his story. "I reached a circle of tall stones and found you on your back within them. I went to you, but you slept on a bed of clean and perfect moss. Then a fog crept toward us and the humming sound returned. That is when the robed men appeared and made me join you in sleep."

"You tell an odd tale."

"There must be another to tell. How did you bring me to this place?"

"Bring you? I brought you nowhere. Like you, I woke to find myself here."

"Then how long have we been asleep and where are we? This looks nothing like the stone-ringed glade."

"Neither question can be easily answered. You slept a half hour beyond my own waking. As to location," the king said, looking around them, "all we can be certain of is that we are no longer in the swamp."

Endrew tested the soil with his boot. "Yes, the ground is far more dry and firm."

"And the trees less laden with moss."

"Then we are safe from the cadwegan?"

"Yes, I should think so."

Endrew nodded, then again stared off into the dim recesses of the forest.

"What is it?" asked the king. "Do you see something?"

"I am sorry, highness. No, I was only thinking of Duke Showann. If he had indeed entered the swamp as you suspected, he—"

"On foot, and probably only lightly armed at best? I fear he could not have survived."

"And that is why you drove us in there with such haste. You wanted to save his life."

The king shrugged. "One hates to lose a perfectly good prisoner. Besides, no man should die in such a manner."

"Yet four of your soldiers did, and we might have shared the same fate. You risked all our lives to save the life of one man."

The king remained silent.

"And an enemy, at that," continued Endrew.

"It is as you said before. Perhaps at another time I would not have found him so."

Endrew's mouth curled in a slight smile. "Highness, you also appear to be a strange man"

"As you, I have also heard that before. My children remind me of it constantly."

Endrew chuckled, realizing he and the king shared much more than their present predicament. "Well, highness, what do we do now?"

"Now? I should think the first thing to do is find our way back toward Talorcan before my daughter is taken with a fit and has the entire countryside out looking for us."

"But which way do we go?"

King Alrick looked up. "It should be evening soon. If we can get clear of these trees we might know our way by the stars."

"Can you find locations thus?" asked Endrew.

"Not really, I assumed you could."

"I am sorry."

"And by the sun?"

"I can tell east from west and north from south," said Endrew, "but even that depends on knowing the time of day. Besides, all of this helps us little if we do not know where Talorcan lies. The hooded men might have carried us far from the swamp."

The king thought a moment, then waved a hand. "No matter. As neither of us is a trained path finder, let us try a related thought."

"Which is?"

"Which is: use our brains. We do not know how we got to this place from the swamp, yet we are here. We do not know how our health was restored, yet we are healed. We have benefitted from the help of, shall we say, persons unknown. Since we do not know where we are, we must assume those who aided us before—whoever they may be—brought us somewhere favorable."

"Would the men in robes have taken us near to your city?"

"Close to it, perhaps. Let us leave these trees that we may look."

"Which way should we walk?"

"Southwest," said the king. "That is the direction to the castle from the swamp. We may stand along that general line."

Endrew looked up to mark the sun's position in the sky, then pointed. "Then that is our path, majesty. At least, I think so."

"Come, then, for we have nothing to carry but ourselves." The king walked off in the direction Endrew indicated, then turned back to note the lad's hesitation. "What is it holds you here?"

"Highness, the sword."

The king waved his hand. "Bring it," he said. "We may have need of two blades."

"Yes, but I thought you placed it there for your safety."

"Oh, tut tut, I found both our swords resting side by side in that location. I merely left yours waiting for you until you woke."

"I did not know if you would permit me arms."

"And why not? If you wanted to kill me, you had ample opportunity earlier when you found me sleeping."

"You did not allow me a weapon when we rode forth from the keep."

"We were guarded then; you had no need to defend yourself."

Endrew walked to where the blade waited and stooped to retrieve it. "You do me honor, highness."

"Oh, stuff and nonsense. It is no more than prudence to have two swords instead of one. Besides, I do not believe you are the type of man to do me harm even if you had the chance. Now, come."

With that, the king turned and walked away as

Endrew hurried to catch up, leaves crushing loudly beneath each step. Alrick walked for several minutes, then looked to where Endrew strode beside him, carrying the blade in one hand.

"Pity you lack a belt for that thing," said the king. "Oh, well, I do not suppose you care to go back and argue with the cadwegan for it, do you?"

"Hardly."

The two men walked through the trees for a bit, then noticed what they first thought to be a clearing ahead. As they neared it, they saw that they were about to leave the woods and enter a vast expanse of meadow. In only seconds more, they stepped through knee high ferns and out of the forest.

"Well, upon my word," said the king, chuckling in recognition.

"Where are we?"

"Halfway to Talorcan. See the line of those hills to the west? I would know it anywhere."

"How far are we from the river?"

"Quite a distance," said the king. "But no matter. We can strike directly for the city."

"Not tonight, surely."

"Of course not. It is too far and we are afoot. No, we shall build a fire here and move on in the morning."

"I will find wood," said Endrew, starting to turn back toward the forest.

"Hold on that," said Alrick. "See there."

Endrew looked in the direction the king pointed, then saw a band of riders top a rise of the undulating grasslands and head toward them. The king waved his arms and Endrew circled the sword overhead.

The horses drew closer, riding faster now, and

revealed themselves to be a group of soldiers struggling to keep up with a smaller figure in the fore. Soon, the lead rider was revealed by a mane of dark, flowing hair as the Princess Briduen.

Endrew and the king lowered their hands, certain now that they had been spotted. In moments, the band of riders reigned to a halt in front of them and the soldiers lifted their spears as if to throw them. Princess Briduen dropped to the ground and ran to her father with swift strides, softer than her boots should have allowed. Her riding cape billowed as she threw her arms around the king's chest and hugged her father tightly to her.

"I was so worried," she said, her eyes locked shut as she spoke.

"Oh, tut tut."

"And you," she said, letting go of the king and turning her attention to Endrew, "drop that sword."

"Now, see here," said Alrick.

"Drop it, I say, or I shall have these men fill you with spears."

Endrew shook his head. "But, I–"

"By the gods, are you deaf? Drop it." Willing to wait no longer for his compliance, she balled up her tiny fist and landed a hard, sudden right square on the side of Endrew's jaw.

The Duke of Chaussey stepped back in surprise. He glanced at the soldiers, then the king, then bent to lay his sword on the ground before bowing slightly to the princess.

"See here, Briduen," said Alrick, "I will not allow you to treat Lord Endrew this way. He saved my life."

"Not really," said Endrew.

"You saw to my father's safety?" asked the girl.

"Only after a fashion."

"Well, you would have," said the king.

"It was not necessary," Endrew told the princess. "The men in robes tended to your father before I arrived."

"Aye, men in robes, he says," said the king as his daughter's face paled, "with their feet all wrapped in fog, just as in the sort of stories people tell to frighten children."

"And their faces?" asked Briduen.

"I saw but one."

"Speak," she demanded. "What was it like?"

"Like the leaves of the forest itself."

"Leaves, pah. Have you ever heard such nonsense?" asked the king. "Endrew was clearly out of his head from his own injuries. Fought and defeated a cadwegan, he did. Now, you men, put down those spears. And Briduen, you be a good girl and apologize for punching the lad."

"It is no matter," said Endrew. "I can see how it must have looked to you, finding me beside your father with sword drawn. I have no sheath for it, you see—"

"Apologize," said the king again.

The princess looked toward her feet. "I am sorry to have struck you."

"Think no more on it," said Endrew.

"There," said the king, "is he not a gentleman?"

Briduen looked again into Endrew's face. "Thank you for warding my father. Where are the guards who rode forth with you?"

"The cadwegan," said Endrew.

"Now," said Alrick, before the princess could ask for further explanation, "what are you doing here? How did you find us so quickly?"

"Quickly?" said the princess, turning to her

father. "You have been gone four days. I have been nearly sick with worry."

"Four days?" said the king, looking at Endrew. "We were attacked on the second day. Why, we must have slept that whole time."

"So it would seem."

"And to think. I doubted your stories of leaf-faced men and circles of stone spires—"

"Quiet," shouted Briduen. "If I hear any more about these things I shall scream."

"Trust me," said the king, moving closer to Endrew, "we do not want that."

The girl gave a loud sigh of frustration, then turned and directed the guards to make camp. The soldiers instantly obeyed.

"I had not thought your daughter so filled with spirit."

"She is quiet most of the time," said the king, "but she does have her moments."

"This appears to be one of them," said Endrew, rubbing his jaw.

"Go ahead, pick up the sword," urged the king.

"With apologies, highness, I think it wiser not to."

Alrick stole a glance toward his daughter, then nodded in reluctant agreement. "You are indeed able to see to the heart of things."

"In this case, I hope so. Another blast from your daughter to equal the first, and I shall have to drink every meal I partake for the remainder of my years."

"Loosened a tooth or two, did she?"

"Nearly so."

King Alrick beamed with pride and memory. "She is her mother's daughter, as well as mine."

10

Upon Alrick's return to Talorcan, he ordered the lords of Wollaire again restricted to their cellar quarters. Endrew found himself unbothered by this confinement, spending most of his waking moments lying on his back and staring at the timbered ceiling. For a time, his fellow dukes pressed him for details on his battle with the cadwegan and his calculation of the odds against Showann's survivals. After that, some of the men gathered into corners and plotted other routes back home that avoided the swamp, but the details of their machinations went unnoticed by their young spokesman. Duke Endrew reclined quietly through it all, lost in his own thoughts.

Several days later, King Alrick softened his stance somewhat and allowed the captives to once again freely roam the keep. He insisted on limiting their visits to the city, however. Only one duke at a time was allowed beyond the fortress walls, and then only under the escort of three armed soldiers. He seemed determined that no other of the nineteen that remained should escape and suffer what he loudly stated and firmly believed to be Showann's horrid fate.

The dukes grumbled at these restrictions but reluctantly agreed this limited freedom was preferable to their dark confinement. A few hours in the morning sunshine with a faint breeze in their hair ended the greater portion of their complaints.

For himself, Endrew mounted the parapets almost automatically. He followed Robear and Jonale to the fresh air that waited above, but his mind remained locked on mysteries he sought to unravel. The sunlight hurt his eyes but he stood facing the northeast, looking off to where the river disappeared from view, with the unseen forest edge and the swamp beyond. Robear and Jonale prattled endlessly beside him but their words failed to reach his ears. Instead, he reached up to touch his face and the fingertips of one hand lightly brushed the line of his jaw, feeling for any last remains of the slight bump that had welled there for a time.

It was she who had stood on the parapet that night, he was sure of it. It was she who had spoken in the unfamiliar tongue with her hands held close to her chest. The gesture had mystified him for the longest time but finally he linked her pose to that of the robed men in the forest. Before they had bade him sleep, they placed their hands in the same position. And "Maelgar," the word that felled him, and the phrase that preceded it; he could not say it was the same language she had spoken, but it contained the same sounds and carried no more meaning to his ears than what she had said. Could it have been the same tongue? What language was it then, and what significance did it hold? He thought of the island of Domnall Ua Cnoba, its name a remnant of some long forgotten race. The riddles circled each other in his head, each one darting in and out to add layers of confusion to the next.

What most puzzled the young lord as he stared into the distance, though, was something she had said just prior to striking him. The remark had passed in the moment, but had come back to him these last few days as he lay on his bunk, and it contained mysteries beyond his comprehension.

"Drop that sword," she had commanded, and when he failed to do so she asked, "By the gods, are you deaf? Drop it," she had said again.

By the gods.

But there were no gods. They had been dead and gone from the world since before the time of their oldest records. True, traders brought tales of distant lands across the western sea where people still worshiped and made sacrifice as of old, but such things were laughed at as the acts of the ignorant. No living soul of Wollaire or Glender or any of the surrounding lands gave the slightest credence to the possible existence of such beings.

Gods that lived? No, it was too foolish, too silly to believe. The gods had been gone from the world for so long that it was as if they had never existed, never even been imagined. Man was the center of all things, the measure by which the rest of the world was compared.

Yet she had said, "By the gods," and said it as if the phrase came easily to her and with familiarity. Who was she truly and what could explain her remark? And who were the men in robes and what was her link, if any, to them? He searched for the meaning of the circle of standing stones, the robed men, and their leader's face of leaves but he found none. The knot of this problem was too tight and the meaning of its riddles beyond him.

During the days that followed, he saw Briduen from time to time in the castle halls and corridors. She always favored him with a slight, shy smile but made no comment beyond a hurried greeting or a perfunctory question about his health before she lowered her gaze and moved on. Endrew tried to catch the princess in conversation, but always she slipped away on one excuse or another.

The days ran on into weeks and the lords of Wollaire plotted their escapes, but the size of the cadwegan grew in the telling and as its stature increased, the urgency of their departure diminished. Gradually they grew used to the routine of their lax captivity until talk of escape ceased altogether.

Endrew enjoyed one privilege denied to his fellows. Alrick often summoned the young lord and requested the pleasure of his company as the king and his companions rode out to the hunt in the now warm weather. Endrew welcomed these moments away from the high stone walls of Talorcan. He found it immeasurably pleasant to ride in the open air, watching the hawks soar through the cloud dotted sky before they plummeted to strike game birds and he delighted in chasing after a pack of baying hounds as they cornered a deer. But more than the other sensations of freedom, he cherished those times when the king ordered that Endrew be given a bow or a spear. He felt less a prisoner and more truly a lord at those moments, almost as if the lands he rode across were his own. The greatest amount of pride that he took, however, was that he had earned the king's trust and the king granted it in full measures.

They stood together in a tangle of trampled undergrowth on one such day, each of them leaning on his spear and breathing heavily from the struggle with the huge boar they had just felled. Alrick shouted occasional directions to the servants who forced the dogs from the still and heavy body with whips while others made ready to transport the creature back to the castle.

"A fine kill," said the king, between labored breaths.

"A noble creature indeed," agreed Endrew. "He gave us a merry chase and a more than good battle."

"More than good," agreed Alrick. "I may be getting too old for this sort of thing."

"Nonsense. You have uncountable hunts in you yet."

The king nodded, silently at first, then said, "One hopes, one hopes." Both men turned their attention again to the boar and the king raised a shout. "You there, tie his legs firmly about that pole. I want him carried back to the city, not dragged. This fellow is bound to the royal table," he explained to Endrew. "Our Summerday feast is at hand."

"A celebration, sire?"

"The grandest in our kingdom. It is a day of rejoicing for the miracle of life and all the world gives us. It is a day of eating and gift giving and, well, we may put a bit of a strain on the wine cellar too."

Endrew smiled in memory of the sounds of music and laughter in his own home and how the smells of roasts turning over a fire sometimes filled every nook of Chaussey keep. "We have a similar day, but we hold it at harvest time."

"We have another then," said the king, "but not to compare with our Summerday." Then his voice grew quiet and his gaze distant. "Though this year," he added, "the merriment may be tempered a mite."

Endrew knew he must proceed delicately. "You have news, sire?"

"Yes, word from Prince Gartnait arrived again this morning. It seems your Giarley is not always so much a fool in battle as he proved himself last year. Your king is providing greater trouble to our army than we had anticipated."

Endrew paused to keep his voice level, lest the mixture of his feelings betray itself. "What is the difficulty, highness?"

"Giarley refuses to enter directly into battle, preferring instead to strike at Gartnait's flanks in small raids and always burning everything in our path as we move to pursue. Our men have little to eat and they grow weaker each day. I may summon the bulk of them home early this year. What say you to this news?"

"I am no minister of negotiation, sire. I know nothing of the legitimacy of your claim to Pollay province. All I know for certain is that many– on both sides– suffer because of it."

The king stared at Endrew for a moment in silent appraisal. "That is exactly the sort of answer I would have expected from you," he said. "Diplomatic, and with honest compassion at the root of it."

"Thank you, sire, but I merely speak my mind."

"And a good mind it is, lad. Come, let us mount and return to Talorcan. There is much to be arranged before Summerday."

"As you wish, highness," said Endrew, walking to where his horse waited.

"And you will, of course, attend the feast with us," said the king.

"Is it proper?"

Alrick took the reins of his horse from the groom. "And who is to say it is not if I say it is? Being king has some good points, eh?"

Endrew accepted the reins to his own horse and swung up into the saddle. "I do not wish to cause you any inconvenience, sire. I have heard it said that you grow too tolerant of me and my fellow dukes."

"My own people say that?" asked the king.

"I have heard it said."

The king sat astride his mount in thoughtful silence for a moment. "Well, then, let us give them something to really set their tongues to wagging. All nineteen of you shall attend our feasts. If people are determined to talk, let them at least have reason."

"Majesty, is this wise?"

"Likely not," said Alrick, "but put it down to royal arbitrariness. Anyway, Gartnait is still abroad. It is he who would make the loudest outcry. Besides, if the people of Glender and Wollaire never meet, how can we have hope of resolving the differences between us."

"You wish to occupy a part of our land, sire. This is a difference of substance."

The king spurred his horse into motion and Endrew followed. "There is more to this than the possession of Pollay province," said Alrick. "Wollaire levied great tariffs against our trade. Your kingdom seeks to isolate us on this island."

"Your pardon, majesty, but does Glender not place the same restrictions on our trade with you?"

"Only in retribution, lad, only in retribution. Were the policy of Wollaire different, Glender might speak with another voice entirely."

"Then is this not something our ministers of trade might settle? Would both lands not benefit?"

"I should think so," said the king. "I will have Rhodri Owain of trade and Caelwin Cyniod of negotiation look into it at once."

"You make me happy, sire."

Alrick turned his attention from the path they rode and looked at Endrew. "Happy?"

"Yes, highness. I find little of war that promises a better world for any of us. Besides, please do not think me ungrateful for the quality of your hospitality, but I fear the people of our provinces will never be able to buy our freedom until the burden of supporting an army in the field is lifted from them."

Alrick tossed his head back and laughed loudly. "I have never seen the like of you, lad. No other man has ever so comfortably couched idealism in such practical terms. Are you certain you lack diplomatic training?"

"I have only such training as I received at my father's fire. He always said that the welfare of our province's people came first. Without them, he said, we who ruled could come to nothing. If this is true for a duke, is it so different for a king?"

"Not the least," said Alrick. "I should like to have met your father."

"You would have been great friends, sire. I see much of him in you."

"If I may judge him by the son he raised," said Alrick, "I shall take that as a great compliment."

"I am glad, sire, for I mean it as one. Now, tell me more of your Summerday."

The two men returned to Talorcan keep, then parted company. Endrew watched the king mount the flight of steps that led into the great castle, then he walked to the gate that gave entrance to the city's merchant quarter.

"Ho, Duke Endrew," said one of the guards on duty, a man he recognized from many escorted trips through the town. "Do you seek some diversion?"

"I do, Feradoch. I have need of some shopping for Summerday gifts."

"I thought you and the other lords were not allowed money," said the guard.

"You are correct, but I must make some

purchases all the same. If you can take me to a jeweler's, perhaps I can turn this into the coin of Glender." With that he raised his left hand that bore the signet ring with the dragon crest of Chaussey etched in onyx. "This should be worth something."

"Is there a significance to the design?" asked the guard as he examined the ring.

"It is my family crest."

"You cannot sell this, Lord Endrew. It is not proper."

"Yet I have nothing else to sell."

"Then I shall take you to a place where you will be well satisfied." With that, he turned and hailed a pair of guards who loitered nearby. The soldier led Endrew down a narrow, winding street the duke had only traveled once or twice before, then stopped in front of a shop. "This place should give you a proper price," said Feradoch, "though you may have to press your case a mite, if you take my meaning."

"In other words, they will have my ring for nothing if they can get away with it," said Endrew.

"Exactly," said the guard, "but if you hold firm, you will not be disappointed."

"Very well," said Endrew, "let us negotiate."

He stepped into the shop, followed by Feradoch, while the other two guards waited out in the street. It was just as well they did so as the tiny chamber could not have held all four men. Behind a small board table covered with delicate tools sat an ancient man with his gaze fixed firmly on a glowing green gem in a gold setting. Endrew cleared his throat after a moment, but his gesture brought no response, nor did a second effort.

"Do you mean to gain my attention by this festival of phlegm," said the old man after a third such attempt, "or are your merely ill?"

"No, not ill at all," said Endrew. "I wish your opinion on the value of a piece."

The old man looked away from his work for the first time. "You are a foreigner by the sound of your voice. Wollairian?"

"Yes."

"This is Lord Endrew," said Feradoch.

"Spare me introductions," said the jeweler. "Let me see the piece."

Endrew held out his hand and the old man waved for him to remove the ring. Taking the object in his hands, the jeweler turned it over and over, looking at it from every angle and in all lights. Finally, he held it close to his face and frowned as he examined the stone.

"It is nothing special," said the old man, handing the ring back to Endrew. "I would give you ten gold royals."

Feradoch shook his head from side to side slowly but without subtlety. The old man looked at the guard and frowned, but said nothing.

"I had hoped for more," said Endrew. "I need to buy two gifts for Summerday."

The jeweler looked a second time at the ring. "Perhaps twelve," he said at last. Again Feradoch shook his head and the old man scowled in response.

"My presents are for King Alrick and the Princess Briduen," said Endrew.

"And would you purchase these gifts here?" asked the old man. "I could give you fifteen in trade if you buy from me." Again Feradoch shook his head and this time the jeweler roared, "What are you, his brains and purse together? What do you know of craftsmanship? Leaning on that damned spear all day qualifies you as nothing but a loafer."

"Now listen, you—" began the guard.

"Never mind," said Endrew. "Perhaps you should wait outside with the others."

"Damn right," said the old man. "Stand around outside; do something you have skill at." Feradoch gathered his dignity around him like a cloak and stormed through the door. "Good," said the jeweler. "Now we can bargain like men."

"He was only trying to help me."

"That lout?" the old man nearly screamed. "He would be hard pressed to help a dead man lie still and stiff." He got up and left the room for a moment through a narrow, blanket-covered door on the rear wall, then returned with a box the size of a small trunk which he set on the floor beside the table. "Now," he said, opening the lid, "let us get down to business."

Sometime later, Endrew stepped again into the street and Feradoch hurried over from where he leaned on the opposite wall. "How did you do?" he asked.

"Well enough, I think. At least, I am satisfied."

The guard nodded. "In the end, that is what truly matters. Is there anything else you need?"

"Nothing," said Endrew. "You may take me back to the fortress now."

"It still troubles me that you sold a gem with meaning to your family."

"It could not be helped."

Two evenings later Endrew led the men of Wollaire into the great hall of Talorcan keep. Bright music filled the air and the place seemed brimming with celebration, laughter, joy, and hope.

"It does not feel right," said Jonale of Quitole, "joining the Glender like this."

"I agree," said Robear of Tushan. "It is one thing to be civil, but this goes far beyond the bounds of mere courtesy."

"I told you," said Endrew, "this may be our first chance to strike down the differences between our two lands."

"Hrrmph," grunted Jonale. "If not impossible, certainly unlikely."

"Ah," said Endrew, "our host."

King Alrick approached with Princess Briduen on his arm. "Good evening, my lords," he boomed.

"Majesty," said the three dukes in unison as they bowed.

"I am glad you could all be with us tonight. It should be a great feast."

"And gift giving," added Briduen. "What did you get me, father?"

"In good time, my dear, in good time. I hope our exchange of presents causes you no embarrassment," he said to the dukes. "No one could expect you to participate in our customs."

"Yet we have done so, sire," said Endrew.

"We have?" said Robear.

Endrew reached into one pocket of his surcoat and pulled out a dagger with an ivory handle. "This is for you, highness."

"Why, Endrew, you should not have done this, lad."

"It is the least we could do to repay your grace and gentility," said Endrew.

"During these months of our bondage," added Jonale.

"And for you, Princess," said Endrew, reaching into another pocket. He pulled out a vase of delicate crystal, every face of the dainty object catching the candles above and dancing with reflected light.

"It is beautiful," said the girl, her face beaming

with obvious pleasure. "Thank you, Lord Endrew."

"How did you manage, my boy?" asked the king.

"We had a little bit put aside."

"I see. Briduen, have we nothing for young Endrew, here?"

"Perhaps," said the princess with a playful smile. "Here." She held out a small box that had been hidden in her hand by the folds of her shimmering gown. "Open it," she urged.

Endrew took the box and pried back the lid. His eyes widened and he felt Jonale and Robear press in upon him from each side. There, within the tiny box, sat the onyx ring with the dragon crest of Chaussey province.

"I do not understand," said Robear.

"Nor I," said Jonale.

Endrew looked first to the king, then to Briduen. "How did you—"

"You treat the guards with respect and courtesy, and Feradoch likes you," said the princess. "Therefore should you trust him the less with such a secret."

"You ought not to be without this ring, lad," said the king. "It ties you to your father and his fathers before him."

Endrew shook his head. "I am without words. Thank you both."

"Thank you, Duke Endrew," said Briduen. "The greater gesture was yours."

"Come, my dear," said Alrick. "We must attend to our other guests."

"Enjoy your evening," said the princess. "My lords. Duke Endrew."

The three bowed as Alrick and Briduen turned and walked away. Endrew felt the two older men follow the king and princess with their gazes for a moment, then turn their attention to him.

"Sold your family ring to buy presents, eh?" asked Robear.

"Nice touch, that," said Jonale.

"Did you see the lad stare at her as they walked away?" asked Robear.

"Oh, yes. A man blind from birth could not have failed to notice."

"Her eyes are a bit too close together," said Robear. "Is that not what the boy said?"

"Aye. That, and her nose is too sharp," added Jonale. "Our young lord here may have to reexamine the girl's features in a new light."

Endrew tried to ignore them, but what they said was filled with the substance of truth. There was no getting around it; the girl's eyes were nowhere near as close together as he first thought and her nose grew more perfect with each consideration.

Two weeks later, in the darkest part of a moonless night, two lantern-lit ships dropped sail and hove to in mid channel while a small boat slowly passed from one to the other. Oars pulled against the force of waves that threatened to upset the tiny craft at any moment. Then it reached its goal and a sailor tossed a rope so the small boat could be made fast. Two hooded men climbed aboard and clomped across the deck with impatient steps. They made their way below and entered a cabin lit only with a single tallow candle.

"What?" demanded Foshay, the Wollaire minister of negotiation, as he pulled his head free of the protective folds of cloth. "What could possibly be worth our risking our lives on such a night as this?"

"Still yourself," said Caelwin Cyniod, his counterpart from Glender. "I would not have summoned you without reason."

"It had best be good," said Pyer, Wollaire's minister of trade.

"Good enough," said Caelwin Cyniod. "Your Duke Endrew of Chaussey has King Alrick's ear. He is urging him to reduce or eliminate tariffs between our lands."

"No," said Pyer, "impossible."

"More than possible," said Rhodri Owain, Glender minister of trade. "Alrick has instructed us to approach you with such reductions as a gesture of reconciliation between our lands."

"This cannot be allowed," said Foshay.

"Our lives depend on it," added Pyer.

"Our livelihoods, at any rate," said Rhodri Owain.

"What can be done?" asked Foshay.

"We must, of course, meet visibly," said Caelwin Cyniod. "Alrick will demand it. We should be able to find flaws with each other's plans, though, and keep matters as they are for a time."

"Yes," said Pyer, "but how long can we hold such gestures at bay. Our King Giarley must also hunger for thoughts of peace. If he gets wind of this–"

"It is this boy, Endrew," said Foshay. "I thought him dangerous from the start."

"I agree," said Caelwin Cyniod. "But what is to be done with him?"

"Some accident?" offered Pyer.

"Did not Showann of Alpenne perish in an attempt to escape?"

"Endrew lives too freely and too close to the king. No one would believe he tried to escape."

"He hunts often with Alrick," suggested Rhodri

Owain.

"Hunting is a dangerous pursuit," said Foshay. "Can you not manage something on your own?"

"Endrew is a lord of Wollaire," said Caelwin Cyniod. "We sought your opinion before taking any action."

"How polite," said Pyer.

"But utterly unnecessary," added Foshay with a thin smile.

11

Endrew saw the princess often in the next two weeks and the girl's countenance grew more beautiful in the young lord's eyes with each brief, quiet word the girl uttered. Every nod of greeting as they passed in the keep's great, sweeping corridors lifted the youth to moments of unequaled joy. On those few times when Briduen stole a glance over her shoulder or took a few seconds from her errand to actually talk to him, Endrew found himself reduced to stammers and an awkward shuffling of his feet. When she eventually turned and hurried away, she always left him smiling as if he'd invented the expression.

None of this went unobserved by all around them. A very few of the castellans of Glender showed new kindness to Endrew while others shut him off entirely, not even acknowledging his bows or greetings when they passed. More were openly hostile, muttering, "Well, did you ever see the like of it?" as he walked by. He also heard whisperings among his own people and eventually a delegation of the dukes faced him with their concerns.

He stood atop the keep's highest parapet late one afternoon, looking out over the countryside and drinking in the still air that promised a calm and beautiful summer evening. Perhaps if he waited long enough, he thought, she would come again in the darkness as she had those long months ago. Perhaps she would speak once more the strange words and he could ask her about the men with robes and leaf faces. Perhaps she— A shuffle on the stone tore him from his thoughts and made him turn. He found himself facing Robear of Tushan, Jonale of Quitole, and Duke Prandwyn of Meersay province.

He stared into their eyes for a moment as if to read their thoughts, then asked, "May I be of help to you, my lords? Is there some errand to the king that requires my attention?"

"Endrew," said Robear, hesitating. "There is a matter of some delicacy we must broach with you."

"I assure you, I will be discreet, as always."

Prandwyn snorted derisively, and Jonale said, "It is your very discretion that appears to be at issue."

"I do not understand," said the young lord. "Have I failed you in some way?"

"No," said Robear, "not at all."

"Yes, he has," said Prandwyn. "His actions show a lack of faith to every one of us."

Again Endrew looked into each duke's eyes, then he said, "I am sorry, I—"

"You have no idea of what we speak," said Robear, "it is plain to see."

"It is the girl," said Jonale, "the Princess Briduen."

"The Glender princess," added Prandwyn, as if it were the land of her origin that needed emphasis. "Do you love her?"

Endrew's mouth dropped in surprise. "Well," he began, "I—" He lifted his hands, but neither they nor his mouth found the words he sought.

Robear put a hand on Endrew's shoulder. "Prandwyn speaks for many among us who feel your affection for the princess brings shame on us and weakens our cause."

"But, I have not—"

"You have done nothing," continued Robear. "We know that, but you wear your heart outside yourself for all to see. Why, the very sight of the girl sets the color to running in your cheek and stills the words in your throat before they can be uttered."

"We have all witnessed it," said Jonale.

"Disgusting," said Prandwyn. "A lord of Wollaire with a girl of Glender. It is the next thing to treason."

"But I have done nothing wrong," said Endrew. "Why, of a truth, I have done nothing at all."

"We know that well," said Robear, "but Duke Prandwyn speaks for many."

"A majority," added the duke.

"A slight majority," said Robear. "Many of the dukes agree with him in that they find you growing too close to the royal family of Glender. They fear you may lose your ability to function as spokesman by growing familiar with Alrick and the princess."

"And you?" asked Endrew.

The lord of Tushan smiled. "There are some few of us who find the matter none of anyone's business. Oh, Endrew, your father should have found you a bride years ago before all this trouble started. That would have made things simple, but young men seem bound to fall in love if matters are not managed for them."

"Love, pah," said Jonale. "I still say there is more to it than that. The lad is working a trick or two to get himself released, perhaps even all of us with him. Clever boy, Endrew."

"I am doing no such thing."

"I told you," said Prandwyn. "His feelings are

genuine and all the more shameful because of it."

"Endrew," said Robear. "We wanted you to know how we feel. Even those of us who support you in your heart's suit wish it were otherwise."

"But, I have made no suit," said Endrew. "I have not breathed a word to Briduen of my feelings."

"Then you must," said Robear, "or it will cause you to burst."

"What advice is this?" Prandwyn nearly shouted. "How dare you urge the lad into our enemy's camp?"

Robear turned his gaze to the Duke of Meersay. "Do you really think Endrew capable of betraying our interests, regardless of this other situation?"

"One never knows."

"With Endrew, one does know. Besides, have you no memory? Were you never the lad's age?"

"I was. Both husband and father was I by the time I was twenty."

"Arranged, no doubt, before you came of age?"

"Of course," said Prandwyn, "as a proper marriage should be among people of our class."

"Ah," said Robear, "then you never knew the fearsome thrill of discovery when you brushed the fingertips of someone who had meant nothing to you the day before and suddenly meant all the world. You never knew the pounding in your heart at the very sight of the girl in whose presence all others paled."

"Yes, exactly," said Endrew. "That is exactly how I feel when she comes near. How did you know?"

Robear looked away for a second. "My own father made no match until I had stumbled upon such a girl quite by accident."

"Your wife?" asked Endrew.

Robear shook his head slowly as if the

movement was as painful as the memory. "I fear not. She was the daughter of a merchant in Tushan, and I thought the sun rose with her in the morning and dare not set until she gave it permission. She was bright, and happy, and clever, and when her hair flowed down about her shoulders, I thought her the most beautiful creation the world had ever known."

"What happened?" asked Endrew.

"My father believed the match unseemly and he sent the merchant away to another province, his family with him. I never saw the girl again. Three months later I found myself married to the second daughter of the Duke of Baretton."

"Then you did your duty as a man of title must. And are you not now happy with the way things happened?" asked Prandwyn.

"Oh, yes," said Robear, "I have come to love my wife. I trust her and respect her, and I have tried to make her life as happy as she has made mine. I am grateful for her having been a part of me for all these years and I hope I have made her feel the same about me."

"Well, then–"

"But there are different kinds of love. If Endrew feels this most powerful of loves now and fails to act on it, he will spend the rest of his years waking in the tiniest portion of the night and wondering what might have been. Endrew," he said, turning to the young duke, "you must go at once to King Alrick and speak to him of these matters."

"This is treason," said Prandwyn.

"How can Wollaire be harmed in this except by slight embarrassment?" said Robear. "It is fitting for a lord to put his fears apart and charge into battle on behalf of king and crown. It is proper to put one's own interests aside and do the king's bidding even when it causes hardship to your own province. But to ignore the whisperings of the heart when neither king, crown, nor country stand to suffer; ah, that would be the greatest folly a lord of principle could allow."

Prandwyn sneered. "I had not thought you so much the romantic, my lord."

"Romantic?" asked the lord of Tushan. "Possibly, but perhaps I am no more than a man who lacks your clear vision of Wollaire's future."

"But it is Endrew's view of the future that is at issue," said Prandwyn.

"My view of the future," said Endrew, "sees the day when Wollaire and Glender will stand together as friends."

"Impossible," said Prandwyn.

"Unlikely, at the least," added Jonale.

"Yet already begun," said Endrew. "I have spoken to the king about lowering the trade barriers that separate our lands by a gulf wider than any channel of water."

"What?" said Jonale.

"Of a truth?" asked Robear. "He would consider lowering the barriers of trade?"

"I found him more than receptive. He instructed the ministers to begin negotiation."

"This could be the first step of many toward peace," said Robear.

"And our release," said Jonale.

"A Glender promise to raise our hopes," said Prandwyn. "Nothing more."

"Perhaps," said Robear, "and you are right to urge caution. But Endrew may have opened a door through which we may all soon step."

"Good job," said Jonale. "Stout lad."

"Go now to the king," said Robear. "He will

hear this new suit of the heart and weigh it next to your suit of the purse already presented. His favor on one will lend weight to the other, and may both these missions find favor in his eyes."

"I do not like it," said Prandwyn.

"You do not have to like it," said Robear, taking the duke by the elbow and leading him toward the stairs. "You merely have to smile and go along with it."

"Clever lad," said Jonale, following the others down, "I knew he was up to some trick or other."

Endrew stood alone on the parapet, listening to the sound of their steps fade as the three dukes descended. Up to some trick? Endrew searched his deepest feelings, then paused as the remembered vision of Briduen's face danced in his mind's eye. No, he decided, Jonale and Prandwyn were both wrong. There was no subterfuge in his emotions, and no treason either. He swallowed once and went to find the king.

Alrick denied Endrew an audience that afternoon and evening, being pressed, the young duke was told, by affairs of the throne. The steward who spoke to him then bowed and asked if the king might have the honor of Endrew's accompanying a royal hunting party in the morning.

"Of course," said Endrew, with a bow of his own in return, "the honor and pleasure are mine."

He slept fitfully and woke several times from dreams where his attempts to speak to the king were interrupted by cadwegan which repeatedly rose from the ground and tore the tongue from his head. Each time he lay awake for a while, listening to the snores of the dukes who slept nearby, and each time he eventually drifted back to sleep only to be assaulted again by the same dream.

Morning finally arrived and Endrew rose to join the king. He climbed the stairs to the main level of the keep, then walked out into the inner bailey where the party was assembling. "Good day, sire," said Endrew as he walked to where Alrick stood.

"Ah, yes, indeed it is," said the monarch. "What say you to a bit of a ride this morning? We seek deer in the forest."

"A hunt sounds pleasing, highness."

"Here," said Alrick, "take a bow and quiver. You can ride that horse there, the speckled roan."

"A fine animal, sire."

One of the lords of Glender walked nearby and raised a flagon in toast of the king, then stared darkly at Endrew before walking on.

"Have you eaten, lad?" asked Alrick.

"No, sire."

"Then help yourself. That table over there groans under the weight of stout food and drink. We cannot have you riding weak to the hunt, now."

"No, sire."

"Oh, and was there something you wished of me? I understand you wanted to speak with me yesterday."

Endrew looked around him at the crowd of people, most of whom stood within hearing of all but a whisper. "Sire, it is a matter of some privacy. These people—"

"Oh, tut tut," said the king with a wave, "the day will afford us some occasion to speak, I am sure. Unless," he added, "it is so urgent a matter as we must withdraw and discuss the problem now."

"Oh, no. I mean, no, I can wait until the moment is right; that is what I mean. There is no need for—I mean, it can wait." Endrew clenched his fist firmly in front of himself as a gesture of resolution. "I can wait," he concluded.

Alrick looked at the younger man in silence. "Hmmn," he said at last. "Good. Now, eat."

Endrew turned on his heel and walked to the table where he chose a roll and a few bits of thinly sliced meat. He doubted his stomach could manage any more than that and he wondered why it churned so.

Soon the party mounted and rode out of the city, across the meadows, and into the forests that stood southwest of the keep. Endrew rode toward the rear of the group, behind the king and lords of Glender, ahead of only the grooms and stewards who followed to mind the horses and do the butchering. The land rose as they climbed higher in the valley, and after an hour or so the king called a halt to the procession.

"Let us leave the horses here and proceed on foot," said Alrick. "We shall travel in threes."

"I like hunting in this manner little," said one Glender lord to another as he swung down to the ground, then brushed his moustache back from his lip with the back of one hand.

"I agree," said the second. "Give me a good chase behind the hounds anytime."

Endrew handed his reins to a groom and turned to face the two men. "Is not any hunt pleasant when you have the freedom to roam under so fair a sky?"

The two lords stared blankly for a second, then the first said, "I suppose it would seem so, especially for one whose freedom is so in question."

Endrew ignored the insult and merely gave the lords a slight nod of his head before walking toward the king.

"Ah, there you are, lad," said Alrick. "I want you to come with me and Lord Wierenn, here."

"My pleasure," said Endrew, then he turned and bowed politely to the lord who had glared so darkly at him back at the keep. Lord Wierenn carried himself erect, looking down his long nose at Endrew as the introduction was made. He wore his hair pulled back so as not to interfere with his shooting and his clothes fit snugly to avoid catching on the brush. The tight fit of his garments revealed a man comfortable in the forest and who took pains to stay fit and trim, despite his years.

The hunting party broke into trios as the king instructed, and small groups of archers walked off into the forest in all directions. Alrick led his own band, with Wierenn and Endrew trailing behind. They walked for some time before they happened on a small trickle of water that wandered among the trees.

"Your highness, mark this," said Wierenn, pointing to the mud that lined the stream's sides. Alrick and Endrew looked where the man indicated and saw the track of a deer.

"Is it fresh?" asked Endrew in a whisper.

"You ask me?" said the king.

"It crossed the stream and went back into the forest–" Wierenn said, pausing to scan the far bank carefully. "There," he said, pointing to a second print.

"But when?" asked Endrew.

"Not long ago," said Wierenn.

"Then it may be just ahead," said the king, quieter now. "You see, Endrew? Lord Wierenn is a fine hunter, a master of the bow and forest lore."

"Let us travel three abreast," said Wierenn, "about twenty paces apart. We will be less likely of missing the deer that way."

"We will be out of sight of each other," said the king.

"No matter," answered the lord. "If one of us has difficulty, a shout will bring the others running."

"Very well, then," said Alrick, stepping across the water. "Let us be off. I will take the center with Wierenn on my right and Endrew on my left."

The three men spread out and walked into the forest, soon losing each other to sight. Endrew paused every few steps to listen, but the only sounds that greeted him were the snapping of twigs and curses as King Alrick fought his way through patches of brush. Endrew smiled at their slight chances of finding the deer with all the royal racket to his right, then forged ahead. He made his way as silently as he was able through a thicket of broad-leafed plants, then used the bow to push aside the last stalks. He froze as he saw a circle of stone spires surrounding a bed of clean and perfect moss.

He stepped out of the entangling mass and crept into the circle. It was nearly the twin of the one he'd seen in the swamp. As he walked between the tall stones and stepped within, he inhaled and marked how clean and pure the air felt here. He hadn't noticed it before, but it came back to him now. The circle in the swamp had shut out the smell of decay and rot that filled the boggy forest. This forest lacked the sense of moldy ruin that filled the other, but as he stared at the pillars of stone he marked the circle's aura of purity.

He slowly turned as he looked from one stone to another, feeling a peaceful calm he hadn't known in days. He thought of shouting for Alrick to join him so the king might see the manner of place where they were cured. He waited a moment though, to savor the circle's perfection. Then as he turned, he thought he saw a flicker of movement from the corner of one eye.

A cry of pain burst from his throat as an arrow slammed into his chest, and he dropped to the ground. His hands rose to grasp the shaft as he rolled about, but he could not draw the slender thing from his body. He thrashed his legs and wordlessly growled his frustration, then fell into a fit of coughing. He put his hand to his mouth, then drew it back in horror as he coughed and his life's blood stained it. He fell back against the moss, with the stones and trees beginning to dance around him in a swirling circle of their own. He shut his eyes to still the movement, then opened them at the sound of hurried footsteps.

"Endrew, my boy," came the king's voice, "what happened?"

Endrew tried to speak but the words caught in his throat.

"Lie still," said the king. "I shall see to this." The monarch rolled Endrew onto one side, and the young lord heard a snap as the king broke off the arrow head that protruded from his back. "Now, then," said Alrick, placing Endrew on his back once more, "hold tight to me, lad, as tight as you are able."

Endrew gripped the king's sides with all the power in his arms, clenching folds of the monarch's tunic so tightly that his knuckles whitened. Alrick put both hands around the shaft, then pulled the arrow from Endrew's chest with a sudden tug.

"Now," said the king, ripping the young duke's stained tunic apart. "Let us see what we—"

His voice tapered off into nothing as his eyes found the wound. Endrew glanced down at his bare chest and saw the blood flowing in streams out onto the moss, then he coughed again and the spray covered the king's tunic with tiny crimson speckles.

"Endrew, my boy, I am sorry. It does not look good for you."

"No," grunted the younger man. "Not yet. Not before I ask you–" He coughed again and his head fell back against the moss. No, not now, he thought, not here. He put his hands over the wound. He was made well in a place like this before; where were the men in robes now? He opened his eyes but the only face that looked back was Alrick's, not the face of leaves. He closed his eyes again. Please, he thought. Please, make me whole.

Then a crackle of magic flashed all around him and his body surged with power. His eyes snapped open and he saw a brief flicker of lights dancing before him, then the tiny points of bright color faded and with their passing Endrew lost all knowledge of the world.

12

Endrew woke first to the clink of crockery, then when he stirred at that sound he heard a woman's unfamiliar voice say, "He wakes. Summon his majesty."

He opened his eyes and found himself in a canopied bed, modest by all proportion but large after so many months on his cellar cot. One servant woman disappeared through the doorway and the other clutched a pitcher to her chest and pressed her back against the wall as if she hoped to pass through it. "Good evening, my lord," she said, her eyes wide.

"Evening?" said Endrew, his tongue forming the word thickly. "Of what day?"

"Of that after the hunt, my lord. You have slept a full day through and a bit more."

Endrew rubbed his eyes and groaned. "Where am I?"

"You are in Prince Gartnait's own chamber. Does it please you, my lord?"

Endrew stopped trying to look at the woman and allowed his head to fall back on the pillow. "As much as anything can right now."

"We were told to comfort you when you woke," she began, but then her voice broke in terror. "Oh, my lord, you will not harm me, will you, good my lord?"

"Harm you? What a foolish notion. However

could you think—"

King Alrick cut the question short as he stormed into the chamber followed by a quartet of spear-carrying guards and an old man in long robes with a grey beard that threatened to match his garments in length. Princess Briduen trailed the procession, staying in the doorway as the room was not large enough to allow her entry with such a crowd already in attendance.

"Well, woken up, have you? Good." The king patted his waist and rocked on his heels for a moment. "Sleep well, did you?"

"I have no recollection. How did I get here, highness? What happened? The last thing I remember was—" Endrew's voice trailed off as he searched his throbbing head for vague and tangled memories.

"The last thing you remember is me pulling a stray arrow from your chest, no doubt." The king paused a moment and cocked one eyebrow, as if waiting to hear Endrew add something. "Or did you recall something else, something after that?"

"Lights," said Endrew, as if reeling in the thought from far away. "Specks of light all around me."

"There," said the king, clapping his hands together and turning to the old man, "is that not how I told you it happened?"

"It is," came the answer, the grey beard barely moving with the words. "It is indeed as you said. May I speak to the boy now?"

"Of course," answered Alrick, gesturing the old man toward the bed. "Endrew, this is Idwal Hir Rhun, royal mage to the court and kingdom. He has a few questions for you, lad."

"That is, of course, if you feel strong enough for talking," said the man with the long grey beard as he moved closer.

"I feel perfectly fine," said Endrew, "now that I am fully awake."

"Good," said Idwal. "May I sit?" he asked, indicating the edge of the bed. "I am a very old man."

"Of course," said Endrew, sliding himself toward the bed's head and sitting up. "Please forgive my lack of consideration."

The mage turned back toward the king. "Polite, as you said."

"Always," answered Alrick, "without exception."

"Hmmn, commendable. Now," said the old man, "let us get down to the matter at hand. Exactly what powers have you?"

"Sire?"

"Powers, lad. Do not play at either words or deafness with me; I am your better in both respects. What powers do you possess?"

"I am sorry, sire, I meant no offense. I must assume you believe me able to cast spells, though, and I have no such ability."

"None?"

Endrew shook his head. "None at all."

The magician raised one white, shaggy eyebrow. "Then how, may I ask, did you heal yourself of a wound that pulled you halfway from this life to another?"

"I do not know the manner of my healing. I remember the king drawing out the arrow. I remember seeing the blood. Then lights danced before me and after that I can remember nothing." Endrew looked from face to face, finally settling on Alrick's. "Highness, did you not cause me to be healed after bringing me back to the city?"

The king leaned slightly toward Endrew at the foot of the bed. "Lad, your wound closed itself before my eyes in the forest. The lights you speak of covered you for a few moments, then when they vanished you were whole. You have slept since then as we did both sleep after our healing in the swamp."

Endrew lifted the collar of the bed shirt he wore and peeped within, then leaned back against the wall. No bandage covered the spot where the arrow entered and no scar, not even the slightest blemish, remained to show that the shaft had ever struck its mark. "I cannot explain," was all Endrew managed.

"We must be careful, you see," said Idwal Hir Rhun. "You have grown close to his highness, our king. If you are a man of enchantment, the king must be protected from you and your powers."

"I have no enchantments, I tell you."

"Yet you healed yourself."

Endrew waved a hand in front of his face. "The circle of stones. It must have been the power of the place that healed me."

"Eh?" said the mage.

"The arrow struck me as I stood within a circle of tall stones that enclosed a bed of moss. King Alrick and I were healed by men in robes in another such circle when we ventured into the swamp."

From the doorway, the princess gasped and her father turned and asked, "Briduen?"

"Nothing, father," she replied. "I was given pause only by Duke Endrew's joyful and mysterious good fortune." With that the princess turned and fled.

Idwal reached into a pouch that hung belted at his waist and drew forth a slender chain from which dangled a pale green gem lined in gold lace around the edges. "This should help us discover the truth," he said.

"What is it," asked Endrew.

"Never mind," said the mage, then he made a gesture over the gem with his other hand and muttered words that passed just below Endrew's hearing. Instantly, the stone crackled with magic and Endrew lifted a hand toward it.

"What spell is this?" he asked.

"You feel it, then? You feel the power of its enchantment?"

"I have always felt the presence of magic."

Idwall looked over his shoulder to the king as if his suspicions had been confirmed. "Detecting the presence of a spell is a skill known only to mages. Let us see of what else you are capable. Tell me the name of the powder that causes sleep."

"I have no idea."

"What root gives a man the strength of many?"

"I do not know."

"What are the words for the spell of silence?"

Endrew shook his head. "I am sorry. I have no knowledge of these things."

The mage's words came faster now. "You feel my spell, yet you say you are not a man of magic?"

"Not in the least."

"A wizard? A mage?"

"No."

"A conjurer, a spellcaster, a—"

"No," Endrew nearly shouted, "I swear it."

The old man paused and looked at the stone that still dangled between them. "And do you mean any harm to his highness?"

"No, I swear it on my honor as a knight and lord of Wollaire."

The old man paused to look at the gem, then twisted his face as if puzzled. "Endrew, listen closely,

I want you to lie in answer to my next question. Do not tell the truth, no matter what I ask. Nod if you understand."

Endrew nodded.

"How old are you?" asked the mage.

The young duke paused a moment at the odd question and the old man's odder request. "Forty-two," he said.

The mage smiled as the gem glowed brightly. "Ah, good," he said. "For a moment I feared the damned old thing was out of order and wanted reincanting."

"What is it, anyway?" asked Endrew again, leaning forward to better see the trinket that slowly faded back to its original state.

"A gem of truth-telling," said the mage. "While activated by spell, it reveals a lie when one is spoken by anyone within its presence."

"A handy thing to have," said the king. Then he turned and looked at the four guards and the servant woman. "You may all leave now."

Endrew watched them go, then asked, "Highness, did you really think I might harm you with magic?"

"Lad, I am a king and ours is a land at war. We decided I could not afford the luxury of trust until we were made sure."

"You must understand," said Idwal. "You admitted to King Alrick that you are able to feel magic, and he saw you heal yourself."

"I know," said Endrew. "I am just sorry that you could not sense–" He broke off and looked away from the king.

"Sense how you care for me?" asked Alrick, to complete the phrase.

"Yes," said Endrew.

"It is plain to see. And I hope my regard for you shows equally. It is only the demands of the throne that forced such caution. My advisors insisted."

Endrew nodded. "They were prudent to do so," he said, without much conviction in his voice.

"You will understand fully some day," said the king. "You were not born to manage a mere province; I see great things ahead for you. Now, come, Idwal. Let us leave this young man to rest and recover."

"No," said Endrew. "Begging your pardon, highness, but there is a matter I would speak to you about."

Idwal rose but stayed where he stood. "Your highness—"

"Oh, tut tut. Your own spell has shown the boy to be pure of heart. You and your bauble are not needed any longer."

Idwal bowed his head and turned to leave the room.

"And close the door behind you," called Alrick. "I think the lad wishes some privacy in this discussion."

The old mage pulled the door quietly shut, then the king walked over and sat at the foot of the bed. "This is the third or fourth time you have sought me in the last few days, lad. You must have some matter of import on your mind."

"I do, sire."

"The war? There is nothing new to tell."

"Not the war, highness."

"The trade barriers, then. My ministers tell me they have scheduled negotiations with their counterparts in Wollaire for—"

"No, sire, not that."

"Well, what then?"

Endrew paused. "Sire, you spoke before of my feelings for you and yours for me."

"Indeed, I did, my boy. You are a man of character. I have grown to love you almost as dearly as if you were my own son. Even more, in some ways." He looked about the room. "It is not by mere whim that I placed you in this chamber."

"I am honored by your words, sire. I trust you know I feel the same about you. You have become almost like the father who was taken from me."

"Then ask what you wish of me; if I can grant it, I shall."

"Do not speak too quickly, highness. I– I wish your permission to–"

The king leaned forward, waiting, but no other words came. "Permission?" he prompted.

"Yes, sire. I wish your permission to... to court your daughter, the Princess Briduen."

The king sat upright, silent for long moments. "Court her, you say?"

"Yes, sire."

"You, a duke of Wollaire, wish to court the second in line to the throne of Glender?"

"I do."

"I see. And do you love my daughter?"

Endrew paused. "I believe so, highness. I think of nothing else but her."

"And you wish my permission."

"Yes, sire, with all my heart."

The king slowly smiled until his grin covered his broad face. "If the gods yet lived, boy, I should thank them that you finally got to the point."

"Sire?"

"Briduen has been asking me about you for weeks, wondering if you had noticed her."

"She has?"

"She feared there was something wrong with her. I told her you bore responsibilities beyond your years, but that you were a bright enough lad and would get around to this sooner or later. I believe she was growing impatient, however."

"Then she cares for me, too?"

Alrick raised his hands, his palms toward the younger man. "Now, I will not put words in the girl's mouth. But of a truth, I think she finds you a very pretty fellow."

Endrew lifted his hands until his fingers touched the sides of his head, hoping to add force to a comment that never came, then let them fall into his lap. He smiled, helpless to do more, then looked to the king and said, "I do not know what to say. You make me too happy, majesty."

"Oh, you need say nothing, lad. Save your words for Briduen, for she will make you use every one of them if you wish to win her."

"I had feared she might be promised to another."

"Briduen? She informed me at the age of twelve that if ever I tried to arrange her life as other fathers managed their daughters', she would find a way to make me itch in places I could not reach, even if she had to pay Idwal or some other mage for the favor. You have seen the strength of the girl's mind," he said, pointing to Endrew's jaw. "I chose to believe her."

Endrew continued to smile in silence for a moment, then his expression faded to one of concern. "And what will the lords and ladies of Glender say, if I am successful in my suit?"

"Say? Oh, plenty I should think. But let their tongues wag. Perhaps through such a union, you can mediate between the two lands to settle our differences. Even my court may come to see the value of such an arrangement in time."

"In time, yes, but—"

"In the meanwhile, let them talk all they want. The exercise will do their jaws good and their words can scarcely harm you."

"It is not their words that concern me," said Endrew.

"What do you mean?"

Endrew paused to find the most careful phrasing. "I mean that I do not believe my shooting was a mere hunting accident."

"What? Not an accident? Of course it was."

"Just before the arrow struck, I saw a flicker of movement among the trees."

"The stray arrow flying in to strike you, and brushing a branch in its path," offered the king. "There were nearly twenty of us lurking about in those woods, firing in all directions. Such things happen."

Endrew shook his head. "This arrow did not come down from a long arc; it arrived on a line. No, I believe what I saw was the pull and release of a bow string."

"From so close?"

"Yes."

"Then the arrow that struck you could not have been ill aimed." The king paused a moment to ponder the idea, then shook his head. "Impossible," he said. "Who would have motive for such a deed? It would take a great reason for one of my lords to purposely stalk and try to kill you, and great skill to do so undetected."

"I have not had time to think it out since waking, sire. Perhaps my very presence offends some. Why, two of your lords made reference to how I should be captive only yesterday morning as we reached the hunting site."

"No, I say. They may resent you, but I know my court better than that."

"Some other reason, then." The young duke thought a moment, then looked up. "My fellow lords of Wollaire say I have worn my heart outside myself for all to see."

"Yes?"

"Perhaps one of your court wishes to woo the princess for himself. Perhaps someone knows my mind and is jealous of my intentions."

"I suppose it is not impossible, but I know of no such person."

"And I know of no other motive."

The king rose from where he sat. "Stay the night in this room, then return to your fellow lords in the mornings. They will become alarmed if you are too long gone from them."

"And the princess?"

"The princess and I dine together in my chamber each evening and will do so tomorrow. If you called at about that time you could join us. I cannot speak for the food, but you may find the company interesting."

"I expect I shall."

"Who knows, I may be weary and feel the need to retire early. You and Briduen can then stroll the corridors of the keep, if you feel strong enough."

"You may depend upon it."

"Then rest now," said the king as he walked to the portal, "in anticipation of a tiring tomorrow." Alrick closed the door behind him, then opened it again to peep inside. "Just to be safe, I shall have a guard posted in the hallway. To keep you from escaping, of course," he added, with a smile.

Endrew spent the night and the following day planning clever bits of conversation that utterly failed him when he entered the king's chamber and saw Briduen seated in a chair working at needlepoint. Her long hair hung down her back in a thick, single braid, and she wore a gown of shimmering cloth that sparkled with the light of candles that lined the chamber and glowed within glass chimneys. He opened his mouth, but only stood staring at her in mute admiration.

Alrick cleared his throat. "Well, up and around are you?"

"Yes, majesty," said Endrew, never taking his eyes from the princess.

"Good, good." The king rocked awkwardly on his heels as he had the day before at Endrew's bed. "Well, what say you both to supper?"

"That sounds lovely," said Briduen. "What say you, Duke Endrew?"

Endrew nodded. "Lovely," was all he could manage.

Servants brought the meal and the three ate in long spans of silence, broken only by the king's vigorous pursuit of particularly greasy pieces of fowl. At last, Alrick ordered the food taken away, and they sat quietly over cups of wine.

"Well, fine weather, eh?" asked the king, to no one in particular.

"Yes, father, the weather has been most fair. Is the weather in Wollaire the like of this?" she asked, turning to Endrew.

"Something like," said the young lord.

The princess smiled and turned her attention back to her embroidery.

The king sat in long silence looking from one of them to the other, then yawned loudly and stretched.

"Well, damn me if I do not feel tired earlier than usual tonight."

"Were you especially busy today?" asked the princess, a tiny smile on her face.

"Not particularly," said the king with a bit of edge in his voice. "But I feel inclined to retire. Endrew, would you be so good as to escort my daughter to her chamber?"

Endrew rose to his feet. "Of course, highness. You have but to ask and I shall—"

"Oh, tut tut. Be off with the two of you then." He flicked his fingers to wave them from the room.

Briduen gathered her handwork and rose. "Goodnight, father," she said, bending to kiss the king on his forehead. "And thank you for everything."

Endrew walked to the door and opened it, holding it for the princess to pass through. Once in the hall, Briduen turned to him and said, "I do not feel as weary as my father. Would you care to take the air with me?"

"Oh," said Endrew, shaking his head at his great, good fortune. "My lady, I should be honored that you would deem me worthy."

The princess looked into his eyes and smiled. "Margid," she said, back over her shoulder. Endrew heard a step and looked past Briduen to see a woman appear around a corner in the corridor. "We cannot walk together without a chaperon, of course."

"Oh, of course," he said, quickly. "It would not be seemly."

Briduen laughed, then turned and led the way toward the battlements, leaving Endrew standing in wonder at how like bells the sound of her laughter was. Then he hurried to catch up, glancing back to see that Margid followed close enough to keep them in sight, but beyond all but the loudest speech. The princess led him up the steps to the castle walls, past a guard, and to a point along the parapet where they could converse undisturbed.

"Oh, my lady," he gushed when she turned to face him, "I have waited for this moment. There are so many things I would tell you."

"Hush," she said, reaching up to place two fingers gently against his lips. "I wish to hear it all, every word you have to say, but there are two things I long to hear above all others. First," she said with a playful smile, "tell me that you love me."

"I do," he said, taking her hand and pulling her fingers from his lips. "I love you as no man has ever loved a woman. And the other thing you would hear?"

"Tell me," she said, leaning close and whispering, "how long have you followed the way?"

13

"The way?" he asked, shaking his head the least amount. "The way where? To what?"

Briduen placed the tips of her fingers to her forehead before thrusting her hands back into Endrew's. "Oh, of course," she said, "I am sorry. Surely in Wollaire you must have your own manner of referring to the worship of the gods. I am taken by the moment or I would have thought of the many differences between our–"

"Gods?" said Endrew. "But there are no gods. They have been dead and gone since before memory. Everyone knows that."

They stared at each other in mutual confusion for a moment, then Endrew felt her hands go limp and slide from his grasp. Briduen shook her head from side to side and backed away, as if in denial of these few moments alone together. "No," she said in a hush, "no." Her face clouded and her eyes pinched with pain, as if he had struck her with a weapon instead of mere words. Then with a half sob, the princess lowered her head and rushed past him as quickly as her gown allowed and bolted from the parapets with Margid at her heels.

Endrew stood for long moments, looking to where she had fled, then he turned to stare out into the darkness that surrounded the keep and he pondered the mysteries that kept slamming against him. Stars filled the sky, tiny points of brilliance that seemed to hint at secrets they would share if only he would listen closely enough. He let his eye run slowly down toward the horizon, allowing it to linger here and there on particularly bright specks, then stopped as his gaze reached the inky blackness that he knew signified the line of forests. He peered off into the unseen distance, and sent his mind flying northward, through the trees and swamp to the circle of stones and the man with the leaf face. His image of the place faded and he sent his memory to the similar glade where the arrow had struck him and, if the king spoke true, he had somehow healed himself. Then he stood erect as the fog-enshrouded riddles that had plagued him for so long cleared with a flash and suddenly made sense. In one brief moment of insight, he realized the inescapable truth.

The gods, he thought; actual gods that still lived were at the heart of these wonders, at the heart of everything, perhaps. The idea went against all he had ever believed, everything he'd been taught, but the notion of living gods was the only explanation that answered all his questions.

"By the gods," she had sworn when she found him with her father in the forest. The remark held no meaning then, because the gods did not exist and no one believed they did. But now... now, he knew that the princess was one who still worshiped the ancient deities, and she was not alone.

And these secret few who hid their beliefs for fear of ridicule or worse were not merely misguided or confused. He thought again of his broken ribs the hooded men had cured. There were other explanations for his healing, but none so ready as the power of unknown gods. And when he lay dying of the arrow wound, had he not closed his eyes and begged to be made well? He pulled memories of the moment from deep inside himself, and he remembered that his arms had crossed over the wound as Briduen's arms had crossed her chest that night she had spoken into the darkness, as the leaf-faced man had crossed his own. But no man in robes acted in that moment of great need, no mage with spells and potions tended him; on his back in a sacred circle he had crossed his own arms, asked to be cured, and he was made well. Only gods could have such power.

He stepped back from the wall, then placed his hands upon the stone, still warm to the touch from the summer sun. He knew what he had to do. Somewhere in the forests that surrounded Talorcan hid a company of people who worshiped the gods. He lacked knowledge of them except that they existed, yet he had to find them somehow and learn what they knew. Endrew shook his head at the size of the task before him. The gods had come rushing into his life in mere moments but knowledge of them would take time, much more time he suspected.

"How long have you followed the way?" she had asked him. He knew he must speak to her again soon, for now he had an answer.

Briduen refused to see Endrew for several days and no matter how persistently he haunted the halls outside her chambers, he never managed to spot the princess. He understood her fears; she thought she had betrayed herself to a nonbeliever, and that was exactly what he had been before that very moment. He had to explain it to her but she denied him even the luxury of a quick glance, much less a word.

On the fourth day of his vigil, he spied Margid, the woman who had escorted them to the battlements that night, approach from the opposite end of the long corridor. She halted when she saw him leaning against the wall, then put on a face of ice and moved forward as if nothing could turn her from her errand.

"Wait," said Endrew, stepping forward to catch the woman at her elbow, "I would have you take a word to the princess."

"Would, eh?" she said, pulling her arm away from the foreigner. "Break her heart again with another bolt of cruelty, would you?"

Endrew shook his head. "No, I would not. I would never—"

"Well, you sent her off in tears right enough last time. I will not see you do so again, you heartless brute, much less be a party to it."

"Please." Endrew again reached his hand out to touch the woman's arm. "Do you know the words that passed between us?"

"I do not. The poor lamb wishes to speak not on it, nor will she listen."

"Then find a way," said Endrew. "You must make her hear these two things."

"Must? You dare tell me what I must?"

"I dare anything that benefits the lady we both love. First, you must tell her that; tell her that I love her with all my heart and that I should sooner die myself than ever again bring pain into her heart."

"A pretty phrase," said Margid, curling her lip. "The sort of thing a young man says when he wants his way. I will not allow my sweet lady to be swayed by such frail and hollow words."

"Then tell her this. Tell her that I was lost, but have found... the way."

Margid lifted her eyebrows but looked at the duke with half-lidded eyes. "And you expect these phrases to work wonders?"

"I dare expect nothing," said Endrew. "I hope everything."

"Hrrmph," snorted Margid. "Oh, very well, I shall give her your message, but only on the condition that you stop loitering about these halls. My lady needs light and air, so away with you for she shall surely not come out while you are here."

"But, I–"

"Be gone now, I say. If she wishes you, she will send word."

Endrew bowed his head to the servant. "Thank you, good Margid. You make two people very happy, though you know it not."

"Hrrmph," she grunted again as Endrew turned and disappeared down the corridor. "We shall see," she muttered to herself when he was beyond hearing, "we shall see. But, by the gods, if you harm my precious lady I shall have your head and serve it to you cold."

Later that night, four cloaked men sat in the cabin beneath the stern castle of a vessel that dipped and swayed with the waves in mid channel. One stared at the flame of the single candle that lit the close, dark chamber, while the other three argued loudly, occasionally pounding on the small table for emphasis.

"But how could he have failed?" asked Pyer, the Wollaire minister of trade.

"I tell you again," said Rhodri Owain, his counterpart from Glender, "he did not."

Caelwin Cyniod nodded in agreement. "He speaks the truth," said the minister of negotiation. "Lord Wierenn is an archer of great skill and he struck the boy fair through the chest."

"Then how—"

"Your young duke cured himself, I tell you," said Owain. "Have you not been listening?"

"Impossible."

"And yet it happened," said Cyniod, "right before no lesser set of eyes than the king's own. He said lights covered the boy's body and he saw the wound close. All of Talorcan knew of the miracle within moments of the party's return to the city."

"How are we to do away with a man who cannot be killed?" asked Owain.

Pyer looked into the two faces for a moment, searching their eyes for any sign of a lie but he found both men too well-studied in that art to reveal anything. "I had never heard that young Endrew of Chaussey had the power of life over death," he said after a moment, "had you?" he asked in a flat voice.

Foshay kept his eyes on the candle's flame. "No," he said coldly, "I had not."

Pyer lifted his hands in a gesture of surrender. "So here we are," he said. "You have failed to remove this irritant as we all agreed should be done. What do you intend next?"

"What can we intend?" Cyniod nearly shouted, rising from his chair and stomping away before turning back. "If the boy can restore his own life, who knows what other powers he may have."

"He has no powers," said Pyer.

"He healed himself," Cyniod screamed.

"So you say."

"We say it because it is so," said Owain.

Caelwin Cyniod placed his palms on the table and leaned across to where the ministers of Wollaire sat. "We are undone, I tell you. Lord Endrew cannot be removed and he has the king's ear. It is only a matter of time before Alrick suspects we have stalled the promised changes in trade policy."

"He speaks no less than the truth," said Owain, walking away from the table with a slight roll as the ship swayed with the swells that passed beneath it. "We may as well pack our profits and head for fairer climes, for we shall surely have to live as honest men henceforth."

Foshay placed both hands on the table and pushed himself away from its edge. "You amaze me," he said with a sigh, and he looked up from the flame for the first time. "I cannot believe that you are the same men we have dealt with all these years."

"The boy has the power of life—"

"Even if that were so," said Foshay, rising slowly to his feet, "it would matter little." He stared into the faces of the Glender ministers, letting his gaze linger in the first pair of eyes before moving to the second. "This equation contains more than one variable."

"What do you mean?" asked Caelwin Cyniod.

Foshay sighed again and tucked his robes around himself. "Men of insight," he said to Pyer.

"Indeed," answered the minister of trade, though his tone revealed he held no greater portion of that quality than they.

"Stop playing at words," demanded Owain, "and tell us what you mean."

"It seems so simple," said Foshay. "Your Prince Gartnait has chased Giarley over much of southeast Wollaire all summer only to find burnt fields and hunger before him as he pursues. Now Giarley has locked himself up in Alpenne Keep to mock and taunt your young hot head from its towers and battlements."

"And so?"

"So," said Foshay patiently, "Gartnait is now summoned home, his army with him, to regroup and take the field again next year."

The ministers of Glender paused a moment. "We have no knowledge of such a decision," said Owain.

"Oh, please," said Foshay, "such deceit is unworthy of you. Do you think me likely to take some military advantage of your admission of what I already know to be true?"

"Very well," said Cyniod as he sat once again, "but of what significance is Gartnait's early return to Glender?"

"Only this," said Foshay, "do you think the prince as open to Endrew's ideas as is his father?"

"Never," said Cyniod, "why the boy hates all things Wollaire with a high passion."

"Such patriotism in the young is admirable and ought to be encouraged," said Foshay. "Thus, Gartnait is the man who should sit the throne of Glender and rule as benefits his land ... and us."

"And so he shall in time," said Cyniod, tossing his hands in the air.

"And that time," said Foshay, "could be now."

"But how can that—" began Owain, then the man's expression changed with the sudden realization of what Foshay implied, and he snapped his mouth shut as if he wished to recall the words that had just fled and he slid back into his seat.

"You cannot be serious," said Caelwin Cyniod.

"Monarchs die all the time," said Foshay. "That is why they have sons."

"But, he is our king," said Owain.

"And your loyalty to his family is duly noted," said Foshay, "but you have admitted that you cannot kill Endrew."

"Since it is not really the boy we wish gone, but rather his ideas, let us then remove the willing recipient of those ideas. Without Alrick's sympathetic ear, the notion of free trade will die, no matter how much our young duke should push his case with Gartnait."

Cyniod slumped against the back of his chair. "But, how–"

"Do not worry yourself about such ugly details," said Foshay, reaching into his robes and drawing out a tiny pouch that he dangled by its drawstring. "I have taken the liberty of procuring a small quantity of a most virulent poison for you. Quite tasteless, I am told, but very effective." With that, he tossed the pouch onto the table between the two men.

Owain and Cyniod looked at the packet, then each other. "I am not sure," said Cyniod, turning back toward the Wollaire minister, "that we can do this."

Foshay turned his palms toward the ceiling. "That choice is yours. You can do what must be done or you can, as you said yourselves, pack you profits and leave."

Pyer caught Foshay's tone and leaned forward. "Of course, you could always once more attempt to remove Duke Endrew."

Slowly, Owain reached out to take the pouch, his fingers creeping toward it as if they feared to touch the thing. Then Cyniod's hand came down to grasp his fellow's wrist and stay it from claiming the poison.

"I do not like this," said Caelwin Cyniod.

"Liking it is not the issue," said Foshay, his eyes locked upon the men of Glender. "But, come," he continued, letting a note of false cheer into his voice, "there is nothing to be so serious about. If the deed repels you, you need not be the ones to do it."

"Truly?" asked Cyniod.

"I have said it," said Foshay, "let us speak no more on the matter."

The ministers drew their hands back from the pouch. "It is good of you to do this," said Owain.

"It is nothing," said Foshay, reaching down to reclaim the deadly powder. He weighed the tiny bundle in his hand a moment, then cocked his head to one side. "Still," he said, "there is one problem."

"What is that?" asked Cyniod.

"With poison," said Foshay, "things are often so uncertain. At a banquet, one cup looks much like another. How can we be certain that the powder finds its way into the king's cup?"

"Well–" began Owain,

"And only the king's cup," added Foshay, "not your own."

Pyer caught Foshay's meaning and said, "Such a tragedy would be most unfortunate."

The ministers of Glender sat frozen by equal measures of fear and anger for several minutes, staring at their counterparts from across the channel, but daring no speech lest it betray their feelings. Then Caelwin Cyniod slowly rose and wordlessly took the deadly pouch from Foshay's extended hand.

"I knew you would see reason," said the minister of Wollaire with a thin smile, "once properly enlightened, of course."

Days passed, and Endrew never heard from the princess nor was he able to find Margid again in the castle, no matter where he looked or who he asked. Every guard, every servant, every possible deliverer of even the slightest message that he sent was soon replaced. Eventually he grew discouraged and sought a more productive tactic.

"Feradoch," he said, putting his arm around the guard's shoulders in the courtyard and drawing him away from his fellows, "do you know the way?"

"The way where, sire?"

Endrew patted the man's back and released him. "That is exactly what I asked," he said softly.

"I fear you got that one by me," said the guard, scratching his head, then moving on to other areas. "Is it a riddle?"

"Yes, but not a very good one. Thank you, Feradoch."

"My pleasure, sire," said the guard. Then, as Endrew walked away, Feradoch shook his head at the automatic response and shrugged before making his usual sloppy salute.

Endrew went to nearly every person he knew within the castle walls, always drawing them aside lest they be embarrassed and reluctant, and always asking the same question. "Do you know the way?" he said, over and over again. Responses varied, but none could be called even remotely positive.

Days went by in this manner and finally Endrew felt he had exhausted the keep's possibilities. He once more sought Feradoch and told the guard he wished to visit the city.

"A bit more shopping, sire?"

"No, not today. I have a mystery I must solve and will need your help to do so."

Feradoch's faced tightened until the stubble on his round cheeks seemed to stick out like quills. "A mystery, my lord?"

"Yes, after a fashion. Tell me, do you know many people in the city?"

"Oh, a great many, sire," he said, revealing several missing teeth as he smiled. "Lived here all my life, I have, and my father before me."

"Good. And do you know any people of Talorcan who others speak of as doing strange things?"

"Oh, a great many, sire. One fellow near my father's house shaved off all his hair and wore his trousers back to front for—"

"No, I mean things like wandering abroad late at night, speaking in a strange tongue, or disappearing from the city for a time. Things like that."

Feradoch stood for a moment, his forehead furrowed in concentration. "Yes, I see what you mean," he said at last. "Now that I ponder on it, I do know of a few such folk, but I had thought nothing of it until you asked. Are they thieves or the like?"

"No, nothing like that, but I would speak with these people if you could take me to them."

"I see no reason why not," said the guard, "but you know the rules."

Endrew looked toward where the gate beckoned. "Is one of my fellow dukes in the city now?"

"Yes, left with his escort just a while ago, he did." Endrew nodded. "Very well, could you please fetch me when the time is right?"

"Of course, sire," said Feradoch.

The guard came to Endrew that afternoon and informed him that Duke Jonale of Quitole had returned to the keep after his wanderings. Endrew immediately joined the man and two other soldiers, and the four of them made for the city's center with Feradoch leading the way.

"I think we should go see Somerled the tinsmith first," said the guard, looking back over his shoulder.

"Why?" asked Endrew.

"Half mad, he is, or so I have heard it said.

With the dark of every new moon he climbs to the roof of his house and sings to the black night in a voice no man can understand."

"That is odd," agreed Endrew.

"And it is a three story dwelling."

"Mercy," said Endrew, feeling that the guard may have struck gold with his first breaking of the soil.

Feradoch led them through winding lanes overhung with the upper stories of houses that perched above streetside shops. The guard raised a hand and halted them where a wagon stood blocking most of the way.

"Here, you see? He has been told a hundred times to keep this cart out of the path, but will he listen? You would as easily talk to the stones that make up the street as speak to his old ears."

"Is he deaf?"

"Deaf, no. Daft, perhaps, but he hears as well as you and I together. Are you sure you wish to speak to such a man?"

"Absolutely."

Feradoch shrugged and walked to a door that stood a few scant inches above the level of the street. "You two," he said to the other soldiers as he grasped the handle and pushed the door open, "you wait out here."

Endrew followed the guard into the shop and focused his attention on a man who sat stoop-shouldered at a bench with his back to the door. The clink of hammer against metal resounded off a thousand hard surfaces which were the tinsmith's wares displayed on shelves around the room. A boy of nine or ten looked up from his own work to stare at the newcomers, especially Feradoch's uniform, but

Somerled kept at his labors.

"Here now, tinsmith," said the guard, "stop that for a moment. My lord Endrew of Wollaire wishes to speak to you, and see you mind your manners."

The man at the bench held his hammer still at the mention of his visitor's name, then slowly turned to face the foreigner. "Endrew of Wollaire?" he asked over the bridge of a long, thin nose. His pale green eyes had a look of madness or wisdom, Endrew could not decide. "Are you not the young man who healed himself?"

"I was healed," said Endrew, "but I cannot say how or by whom. Perhaps," he ventured, "you can tell me ... the way."

Somerled stared into the young man's face without changing his expression. "Yes," he said at last, "perhaps I can." Then the smith's eyes shifted to where Feradoch stood. "And does your friend here wish the same information?"

"Oh, yes," said the guard, "I should very much like to know how the miracle occurred."

"Good Feradoch," said Endrew, leaning close and whispering to him, "would you be so kind as to wait outside for me? I will share what I can with you later, but I think this man will speak more freely if he believes the words are for my ears only."

"Good thinking," said the guard with a wink that could only have escaped the blind or dead. "I shall be right out here with my fellows."

Endrew and Somerled watched as the guard stepped back into the street and closed the door behind him. Then the lord of Wollaire turned to again face the tinsmith.

"What can you tell me of the way?"

"I am able to tell much about many things, but I am not certain I shall."

"Do you distrust me?"

"I have reason to distrust many."

"Then send away the boy. You shall have my word as a knight and lord that what you tell me will be kept private for all time."

"The boy is my apprentice," said Somerled patting the lad on the head. "In everything."

"Then speak," said Endrew. "I would know of the way."

"You must already know much," said the smith. "You healed yourself."

"But without knowing how I did what I did. Please, help me to learn."

"Some things are not to be spoken of; it could be dangerous for me. A common prisoner fares less well in the keep than a noble one."

"But I must know."

Somerled thought a moment. "And so you shall," he said, raising a hand and pointing it at Endrew. "Maelgar," he said, with a wave of his fingers.

Endrew felt a crackle of magic at the familiar word, the word he had played over and over in his mind since the man with the leaf face had spoken it, then sagged to the floor in sleep.

Somerled reached out a hand and tousled the hair of his apprentice. "Go out the back way and tell the others to spread the word that I have him," he said.

"Will you meet in the usual place?" asked the boy.

"Yes, now go. The soldiers outside await me and I believe they are showing signs of growing as sleepy as our young lord here."

14

The heavy splash of cold water in his face roused Endrew from the enchantment. He shook his head and struggled back to consciousness as a nearby voice said, "There, you see? A full pail works as well as any spell could."

"And spends less effort," answered another.

Endrew blinked his eyes open to find himself propped on his elbows at the center of a circle of tall stones. The last light of day peeped through the surrounding trees and revealed a robed and hooded man in each gap between monoliths, with more people waiting beyond. Every cloaked figure now stood as silently and still as they had that day in the swamp.

"Who are you? What do you wish of me?" asked Endrew, scrambling to his feet.

"The question, young lord of Wollaire, is what do you wish of us?" came a rich bass voice from deep within the folds of one man's hood.

Endrew turned to scan the circle. "Somerled? One of you must be Somerled the tinsmith."

"Who we are," said a figure, his voice half muffled by the layers of cloth that hid his face, "is of no concern to you. Now we ask again, what do you wish?"

"I wish to know of the way. I would have you

tell me of the gods."

"There are no gods," said a voice.

"Everyone knows that," said another.

"It has been generations since anyone has spoken of the gods."

"Many died for doing so."

"None even dare speak of them now."

"None."

Endrew raised a hand to still the chorus. "Yet they live and I dare talk of them," he said. "I have felt the power of the gods and would know their names."

"Names are easy, young lord," said the deep-voiced figure. "It is knowing the truth behind those names that is difficult."

"Then instruct me," challenged Endrew.

The hooded figures stood motionless for long moments, then the deep voice spoke. "Niall aed donnchad," he said.

"Bonnal cenn faelad caillen."

Other voices answered and Endrew twisted his head from side to side to follow the conversation. The words flew around him without his comprehending them but he recognized the sounds of the ancient tongue: the sounds that named the mysterious island of Domnall Ua Cnoba, the sound of the spellword "Maelgar" that had twice sent him to sleep, the sounds of Briduen's prayer delivered into the night sky from a dark and deserted parapet. Endrew heard these sounds whiz past him and knew that every unknown syllable debated his fate.

"Hold," he called, lifting his hands over his head. Slowly he lowered his limbs as silence again filled the clearing. "Please, if you mean to speak of me and of what you plan to do, I would ask the privilege of understanding what you say."

"You may not like what you hear," said a figure.

"I prefer that to not knowing," said Endrew.

"Very well," said the man with the deep voice, "let it be as our guest has requested. Continue."

"I say again, then," said another figure, "this man is a spy of some sort, sent to ferret us out and cause our ranks to be destroyed as of old."

"Impossible," said another, "he is already a priest of one god or another."

"And that is itself impossible," said a third. "The Wollairian denies any knowledge of the gods. You heard him ask for that knowledge."

"Yet he healed himself," said the figure who had just spoken, "and in this very clearing."

"He could be a mage with healing spells of some sort," said a man who had not spoken before, "hoping to fool us into believing he is a priest."

"How are we to know?" asked the man with the deep voice.

"Wait," said a figure who stepped forward from his place between the stones. Hands slowly rose to grasp the edge of his hood and pulled the cowl back to reveal a face of leaves.

Endrew started at the sight. "Are you the man who healed me in the swamp?" he asked.

"Swamp?"

"Your face. The man who put me to sleep in the swamp had a face of leaves."

"Ah, these," said the man, the tips of his fingers brushing the leaves. "Join me," he said to the men around him, his hands twitching in small gestures of beckoning. A half-dozen hoods drew back to reveal similar faces. "Masks, you see," said the figure. "Our survival often depends on our anonymity."

"He knows nothing of us or the gods," muttered someone.

"No, he is pretending his ignorance," said another. "But why?"

"Silence," said the man who had stepped forward, as he lifted a hand to still the murmurs. "I think I may have the solution."

"And that is?" said the deep voice.

"Simple. We must put the lad in danger of his life. If he was able to cure himself of one wound, he should be able to manage another. All we need do is stand by and wait to see whether he uses the spells of a magician or the power of the gods."

The figure with the deep voice shook his head. "It would not prove everything."

"Perhaps not," said the priest who had offered the idea, "but it would go a long way."

"No," came a new voice, higher in pitch than the rest.

"It must be done," said the figure with the deep voice, speaking sharply to still the objection. Then he turned toward Endrew and pointed. "Hold him."

Before Endrew could react, robed men rushed forward from every direction. Hands grasped him from all sides and held his arms out so he could neither flee nor fall. Another figure stepped toward him and grabbed his tunic at the throat, then tore it open so the young duke's bare chest shone in the dusk.

"Now," said the deep voice, "bring the Bec Artgall."

"Is it fit for such a purpose?" asked another.

"I can think of none better," said the deep voice. "I believe this man speaks the truth and I trust the Bec Artgall to reveal it to us."

Endrew watched as the leaf-faced priest who had proposed the test left the circle, then returned holding something in his hands that was hidden by the draping of a thin cloth. The figure with the deep voice walked to where the priest stood and spoke too quietly to hear, then he pulled the fabric aside to reveal a thin, long-bladed knife with a gold and jewel-encrusted handle.

"Now listen closely, young Endrew," said the man with the deep voice. "Stand as still as you are able, else the blow of the Bec Artgall may be badly aimed and instantly fatal, denying you the chance to prove you have the powers of the gods."

"I have made no such claim," said Endrew, feeling other hands grasping his legs now and pinning him where he stood. "I have no idea how I was cured before in this place."

"Then we shall solve the mystery together."

"Can you not see the truth by magic?" asked Endrew. "The king's wizard did."

"We know nothing of sorcery," said the deep voice as the man folded the cloth that had covered the knife. "Our spells flow from the gods themselves."

The priest who carried the blade held it aloft and moved toward Endrew. "No," came the cry of the high voice again, followed by, "Silence, we must know."

"Ainmuire menn boruma," said the priest, ready to strike.

Every fiber of Endrew's body sought to fight back, every minute of his knight's training told him to strike before the knife blade landed. The multitude of hands held him firm though, so he lashed out with the only weapon left to him.

Endrew looked straight into the eyes that peeked from the priest's leaf mask and shouted, "Maelgar!"

The word had only half escaped his lips when

the circle of stones resounded with the crackle of magic. The priest wobbled for a second, then dropped to the ground with the ceremonial knife falling harmlessly to the moss beside him. The priest rolled as he landed and his mask slid aside to reveal him as Somerled the tinsmith.

A hush fell over the clearing, broken only when the man with the deep voice looked at the fallen priest and said, "Well, it seems that turnabout is, indeed, fair play."

Endrew had no time to reflect on the poetic justice of the situation. Instead, he felt the hands slide free of his body and limbs and he turned to look at the figure with the deep voice. "I am sorry," he said. "I did not even know if it would work."

A robed figure knelt beside Somerled and listened at his chest for a moment.

"Is he well?" asked Endrew. "I meant no harm."

"He sleeps. That is all."

The man with the deep voice drew back his hood, then lifted his own leaf mask from his face to reveal a lined and craggy visage. "Light torches," he said to the others, without taking his eyes from Endrew, "then see to Somerled and the Bec Artgall." He held out the cloth that covered the knife, and robed figures scurried about to do as he instructed. Then he said, "Truly now, young lord, which god do you serve?"

"Truly asked and truly spoken," said Endrew, "none. I have only the truth in saying I seek knowledge of the gods, for I have none."

"Then how did you learn this spell?"

"It has been twice used on me, once when I was cured of the cadwegan's crushing wounds and again by the tinsmith in bringing me here. I remembered the word, that is all."

"Kineth, he still lies," said another. "One cannot call upon the power of the gods by the mere use of a spellword. Even true followers of the way need more than just that."

"Normally I would be inclined to agree," said the deep voice, "but I believe our young friend here may be favored, even chosen by the gods. Would that not explain his healing himself and his use of the sleep spell without greater knowledge?"

"And why should the gods select such a one as he, a non-believer and ... and a Wollairian?"

"They have their own reasons for all things. It is not for us to question."

"I tell you, Kineth, you will one day regret the making of this choice."

"Each man regrets many things in his life. One error more or less should not matter greatly. Now, come." He pointed to several members of the masked and hooded company and bade them follow, then he put his arm on Endrew's shoulder and drew him out of the circle of stones and along a dark trail to a ring of fallen logs where he motioned for the people to be seated.

Torchbearers stood just behind the group and someone draped a cloak over Endrew's wet and torn tunic. The young duke pulled the cape close around himself, then strained to see Kineth in the flickering light. The man with the deep voice looked back at him, his gaze peering into the youth's eyes, if not his soul.

"May I not now see all your faces?" asked Endrew.

"Not yet," said Kineth. "I live in these woods and have no reason to fear your knowledge of my face. But these others who sit with us," he said, gesturing at the five figures who shared the logs, "dwell in the city of Talorcan. If you prove false, you could cause them great harm, were their faces known."

"I am not false."

"So you said," Kineth replied, "but proving it may be difficult."

Endrew looked at the ground for a moment, then raised his eyes to look into Kineth's. "Have you ever seen the gods?"

"Seen them?"

"Yes, have you ever sat face to face with the gods as we sit now?"

"Of course not. No man is granted such a privilege."

"And yet you know they exist."

"I do."

Endrew leaned forward. "Then you take on faith that which you have never seen, never touched, never heard."

"I see what you mean," said Kineth. "Your point is well taken."

"I had hoped it would be," said Endrew. "You may have to take the truth of what I say with the same unproven faith you place in the gods."

"Your argument is eloquent," said a man to Endrew's right, "but it does not persuade."

"I agree," said another, directly across. "Such faith does not come easily."

"Especially," said a third, "in an enemy."

Kineth lifted a hand to his face and held two fingers against his lower lip for a moment. "Perhaps," he said, "we might find it easier to grant the faith you require of us if we knew you better."

"Yes," said the man to Endrew's right. "Tell us of your background."

"Your family," added the man directly across.

"And speak nothing but the truth," warned

Kineth, "for we know more about you already than you may think."

Endrew told them of Wollaire and his home in Chaussey province. He spoke of his father and how Duke Endron's title had been thrust upon him after the battle of the vale. He went on to his journey and imprisonment, then a figure to his left interrupted.

"And do you not hate the people of Glender for what you have suffered?"

"Suffered?"

"The loss of your father."

Endrew looked to the ground for a moment, then lifted his face in reply. "Such things happen in war. Some of those same people of Glender you speak of may yet grieve for fathers and sons and brothers lost to my hand. No man can say such things are fair."

"But your imprisonment—"

"It has been most gentle," said Endrew. "Your King Alrick is a fine man, a man of honest and reasonable nature."

Kineth narrowed his eyes slightly. "An odd statement, for one in your position."

"Not so odd as it may seem. King Alrick and I have talked long hours about ending this conflict. War is an evil business that profits nobody in the end."

"So," said the man on Endrew's left, "you have come to look on him with kindness."

"I have. It was with great pleasure that I was able to serve him when we faced the cadwegan."

"I heard it told that you killed one of the beasts with only a sword. Is this so?"

Endrew nodded. "Luck was with me. And the gods, perhaps," he added, "though I knew nothing of them at the time."

"Tell us more of that encounter," said Kineth.

Endrew told how they had ridden from Talorcan in search of Duke Showann. He detailed how the guards were lost to the great beast and how he prevailed over its strength. Then he spoke of pursuing Alrick into the forest and finding him asleep in the stone circle. "That is where I first felt the power and magic of the gods," he said. "The glade fairly shook with it."

"You felt the magic?" asked Kineth.

"I have always been able to feel magic," said Endrew. "I do not know why it is so."

"Most unusual," said the man on his right.

Endrew went on with his story, telling how he puzzled over the leaf masks and the spellword, "Maelgar." He then told of the night he sat on the battlement in darkness and overheard Princess Briduen's prayer.

The man across the circle lifted his hand at the mention of the princess' name. "I have heard," he said, "that you have paid some attention to Briduen."

"I have heard the same," said Kineth. "Tell us, what is your intent."

"My intentions are private, between the princess and myself."

"You must hold nothing back," said Kineth, his deep voice rumbling in warning.

Endrew paused and sighed. "I suppose it matters little," he said at last.

"What do you mean?"

"I spoke to her father, expressing my feelings for her, and I sought permission to—" His voice trailed off in embarrassment.

"Do you love her?"

"With my last breath, but she will no longer receive me. I fear I may have put myself from her mind for all time."

"Why?"

Endrew explained their moment alone on the parapet and his answer to her question. "I had not yet seen what was so obvious," he said. "I had not realized until she fled my stupid presence that the gods lived. I had felt their power without knowing what it was."

Kineth nodded. "Then you seek knowledge of the gods that the princess may hold you in higher esteem."

"Partly. But another portion of me wishes to know the cause of what I have done. You have heard how I healed myself and tonight I felled Somerled with your spellword." Endrew shook his head. "I must confess that I am puzzled by these things."

"It appears that I was right," said Kineth. "The gods have indeed chosen you for some great and mighty purpose after all."

"I would give all I have to know what it is," said Endrew.

"And the princess?" asked the man on his left.

"I would give it thrice over if she would be mine and make me hers."

"She will," came a voice from within the robes of one who had not spoken yet. The figure slowly lifted a pair of small hands and pulled back a hood to reveal the princess' face looking shyly at Endrew.

The young duke stuttered for a second. "My lady."

Briduen lifted a finger to her lips as she stood. "Say nothing," she gently commanded. "Do not spoil the moment."

"Something of which I am easily capable," said Endrew, rising to his own feet.

They stared into each other's eyes for what seemed an eternity, then Kineth rose to his feet and slapped his stomach. "Well," he said, "I suspect this conversation has produced all that we are likely to learn for the time being."

"So it would appear," said the man on Endrew's right, his words filled with amusement.

"May I suggest we withdraw," said Kineth, "and leave these two to their own thoughts. I think Endrew's instruction in the way of the gods will have to wait just a bit longer."

Endrew heard the men begin to move away, then tore his gaze from Briduen's to look after them. "Kineth. Gentlemen. Is it proper to leave us here alone together? I wish nothing to reflect upon–"

"You are not going to be alone together," said a woman's voice. Endrew turned to where one of the torchbearers still stood. The figure lifted a hand to pull back her hood, revealing Margid's harsh stare. "And let me warn you, young lord," said the servant, "that despite favor of the king and any powers the gods have granted you, if you harm one hair of this girl's precious head or give her even the slightest reason to be upset again, I will flay your hide until even the hounds will refuse you."

"I should take her seriously, were I you," said Kineth, laughing as he turned to depart.

"Believe me," said Endrew, looking at Margid waving the torch like some flaming club, "I do."

15

Endrew listened late into the evening as Kineth spoke of the gods, the priest's rich, deep voice filling the night air with tales of both wonder and sorrow. The power of the gods had diminished, he said, as men ceased to believe, and each successive drop in might had sped the decline in faith ever downward until now only a handful of people worshiped the nearly-forgotten names and memories.

"But, how can the gods be weakened?" asked Endrew. "Are not the abilities of beings so mighty fixed for all time?"

"Even one so great as a god must draw their power from somewhere," answered the priest. "Is not a king, or even a duke like yourself, limited in power by the combined strength of those he rules?"

"Yes, I suppose. But a god—"

"It is exactly the same. The might of a god relates to the power of the faithful. Across the sea, to the west, I am told that gods still roam the world as of old because all men believe."

"

Endrew shook his head. "Then the state of our gods is sad beyond the telling."

"Yet we continue to worship in our desire to turn the tide." Occasionally, the priest went on, some individual appeared in whom the remaining powers of the gods flowed especially strong. Such a person was the hope of those who followed the way. Such a person might demonstrate the deities' latent powers and bring people back into the fold, causing the gods' might to grow with the added strength of each new worshipper.

"Such a person," said Kineth, "you may perhaps be."

Endrew shook his head. "I do not see how. Until this night I knew practically nothing of the gods."

"That matters little," said the priest. "If one is chosen by the gods, that is all we need to know, not how or why the choice was made."

Endrew looked away from the priest and stared into the flames of the torch Margid still held. "But what am I to do?" he asked.

"Perhaps nothing," said Kineth, with a shrug, "perhaps a great deal. If the gods require something of you, they will tell you when they are ready."

"To serve the gods would be a grave responsibility," said the young lord.

"One of which you shall surely be the equal," said Briduen, reaching out her soft hand and resting it gently on his arm.

Endrew looked down at the dainty fingers that lightly brushed his flesh, reveling in the thrill this slightest touch caused in him. Then he watched the hand flit away as he felt, rather than saw, her blush in the near darkness.

Kineth cleared his throat. "Well, I see that it has grown late. Many of the others have made their way back to the city already. You must also be off before you are missed and discovered."

Endrew joined the group in rising to his feet. "How do you manage your coming and going?" he asked. "There are guards at every city gate."

"And one of them follows the way," said the princess. "He arranges to occupy his fellows and look conveniently aside as we pass through the shadows."

"I suppose," said Kineth, "you would prefer to ride back to Talorcan beside the princess."

"Compared to the way in which I was brought here? Yes, I should think so."

"Then here are horses," he said as a robed man stepped forward and handed over the reins of a pair of mounts. "Briduen will guide you back." Kineth watched as the couple climbed into the saddle, then lifted his arms wide. "Go in the comfort of the way."

"We shall," said Briduen, then the pair wheeled their horses and returned to the city, leaving the mounts with a hostler among the shacks that lined the walls. As Briduen had predicted, they crept past the guards without notice.

Endrew found time taking on a life of its own during the next two weeks, and he gradually felt events slipping from what little control he held over them. Briduen's acceptance of his love seemed to dovetail neatly into his early instruction of the way, and several times he found himself in the forest with the princess beside him, listening to Kineth speak of the gods. At last, one night he felt her hand creep forward until it tightly clasped his own, and this time she neither blushed nor pulled away. From there, it seemed only natural to find himself among a crowd in the great hall of Talorcan keep the following evening, staring up toward the raised platform where King Alrick sat.

The monarch traced small circles on the table's white linen with one finger and looked down at his lords and ladies with an expression of forced solemnity that utterly failed to hide his glee. Then he turned his eyes to where the dukes of Wollaire stood in a tight knot before looking back at his own people. "I have called you all together here to make an announcement," he said.

"Is Prince Gartnait home?" called a lord of Glender.

"Is the battle won?" shouted another.

Alrick waved his hand slightly and got the silence his gesture requested. "My announcement has nothing to do with the war. Yes, my lords and ladies, Gartnait is indeed bound home for the year. And when he arrives, I suspect he will be surprised to find his sister, the Princess Briduen, newly betrothed."

A wave of hushed speech swept the room and heads turned to where the young woman stood with Endrew by her side. Slowly, the speculative voices faded until silence again filled the great hall, this time dripping from the walls in mute protest of what the king was about to announce.

"Yes, betrothed," said the king, his smile now beaming broadly across his face, "and, as you have guessed, to Lord Endrew of Chaussey in Wollaire, as fine a knight as ever sat a horse."

Caelwin Cyniod and Rhodri Owain exchanged looks, then Cyniod bowed to the king and asked, "Begging your pardon, highness, I believe we are all of one mind. Is such a match proper?"

"You are minister of negotiation, not protocol," snapped the king. "It is up to me to decide what is proper and what is not. Endrew and Briduen have shared their feelings for each other with me and I approve of this marriage with all my heart. I may be at war with Endrew's king, but I could not love this young lord greater if he were my own countryman, nay... my own son."

A few murmurs rose in protest and the king nearly shouted, "Stop that at once. I have made up my mind. If any persist in this whispering, I shall have Idwal Hir Rhun turn the offenders into hogs. At least then they shall be of some use."

Endrew leaned close to the princess. "Could the old mage really do that?"

"No more than fly," answered Briduen, smirking at the silence that answered her father's threat. "Why, casting a spell of light no brighter than a candle puts him out of breath."

Alrick clapped his hands and the doors of the great hall flew open as servants entered carrying trays filled with glasses and bottles of wine. "Now," said the king, "I will hear no more of the propriety of such a union. Who knows? Perhaps through this bond our two lands may become as one and the differences that rose between us in the past will vanish. Now, a toast."

Every hand in the room raised a goblet toward the king as he licked his lips and stared at the ceiling for a moment in thought. "May these two live long and happy lives together," he said at last, "and may they be blessed with children that know both Glender and Wollaire as home. To Briduen and Endrew."

"To Briduen and Endrew," answered the crowd, somewhat reluctantly, and they raised their cups to drink.

"Here," shouted the king, "fill the glasses again. Let us have another toast."

Servants passed through the crowd and each man and woman present held out a glass to be filled with the wine of Glender. So intent were they on their goblets that no one saw Caelwin Cyniod's hand creep into the fold of his robes, nor did anyone notice Rhodri Owain reach out to touch his fellow minister on the arm, then shake his head slightly from side to side. Owain cast his eyes around the room, taking in the size of the crowd that filled it. Cyniod's gaze followed, then he drew forth his empty hand and smiled as a servant passed by with a bottle.

"To peace," said the king, and the crowd answered.

"Peace?" asked a lord of Glender. "Do you not mean 'victory'?"

"I mean what I say," said Alrick. "At Endrew's suggestion, I have opened negotiation with the ministers of Wollaire with the easing of trade restrictions our first target. Is that not so, Caelwin?"

The minister bowed. "Truly, sire. Even now we strive toward this goal, but it is slow and difficult ground to travel. One should tread with care."

"Oh, posh," said the king, grabbing a servant and holding out his goblet for a refill, "you ministers always make everything at least sixteen times as intricate as it need be. If we kings could meet face to face it would be one, two, three, and done."

"The language, sire," said Rhodri Owain, "must be very precise to protect all parties, yourself in particular."

"Hrmph," said the king, into his cup. "I suppose."

"When will this wedding take place?" called a voice from the crowd.

"Ah, at last," said the king, brightening. "A question with substance. Briduen and Endrew will be wed two weeks after her brother returns."

Robear eased his way through the crowd and clapped Endrew on the shoulder. "Congratulations, my boy. You have picked a beauty for your bride."

Jonale leaned in from behind his fellow. "I must say, though, this is a bit of an extreme action just to be out of that basement."

"Even if I thought that was all he saw in me," said the princess, smiling, "I should still marry him."

Robear took the girl's hand and kissed it. "Then you are indeed a gem of great price to see the value in this lad of ours. Please accept our warmest wishes for your mutual happiness."

Jonale also took her hand and kissed her fingers. "Indeed," he said. "As you come to know each other better, may you always be fond of what you find."

"Thank you, my lords," said Endrew. "Briduen and I have already discovered we have more in common than you can imagine."

With that, the doors of the great hall burst open and all heads turned at the sudden noise. "Majesty," called one of a pair of guards who stood in the portal.

"What is it?" answered the king.

"A messenger from the coast has just arrived. Your noble son and his army have returned. His ships have begun to land in Cinioch and he should again stand beside you, in two days at the most."

"There you have your answer," said the king, beaming at the crowd. "Make your wedding plans, for in one brief fortnight these two will be as one."

Briduen leaned close to Endrew and whispered, "Then we must act quickly and be wed by Kineth before that date."

"Is it necessary?"

"My father's ceremony would mean little without being wed—" She paused to look around, mindful of who might hear. "Without being wed—properly."

Endrew could see how much this meant to her and he reached out to take her hands. "Then it shall be as you wish. Do we need to send a message or make some sort of arrangements?"

"Margid will manage it."

Endrew nodded and smiled. "Then you have only to tell me when and where. I shall marry you as many times as you wish."

The princess beamed back at him. "Twice should more than manage."

Thus it was that six nights later Endrew stood beside Briduen within the circle of tall stones, their heads ringed by bands of interwoven flowers. Kineth faced them, his countenance hidden by his mask of leaves, and all around stood a ring of robed figures. Each person held a torch, and the whole forest seemed to dance like the fire of a gem in the flickering light.

"This will be like no ceremony you are familiar with," Kineth's said to Endrew, his deep voice seeming even richer than usual with the solemnity of the occasion. "What we perform is a rite of the way and it is called a hand fasting."

As if on cue, the circle of watchers chanted in the ancient tongue, their voices uniting in words that largely escaped Endrew despite his efforts at learning the language of the gods.

Kineth clapped his hands, then lifted his arms to the level of his shoulders, palms up. Two robed and hooded figures stepped from either side of the clearing and walked toward him. Each of them stopped, bowed, then placed a bright scarlet ribbon in the priest's upturned hands.

Kineth closed his fingers around the ribbons and lowered his hands as the two stepped back into the circle. "These ribbons symbolize your lives and the blood that courses through your veins," he said. "They have been separate; indeed, they are separate, but they shall function as one to bind you together if the gods will it."

Endrew felt Briduen's hand slide into his own and he gave his bride's fingers a gentle squeeze without taking his eyes off Kineth.

The priest looked to both sides of the circle, and again a pair of figures stepped forward to join them. This time, each of them carried a goblet.

"This is a special wine," said Kineth. "It comes not from the vines of men, but from the wild grape of the forest." He took one cup and handed it to Briduen, then gave the second to Endrew. "Drink, and be truly blessed," he said, "for this wine exists only by the will of the gods."

He crossed his arms over his chest and the couple lifted the goblets to their lips. Again, the circle of watchers chanted what Endrew knew to be both a blessing and a request for favor. They emptied the cups, then followed the priest's gestures and handed them back to the waiting figures.

"When a couple marries in the presence of the gods," said Kineth, "they need make no promises, state no vows, speak no empty words of men. For what is in the hearts of this couple speaks louder than anything they might say, and the gods hear these hearts. They, and only they, are able to see how much love Briduen and Endrew bear for each other."

Again, Kineth raised his arms out at shoulder height, showing the ribbons to the crowd. Then he nodded once more to the sides of the circle and another pair of figures stepped forward to join them. The priest took Endrew's right hand and wrapped one of the ribbons loosely around his wrist, then he took Briduen's left and did the same. He put their hands palm to palm together, then tied the ends of the two ribbons to one another. The crowd chanted and

Kineth stepped back.

"Let us see," said the priest, "how tight the bonds of this couple are to be in their life together."

With that, the two waiting figures grasped the couple's free hands and pulled. The young lord's fingers began to slide past those of the princess, then he felt the ribbons hold. The two people in robes pulled harder, and Endrew turned to look at the knot, hoping to the gods that it would stay together. Then the tingling crackle of magic filled the circle of stones, and a point of blue luminosity coldly burned where he looked. It flared for a moment between their hands, almost brighter than his eyes could bear, then it ebbed until its glow was no more than a memory shared by all in the now-murmuring circle.

"Kineth," said Briduen as the robed figures stopped pulling, "what was that light?"

"A sign," said the priest, stepping closer and looking at the ribbons that still bound their wrists. "A great sign. Look."

All eyes turned to where he fumbled with the ribbons, then a new wave of wonder swept through the clearing as Kineth held the shiny bands aloft for all to see. No longer were they tied with his knot, but fused now into a single, slender strip.

"It is the work of the gods," he said, turning so all might witness the miracle. "This pair is not only blessed as a wedded couple; their lives are truly fated for special meaning as they follow the way."

"But what?" asked Endrew.

"It is as I said before," said Kineth. "No man can tell. But when the gods wish something of you, you will surely know."

"But, Kineth," said Briduen. "Are we now married?"

"Married?" repeated the priest, looking down

at what had been two ribbons and were now one. "Why, my dear, you are the most thoroughly married couple in all the world."

As she had on other nights, Briduen led Endrew back to the city. This time, though, they paused on a crest that overlooked Talorcan's walls and towers and stared at the tiny points of light that marked where torches and lanterns hung. The horses nickered and pawed the earth, anxious to be in their stalls, but Briduen caught Endrew's arm and reached up to kiss him for the first time. The young lord's lips tingled at her touch and he reached one arm around her to draw her as close as the horses allowed.

"It is a shame we cannot now live as a wedded couple," he said, after a moment's embrace.

"Soon," she answered. "After father's ceremony."

A little over a week later, Endrew and Briduen stood again before a crowd. This time the great hall of Talorcan was filled with the light of hundreds of candles and the forced and fragile gaiety of onlookers less sincere in their well-wishing than those of the stone circle. King Alrick wandered through the mass of people slapping backs and laughing more loudly with each goblet of wine he consumed. The lords and ladies of Glender shared his merriment in his presence, but each time the monarch turned his attention elsewhere, the faces of the nobility hardened. Only one man in the room dared not to put on a bit of a show for the king. Prince Gartnait sat on the dais, his chair tipped back on two legs and his feet crossed at the ankles on the table, and glared at Endrew with the same unblinking ferocity that had been present in his face since returning to the news of his sister's engagement. The prince drained goblet after goblet of wine, never taking his dark gaze off the young lord of Wollaire as he did so.

"Alright, quiet now," shouted the king, waving his arms for silence and spilling a measure of wine on himself in the process. "We are here tonight to share in a joyous occasion," he said, as the crowd stilled, "the wedding of my daughter, Briduen, and Lord Endrew of Chaussey."

"In Wollaire," added the prince.

"We all know where he hails from," shouted the king, whirling to face his son. The two men stared at each other in silence for several moments, then the king lifted his cup to his lips and drained it. "Now, where was I," he asked, running the back of his hand over his beard and holding out the goblet for more wine.

"The wedding, sire," said a servant, rushing forward with a bottle and tipping it up over the cup.

"Oh, yes. Give us room here," he said, weaving toward the table that sat upon the platform and moving people out of the way as he went. "Now, you two," he said to the couple, "come over here so we can do this thing and get on with the celebration."

Endrew and Briduen walked forward, conscious of the stares that followed them, and stood before the king.

"Weddings are a simple matter in Glender," said Alrick. "We make marriage easy enough to get into because it is so damnably hard to keep at, eh?" The king laughed at his own joke and raised his eyebrows to the crowd until they joined in. Then he turned back over his shoulder to set his cup on the table and saw the prince. "Put your feet down," he nearly snarled at Gartnait.

The prince let the command hang in the air for a moment, then lowered his feet and stood. He put his cup on the table and walked to one side of the room, blending into the crowd to watch.

"Kneel before me," said Alrick, and the two dropped as instructed. "Coming to love the husband or wife that is picked for you is rare enough," he said, "but to be able to wed the person you truly love is even rarer. Briduen and Endrew have the good luck to have met here, under trying circumstances to be sure, and to have fallen in love. How can any one of us, whatever our motivation, say that this match is ill suited?"

He paused to look at the crowd, staring into the faces of lords who stayed with ladies in marriages of convenience while they dallied with women who more suited their tastes. He glared at ladies who had been bonded to lords for the sake of some transfer of land or the guarantee of some right of access. Each time he met someone's gaze, they tried to look back at him, but each time they ended up staring at their feet.

"How can any one of us," he continued, "wish these two anything but the best? If we search our hearts, if we are truly honest, we cannot."

The king put his hands on the pair's shoulders.

"Briduen, is it your intention to declare here, in front of these witnesses, that you wish to live with Endrew as his wife?"

"It is, father."

"And Endrew, is it your intention to declare here, in front of the lords of your own realm as well as the nobility of mine, that you wish to wed Briduen and be her husband."

"It is, indeed, my lord."

The king patted Endrew's shoulder. "Then as king of Glender, I do declare you to be wife and husband to each other, with hope that you make each other's life the better for your being in it."

He paused and looked at them both in silence for a moment, then he raised his head to the crowd. A smattering of applause began, then grew as one by one the people of Glender and Wollaire joined in wishing the young couple their belated but sincere good wishes.

Alrick lifted his hand from Briduen and waved it to still the crowd. "There is one other matter. As everyone must be painfully aware, Endrew is technically my captive here. Well, it simply will not do to have my daughter married to a prisoner, so I do hereby declare Endrew free of his obligation and able to come and go as he pleases, even to Wollaire should he so choose."

"My lord—"

"Oh, father," said Briduen, hugging the king so firmly about his left leg that he nearly toppled.

"Wait, I have more," said Alrick.

"More than that?" came Gartnait's voice from the back of the crowd. "What other insult do you wish to heap upon your own people?"

"The insult is in the hearing," said the king, "not in the speaking. Are there any here, save the prince, who still feel this an ill match?"

Every voice but one muttered, "No, sire," even those that lacked enthusiasm.

"Sheep," said Gartnait. "What else have you to tell your flock?"

"Only this. Not only is Endrew free, but I grant him the unoccupied land northwest of and adjacent to the great swamp. I know of no man better able to tame and defend it. With this land comes the title of Baron of Anarad, if he wishes it."

"Sire," said Endrew, words failing him utterly. "Is it not—"

"He is a Wollairian," Gartnait nearly screamed. "That land is a third of your kingdom."

"And one day you shall have it all," Alrick shouted back, "but Endrew will govern this one part for you. He is my daughter's husband, and you should think of him as your brother."

"Never."

"Then that is your loss, not his."

Gartnait nearly sputtered in his fury, then wordlessly turned and walked to the platform where he once more claimed his goblet and pointedly slouched back into his chair.

"Now, come," said the king to the crowd, "let us have no more of this bickering. Play, play," he shouted at the musicians. "Let Briduen and Endrew lead us in a dance."

The couple rose to their feet, painfully aware of the awkward silence that followed Gartnait's protest and the glare of hostility that still poured from where the prince sat. The plunk of lute and harp soon joined with the whistle of pipes, though, and the crowd clapped with the tempo as Endrew led Briduen back and forth across the room in a shuffling step that sent the fresh flowers scattered about the floor flying into the air in tiny, aromatic clouds. Alrick downed another goblet of wine and soon shouted for the others to join the dance. Men, their long sleeves standing nearly straight out from their bodies, and women, their loose hair billowing around their heads in perfumed halos, spun and whirled in the dance. In no time, laughter filled the room and no one roared louder in his glee than King Alrick Nectu.

The great hall was a blurred whirl of color, music, and movement as the celebration built. Alrick waved his arms over his head as if conducting the revel, then drained his cup and walked around the table to sit beside his son. The dancers scarcely noted the king put his arm around the prince in a gesture of reconciliation. Nearly no one saw him coax a nod and the least smile from Gartnait's lips. Few took notice of the king's broad grin of victory as he turned from the prince and called for another wine. Fewer still gave a second thought as Caelwin Cyniod stepped forward to fill the royal goblet.

The dancers continued in their movement and the light music joined the candles' glow in filling the hall with mirth. Then the musicians ended their music with a flourish and the dancers broke into loud applause. King Alrick rose tottering to his feet, his mouth gaping wide as if he wished to speak.

"The king," called one lord of Glender.

"Attend the king," shouted another.

Alrick gasped for air and lurched forward, catching the tabletop with both hands to steady himself. The crowd laughed at the effect of so much wine and cheered him, calling for him to speak. The king's eyes bulged and he opened and closed his mouth several times, as a caught fish on a dock does while waiting to die, then he toppled backward, missed the chair, and landed flat on the platform.

Everyone present laughed and Gartnait shook his head, then rose to help his father to his feet. Lords and ladies called for Alrick to get up and outdo them all in drink and dance, then Gartnait stood, his face pale.

"The king–" he began.

Everyone hushed, their smiles still frozen on their faces but their eyes suddenly tight with confusion.

"The king is dead."

16

Briduen screamed at her brother's words and buried her face in Endrew's tunic. The crowd stepped back, stunned by the unexpected nature of the king's death, and drew in its collective breath.

"Call for the guards," shouted Gartnait. Servants pulled the two huge doors open and a squad of spear-carrying men rushed into the room. "Take the prisoners back to the basement," he commanded, pointing to the men of Wollaire. "Except this one," he added, turning his attention to Endrew. "Drop him into the deepest hole our dungeon offers and clap him in irons there."

For a moment, no one moved, then Gartnait shouted, "Am I not the king?"

"You are, sire," said a nearby lord, "but your father declared Endrew a baron of Glender no more than mere moments ago."

"Even a real baron may be a traitor, much less a false one such as this. Besides, my father is dead."

Briduen faced her brother and pleaded, "But, why the dungeon, Gartnait? Why must he be imprisoned?"

"Our father was a strong man, too strong to fall over dead without the merest hint of illness. Will any deny it?"

He scanned the room but received no rejection

of his statement. "Therefore, I suspect these foreigners of killing the king, by poison probably. Furthermore, I suspect Endrew of causing the deed to be done, if he did not do it himself. I want him where we can be safe from the danger he presents until we learn the truth."

"But—"

"No more protests, Briduen," Gartnait snapped. "Now, you," he said to the soldiers, "do as I have instructed or I will see your heads on those spears you carry."

With that, several of the guards ushered the lords of Wollaire from the room, then four others surrounded Endrew. Briduen wailed and clutched at his clothing, but the guards pried her fingers free and led the bridegroom from the chamber. As he reached the portal, Endrew turned back and snatched one last look at the princess. For the slightest moment their eyes locked together, then the guards pulled Endrew toward the stairs. He went without struggle, but his heart stayed behind in the great hall.

They led him to the basement room where his fellow dukes stood watching, their tongues silenced by the sudden turn of events and the spear points that waved inches in front of their faces. Two soldiers pulled a thick, wooden panel aside, revealing a dark hole in the floor, then one took a torch from the wall and climbed down a ladder that led below. A second guard followed, then a third.

"Now you," said a soldier, prodding Endrew a mite with the tip of his spear.

Endrew swung a leg into the hole and climbed down the ladder. The three guards waited for him at the bottom in a tiny chamber without feature except for a half dozen small metal doors, each no more than waist high. One of the men pulled an iron ring of keys off a peg on the wall and tried several in a lock before he found a match.

"In you go," said the guard, holding the door open. Wordlessly, Endrew stooped and entered the cell in a half crawl.

The guard who held the torch crouched behind him so its flickering light flooded the chamber. "Not enough room to stand, is there?" said the soldier.

"Gartnait said to put him in irons," reminded one of the guards outside.

"How is he going to escape if we lock him in here?" asked the man with the torch.

"How should I know?" said the other. "Only, Gartnait said to do it."

"That boy has a temper like a stuck boar," said the third. "Always has had."

"Well, no matter his temper," said the second, "best do as he said."

"Oh, all right," said the guard with the torch. "Here, hold this thing so I can see."

He handed the torch to another man, then crawled in after Endrew and picked up a manacle that lay on the floor at the end of a short chain. He gave it a tug and found the chain fastened tight to a ring embedded in the stone of one wall. "One of these ought to do," he said, looking Endrew in the eye. "I expect if part of you stays here, all of you will."

"I expect so," said Endrew, his voice barely more than a whisper.

The guard closed the device around Endrew's wrist and squeezed it shut with a click. "Well," he said, sitting back on his haunches, "that does it."

"Get out of there, then," called one of the others.

The guard ducked his head in a tiny gesture of

respect or contrition, then backed out of the cell. Endrew saw the door close and heard the key scrape within the lock. A thin line of golden light showed where the cell's door was and he listened to the ladder's groan as the three men climbed up. The line of light grew pale, then the wooden panel fell in place with a thud and he was alone in complete, damp, suffocating blackness.

 He sat for what must have been days in a darkness so thick it seemed to have depth and layers like the winter fur of a wolf with its undercoat. No sound marred the silence, no speck of light broke the black, except for those few times when someone crept down the ladder and a moment's flash of golden light showed where a hand thrust food into the cell through a small, hinged section of the door. No word was ever spoken, just the offering of a few scraps and some water, then silence and shadow reigned.

 At first he had crept around the tiny chamber as far as the length of chain allowed, his fingers prodding every crevice in the rock and grasping every speck of dirt on the floor. This exploration had offered no result and had not continued long. Now, Endrew sat endlessly with his back against the wall, his eyes open and staring into the pure ebony that surrounded him. Occasionally, he found himself waking from the nightmare of being entombed, and he drew in his breath with a rush and struck out a hand to force the blackness away. Then calm returned and he resumed his waking dreams.

 He thought of Briduen and wondered if, though twice wed, they would ever live as one. Always her face seemed to hover there in the dark, a presence just beyond his senses that could be felt but not seen. He thought of Chaussey and his river valley, longing for their openness. He thought of the gods—

Perhaps he had imagined them all, he thought. Perhaps a healer had treated the arrow wound and the broken ribs. Perhaps the merging of the ribbons was no more than a sleight of hand trick like those of the wandering magicians who appeared at market fairs. Perhaps Somerled had only pretended to fall asleep at his speaking of the spellword as part of some elaborate hoax. Endrew sat in the dark, turning these thoughts endlessly over and over in his mind, and always in the same sequence: from Briduen, to home, to the gods, then to doubt. In this manner, he passed the long, endless hours of smothering confinement.

He woke with the feather touch of some insect crawling over his hand and swatted wildly at what he could not see. He flailed in total blindness for several minutes, then stopped, breathing as heavily as if he'd just fought a long bout in full armor. He pulled himself to his seated position and began the sequence again: Briduen, to home, to the gods—

But this time he felt no doubt, not the least particle. He had probed what he'd seen and felt from a thousand different directions in previous examinations and he found no way to deny the truth of his healing nor the strength of the magic he had sensed. Try as he might, he could not help but believe. The gods were there, waiting to hear from him, and he began to spend more and more of his time in trying to reach them.

He crossed his hands over his chest and spoke the words of the ancient tongue as best he could. Briduen and Kineth had taught him a great deal, but there was so much more he lacked. He struggled with the speech of the gods, sometimes aloud and sometimes in mere thought, and always he found himself waking to begin the process again without answer. Their silence became a challenge, another reason to live. He addressed his questions and pleas to the gods, calling them by name, then waited. He listened for any sign of answer but heard and felt nothing. Always he waited, then always he began again.

Day after day passed until he no longer guessed at their number. His waking thoughts were only of Briduen and the gods and soon his dreams were the same, so he could never be certain which was which. Darkness was all he knew except for the occasional line of gold when an unseen hand brought food.

Gradually, his thoughts became more bizarre and, though he realized his incredulity at his imagination, he was powerless to control it. He fancied he heard rats tunneling toward him through the solid stone walls. He imagined water seeping down until it filled the chamber and drowned him. He pictured a thousand other horrors, and which were dreams and which were fostered by his waking mind, he could not say.

He sat with his back to the wall, staring into the blackness and choking back the image of death by slow torture when he first heard groaning. Spirits of the dead, he thought, as the sharp wail touched his ears. The spirits of men who had died in this cell must be rising to see who now came to join them. His ears, keen to every sound in the sightless world he'd come to know, listened and heard the rattle of fleshless bones from the direction of the cell door.

He crawled away, toward the fouler end of the tiny chamber, staring in horror at the ghostly light that lined the entrance. Then the door swung wide open and a face leaned in, backlit and surrounded by the golden glare of a world on fire.

"Endrew," came a voice like Briduen's.

"Away, spirits," he shouted, putting his hands over his face to shield his eyes from the sudden brightness.

"He is mad from his confinement," came a man's voice.

"No," said another voice, deep and rich, "it is too soon for that. He is confused, that is all."

"Endrew, my love," said the woman's voice again. "It is I, Briduen, your wife. We have come for you."

Endrew made no reply, but only ducked his head behind his waving hands. The chain that bound him rattled with each movement of his arms.

"Get in," said the deep voice. "Undo that manacle so we can be off,"

"Right," said the other. "This smaller key must do the job."

A dark figure filled the doorway, crawling toward Endrew who threw his arms across his face and froze.

"What if he shouts and gives us away on our way out?" asked a voice as Endrew felt a movement at his nearly numb wrist.

"He shall be well enough when his eyes adjust to the light and he sees who we are. Poor beggar has a right to be a bit taken aback after these weeks alone in here."

Endrew heard a clink of falling metal and felt a gentle hand tug him toward the door. He made no effort to resist.

If spirits wished to take him, he was powerless to stop them. Still, he felt no magic. He had always assumed that spirits would carry with them the crackle of power from other worlds.

He felt the hand urge him to his feet and he

stood, his muscles screaming at him for putting them in this long unfamiliar position. He weaved slightly to one side and put out a foot to balance himself, but he seemed to half sag under the weight on that leg. Hands caught him and held him from falling.

"Endrew, do you not recognize me?" asked a face that drifted into his view.

Endrew squinted, his head half turned away, his eyes fighting to focus in the glare that filled the room. It was the face that had danced just out of view so many times when he stared into the darkness. "Briduen," he said, and he reached out to softly brush her features with the tips of his fingers. "Is it truly you?"

"Truly," she said, and she threw her arms around him and held him for long moments.

"Highness, please," came a voice, "not until we clean him up a bit."

"He is clean enough for me," she replied.

"Come," said the deep voice, "we may be discovered."

Endrew patted his bride weakly on the shoulders. "I am so sorry. I thought you were–"

"Spirits, yes, so you said."

"I heard groaning."

"The ladder as we descended, my love."

"And the rattle of bones."

"These keys," said the deep voice.

Endrew fought to focus on the man who spoke. "Kineth?"

"Yes, and that is Somerled who holds you. Now, hurry, we have put those above us to sleep with the help of the gods, but the spells will not last forever. Can you climb this ladder?"

"I think so."

"Good. We have only to reach the city gate, then horses wait for you to escape."

Somerled placed the torch in a stanchion on the wall, then scrambled up the ladder, pausing only to peek out into the basement room before he climbed out of sight. "Hurry," he said, his head popping back into view. "There is no one about."

Endrew felt himself led to the ladder. Its rungs seemed to swim in front of him for a moment, dancing back and forth as if they sought to deny him access to the room above, then he put out a hand and gripped the ancient wood with all his strength and resolve. Slowly the ladder stilled and Endrew climbed hand over hand, one step at a time, to the next level.

Somerled helped him over the edge, then Briduen and Kineth scrambled up. The two men pulled the hatch cover back into place while Endrew scanned the room and saw the cots filled with his sleeping fellows and a pile of four guards at the foot of the stairs that led above.

"Are they–"

"Dead? No," said Somerled, "only asleep. When they wake, they shall be the ones who will think spirits have been here. Been here, and taken you away, that is what they will think."

"Not for long," said Kineth. "When they find Briduen missing as well, they shall put the truth together soon enough. Now, hurry, and keep to the shadows."

The priest led them up the stairs, his back hugging the stones as they curved toward the main floor. Behind him, dressed in trousers and cloak instead of a gown, came Briduen with Endrew's hand locked in her own. Somerled brought up the rear of the procession, glancing backward with every few steps to be certain they were not followed.

Kineth held up a hand and they stopped at the signal, each of them holding their breath to listen. Then the priest's fingers beckoned them onward and they hurried into the broad space at the head of the stairs and made directly for the open door that led to the inner bailey. Endrew looked to where two more guards lay sleeping against each other, their spears fallen to the floor at odd angles. As Kineth paused to look outside, Endrew bent to grasp one of the long weapons.

"We shall have no need of that," whispered Somerled. "The gods are with us."

"I spoke to the gods from my cell constantly," returned Endrew. "They never answered."

"Of course they did," said Somerled. "When the time was right, they sent us."

"Put the spear down, my love. We have no need of it."

"But—"

Briduen gripped his hand a bit more firmly. "It will only catch on something as we creep away and betray us with noise. Besides, once we are outside the city you will find I have a weapon for you that will better suit your hand."

"Come," whispered Kineth.

"Very well," said Endrew, putting the spear back on the floor, "since you wish it."

"Thank you, love," she said, then they hurried outside into a stillness that spoke of a night at its deepest point, no more than an hour or two before the first hint of dawn.

Two guards stood at the gate, but Endrew saw they were asleep, propped against the wall carefully so as not to drop to the ground. One of the two stood with his head tipped back and he snored softly as the group hurried by. The other's eyes were hidden by his helmet which had slipped forward to half cover his face.

"You two were busy with your spells," whispered Endrew as they hurried past.

"It did provide a certain level of satisfaction," answered Somerled.

Once outside the walls of the keep, they turned and rushed into a narrow lane that Endrew had traveled many times with Briduen when they sought the company of others of the way. The alley led into another which took them to a third, and so on, winding them toward the gate by which those who worshiped the gods left and entered the city at night. They crept carefully past a shop so the money changer's dog would only growl and not bark, then froze at the sudden yowling of cats fighting in an alley.

They continued on when the noise ebbed, swept through two more narrow lanes, then crouched behind a merchant's wagon and looked to where a quartet of guards leaned on their spears beneath the light of a torch near the tower guarded gate. Somerled raised his hands to his mouth and let out the muffled cry of a hungry cat, then twice again in rapid succession.

Moments passed, then one of the guards looked behind himself and pointed into the dark in the direction opposite from where the four hid. "Did you hear that?" he asked the others.

"Hear what?" came a sleepy reply.

"I thought I heard something over there," said the first soldier.

"Oh, if you are not the greatest one for hearing things," said another. "That was only a cat."

"No, not that," said the first, "afterward. I thought I heard the sound of a moan, like somebody calling for help."

"Calling for help?" said another. "Oh, give it a rest, will you?"

"I heard it, I tell you. Do you want the sergeant to find a body over there someplace and start wondering why we did nothing about it?"

"Oh, all right," said one of the soldiers. "Have it your way."

The four men straightened their helmets and walked off into the blackness. Kineth rose from behind the wagon and led the others out the gate in a sudden rush.

"Why did you not use a spell?" asked Endrew.

"There was no need," answered the priest. "Our ally is as reliable as ever."

"Besides," said Somerled, "we both nearly exhausted ourselves putting all those others to sleep. If we tried it again, you would likely have had to carry us out the gate."

"But the power of the gods—"

"Is extremely tiring to those who act as conduits for it," finished Kineth. "Remember, overuse of a spellword is as like to leave you helpless as not."

"Then I should have brought the spear," said Endrew. "We were defenseless."

"Hardly that," said Kineth as they hurried along the lane that led to the hostler's where their horses waited, "the gods were with us."

They reached the stable and rushed through a gate into a corral where three mounts stood saddled and waiting.

"Who stays behind?" asked Endrew.

"I do," said Somerled. "Once they discover something is amiss, someone must create enough confusion to occupy a portion of Gartnait's soldiers."

"Take care, old friend," said Kineth, grasping the tinsmith's hand, then swinging up onto the horse's back.

"And thank you," said Briduen, hugging him.

"May the gods guard your way," said Somerled, helping Endrew as he rose into the saddle. "Now, quietly, walk these beasts away from the huts, then be careful when you reach the meadows. You will not even begin to have enough light for proper travel for an hour or more."

"It will be midday before they notice anything," said Kineth. "We will be far away by then."

"Good," said Somerled. "Now, be gone."

The hostler opened the gate to the corral and Kineth led Endrew and Briduen away from the outskirts of Talorcan and toward the west.

"Are we not to seek the shelter of the forest?" asked Endrew.

"It would be dangerous for others of the way. Besides, Gartnait will leave no scrap of this land unsearched," said Briduen. "You and I are bound for Wollaire."

"Wollaire?" asked Endrew, pronouncing the word as if it represented a goal long thought unattainable. "Home?"

"Yes," she answered. "We travel to the safety of your own lands of Chaussey province."

"But, the port is the other way."

"You would have little luck leaving Glender by way of Cinioch," said Kineth. "That is the first place Gartnait will send his troops and if you did not have the good fortune to arrive in the town and leap aboard a ship just as it was pulling away from the dock, well ... the odds against—"

"Your point is well made," said Endrew, "but why do we flee to the west? I thought Glender was bordered on that side by mountains that ran right down into the sea."

"Indeed, our land is as you say," said Kineth.

"There are a few coves with fishing villages," said Briduen. "They have little enough contact with the rest of Glender because they are so hard to get to. Father let them alone so long as they paid their taxes."

"And we can take passage from one of those towns?"

"I should think so," said Briduen, patting a purse that hung at her belt and jingled as she jostled it. "I have a suspicion that one fisherman or another will be only too happy to sail us across the channel."

"They may fight for the honor," said Kineth.

"Here," said Briduen, taking a pouch that hung from her side and handing it to Endrew. "You need something to eat if you are not to fall out of that saddle."

"I have no appetite."

"Yet eat you must if you are to make good this escape."

Endrew took the pouch and lifted a handful of its contents to his mouth. Then he hesitated. "Will you not eat with me?"

Briduen chuckled in the dark. "By the gods, do your manners and courtesy know no bounds? We ate before fetching you, now it is your turn. Eat, and drink this," she said, handing him a flask.

Endrew did as he was instructed, forcing down bread and smoked fish, then following it with water so pure that it tasted as if it had fallen directly from the sky. "It is good," was all he could manage to say.

"Then, here," she said, an unseen smile clear in her playful pronunciation of the words. She turned in her saddle to reach behind and loosen an item from the bundle that sat there. "Perhaps you now have enough strength to manage this."

"Hold, my lady," said Kineth. "It would be better to wait until we stop."

"But—"

"In this darkness he will hardly be able to appreciate the thing," said the priest. "Ride on."

"What is it?" asked Endrew.

Briduen patted the bundle, then turned back to once again face forward. "It shall be as Kineth requests," she said. "Wait until we stop. Then you shall see."

Her words seemed to tease him through the darkness. He rode on in silence with his eyes half closed and, as in his cell, her face danced in his mind's eye. Only this time, it was smiling.

17

Slowly the sky changed in tone, rolling back the gloom until the first pink rays of sunrise struck the tips of the mountaintops ahead, making them shine with wine colored light. The summits seemed to dance with life as bits of cloud swirled around them, playing tag against the still dark western sky.

"Is that snow on the tallest peaks?" asked Briduen, noting how the light reflected from the heights.

"Yes," said Kineth. "It is a trifle early this year." He turned to look back at the princess, then said softly, "Fear not, we shall be safe enough."

"What is the matter?" asked Endrew. "Must we ride through the snow?"

"No, not likely," she said, shaking her head, "forget it. I was thinking of something else."

Endrew rode in silence for a moment, not wanting to press her on a topic she obviously did not wish to discuss. He found her expression of fear bothersome, though, and remembered Alrick's reluctance to tell him about the cadwegan. And after all, he thought, Briduen was very much her father's daughter.

He turned in the saddle and looked back into the bright glare of the rising sun. The city was not to be seen. The fields of Talorcan lay far to the rear and the three had nearly ridden across all of the wild grasslands that led to the hills. Already, small stands of trees had begun to dot the landscape.

Endrew scratched at his cheeks and felt the unfamiliar growth of beard his confinement had left there. "Are we to stop soon?" he asked. "I should like to clean up for—"

"Briduen has a change of clothes for you," said Kineth, "and we may spare enough time for you to wash."

"By all means," said the princess.

"As for the beard," said Kineth, "keep it. If we are pursued, it will make you more difficult to recognize. Of course," he added, "that assumes the lady has no great objections."

Briduen eyed her husband carefully. "I cannot honestly say it improves you, but Kineth is right. The beard should stay until we are safe."

They rode for an hour, passing across tree-littered slopes that led up into the hills, then paused beside a stream to rest the horses.

"This is where the climb begins in earnest," said Kineth. "I will prepare something to eat. Briduen, would you fill our flasks while Endrew bathes and changes?"

"Of course," she said. He made the request without the least hint in his voice that such a chore was beneath one of her rank and she replied as cheerfully as if the slight had not existed.

"Oh, and Endrew," said the priest, "by all means, go downstream to bathe."

Briduen nodded. "You will foul the water otherwise."

"In the dungeon," reminded Endrew, "you said I was clean enough."

Briduen giggled. "In the dungeon, your own

particular odor was lost among the crowd of other smells."

Endrew wordlessly shook his head in mock disappointment at her betrayal, then walked away from the campsite. At the stream he removed his filthy clothing, then doused himself with cold water and scraped the layers of grime from his skin. The chilling wetness brought his senses back to full strength and he marveled at how dulled his mind had become in the cell. Somerled had thought him mad, and perhaps madness lay not too far from where he had been. To be deprived of family and home had been bad enough. To see Alrick die and be wrested from his wife's grasp had been worse. To spend weeks deprived of his very senses had been most painful of all, and his heart swelled with joy as he listened to the morning chirp of birds that flitted among the leaves, saw the rush of water bubble over the stones of the stream bed, and felt the cold morning light upon his skin. He smiled at the miracle of being alive, then dressed in the fresh clothes Briduen had provided. He walked back to where Kineth and the princess waited and both smiled broadly as he approached.

"Well," said the priest, standing with his hands on his hips, "you do look refreshed."

"And ever so much more presentable," added Briduen.

"I feel infinitely better," he said. "Thank you for the clothes."

"Did you bring your old ones?" asked Kineth.

"Here," he answered, holding up a filthy bundle. "I thought we ought not to leave them to betray our passage here."

"Exactly what I was thinking," said Kineth. "Now, seat yourself and enjoy a proper meal, not like those scraps you had earlier."

"They filled me," he said, patting his stomach. "I have grown used to having little."

"And again," said Briduen, "I must insist that you eat, your lack of appetite not withstanding. Your strength depends upon nourishment, and I will see you eat this, whether you wish to or not."

Endrew looked at his wife's face and smiled. "I see."

"Now you know what it is to be married," said Kineth. "For the rest of your days you will have someone else to do your thinking for you."

"Oh, posh," said the princess, "I intend no such thing. Now, here," she said, taking Endrew by the hand and pulling him to the ground beside her, "eat this." She handed him a small platter of food.

"Of course," he said, "I was probably hungry and did not know it."

"Probably," she said.

"Has the food been blessed?" he asked.

"It has," said the priest.

"Then thanks be to the gods," said Endrew and he began to eat.

Briduen watched him chew and swallow every bite with all her attention, apparently as happy as if she sat in her father's court watching the greatest minstrels in the land perform. At last Endrew finished his meal and the three of them cleaned the spot so no sign of their passing remained. Kineth mounted his horse and Endrew moved to do the same, when Briduen halted him.

"Here," she said, taking something from the bundle that sat behind her saddle, "I told you before that I had a surprise for you."

She held out a long thin object, wrapped in cloth. Endrew took it and felt its weight, then slowly peeled the fabric from the thing. There in his hands lay a great sword, its hilt wrapped in golden wire, its scabbard and belt dotted with gems.

"It was my father's," she said. "I know he would have been happy to see you carry it."

Endrew stared at the blade in silence for long moments. "I– I do not know what to say. My father's sword was lost in battle and I put my own blade upon his breast when we placed him in our family tomb." He felt the beginnings of tears well up in his eyes. "This is too great a gift."

"It is what he would have wanted."

"But it should be Gartnait's."

Briduen shook her head. "Gartnait would never use it as my father would have. You will. Gartnait would use it to conquer, while you will use it to defend. That is the difference between you and he, and that is why my father loved you as his own."

"I shall wear it in his memory and hope to honor him in doing so," said Endrew, fastening the decorated buckle so the belt hung around his waist with the sword dangling from his left hip.

"Now," said Kineth, "come. We must push these horses hard if we are to gain the summit before nightfall."

"Must we spend the night at the highest places?" asked Briduen as she climbed into the saddle. "The snows."

"Perhaps we will be lucky enough to start down the other side. Besides, in any event we shall stay well below the snow line."

"Wait," said Endrew, standing beside his horse without mounting. "In giving me this great blade, you must think there is the possibility I will use it. I would know what troubles you both before moving on."

"Nothing," said Briduen.

"Nothing at all," echoed Kineth.

"You are both too well practiced in the truth," said Endrew. "Deception comes hard upon your lips."

"I–" began the princess.

"No," said Endrew, waving his hand and speaking over her objection, "your father did the same thing to me when we pursued Showann of Alpenne into the great swamp. He and his men held knowledge of the cadwegan from me until the creature itself burst upon us. I do not know if he then found me unworthy of trust or feared I might lack the courage to follow him if I knew the truth."

"But, husband, you have had to endure so much these last weeks. I sought only to protect you from one more thing that might weigh heavily upon your mind."

"Its weight will be greater if I do not know what it is."

Briduen looked at Kineth, then turned her gaze back to Endrew. "The batu men."

"The who?"

"Batu men," said the priest. "Solitary creatures of the peaks, they are, more animal than man, really. They live in the highest places and descend only when snow covers the land."

"Dangerous, I assume?"

"They can be," said Kineth, "though I think it unlikely we should encounter one."

Endrew looked at them both for a moment, then turned to glance up at the peaks that still loomed ahead of them. "Batu men, eh?"

Kineth and Briduen nodded.

"Well then," said Endrew, swinging up into the saddle, "let us be off to meet one."

Kineth spurred his horse toward the west. "I

hope you will not be disappointed if we fail to do so."

Endrew smiled as he and Briduen followed. "I shall try to deal with the loss."

The priest led them ever upward, passing through stands of trees and across meadows where tall grass waved in the wind. They stopped every now and then to rest the horses but always hurried on, mindful of the frenzy that would arise when Endrew's escape was discovered and wondering if it had already begun. By mid afternoon, the trees had grown shorter and were covered with a frosting of grey lichen while all around them, fields of barren rock had replaced the grass below.

"Not the most pleasant of places," offered Kineth, turning to look back at the duke of Wollaire.

"Compared to the northern swamps or Gartnait's dungeon, I find little to complain of."

"Will we have hard lands to travel in Wollaire once we cross the channel?" asked Briduen.

Endrew shook his head. "No, low hills at the worst, depending on where we arrive on the coast. If we find the proper boatman, we can sail around the northern headlands and go up the river to the very gates of Chaussey Keep."

Briduen said nothing but nodded as if she felt they deserved an easy passage after what they had done, or were about to do. She glanced upward into the rocky outcroppings and clefts where shadows lurked, and Endrew noted her attention there. He kept his head facing forward, but he allowed himself to scan the terrain above them from the corners of his eyes.

Eventually the sun dropped from sight behind the line of mountains and the air grew immediately colder with its passing.

"How near is the summit?" asked Briduen.

"Not far," said Kineth. "We shall have light for a while yet so we may reach the pass."

"But not descend?"

The priest shook his head, then pointed to the peaks. "No, but fear not. You see how the snows still sit far above us."

Briduen shivered, but whether from the chilled air or dread, Endrew could not say. "But do not the batu men come below the snow line if the weather is cold enough?" she asked.

"None know with certainty," said Kineth.

"Then why can we not stay here," asked Endrew, "lower on the slopes and less vulnerable?"

Kineth spread his hands in a helpless gesture. "We are surely pursued by now. Were it not for that we would have the luxury of–"

Endrew cut him off. "I do not like the idea of taking Briduen into danger if it is unnecessary."

"But it is," said the princess.

"No," said Endrew. "Only I am in peril if we are overtaken."

"Do you think Gartnait would let Kineth live after helping you?" she asked. "Or me?"

Endrew's head shifted back at the suggestion. "He would not dare harm you, his own sister."

"Oh, husband, you knew my father so well you think you see his shadow's passing in my brother. Gartnait would not hesitate to see all three of us in his dungeon cells or decorating the keep's walls on the ends of pikes. We must press on. We cannot spare even a single hour's progress."

Endrew rode in silence for a moment, then turned to scan the steep slopes above the trail. "Very well, but let us keep on guard all night." He tried to resume his forward-facing pose of calm, but found his fingers drifting frequently to the hilt of Alrick's sword.

They rode to what Kineth labeled the summit of the pass, though no immediate downgrade presented itself on the far side. Another half hour finally brought them to a windswept place with a view of the last glow of a distant sunset.

"Is that Wollaire on the horizon, or the channel between?" asked Endrew.

"You could not see Chaussey from here," said Kineth, "but that roughness to the south is the hill country around Kauley. Are you glad to see your homeland, even from such a distance?"

"I shall not believe it until I truly stand on its soil."

"I fear further progress to that end is impossible for the moment. The trail is too dark for safe passage," said Kineth.

"Here is where we rest then," said Endrew.

Briduen dismounted and scanned the area. "There is no water here."

"We shall have to make do with what we brought in the flasks," said the priest. "Now, scatter about and find what wood this place may provide. We shall have fire to push back the night and cook our supper."

Endrew watched as Briduen turned to go. "Be careful," he said.

She gave him a look that said his warning was unnecessary, then disappeared.

Endrew tethered the horses where they could stand out of the worst of the wind, then followed Briduen among the rocks. He called her name, heard no answer for a moment, then shouted louder.

"Here I am," she said, stepping from behind a mass of rock with a bundle of sticks crooked in one arm. "There is no need to make so much noise."

"I did not hear you answer."

"It is this wind," she said. "It carries the sound away with it. Now, come help me; there is wood aplenty over here."

Endrew helped her gather enough wood to keep the fire burning until dawn, then the two of them returned to the path and found Kineth crouched over a pile of tinder and sticks, striking flint against steel and muttering to himself as the sparks blew uselessly away. Briduen and Endrew crouched and spread their cloaks to keep the wind from his work, but the swirling air continually frustrated his efforts.

"It is no use," he said at last. "We might as well be under water."

"Perhaps godfire," offered Briduen.

Kineth nodded. "I had hoped to save the spell, but I see no other choice." The priest put his tools back into a pouch that hung at his side, his movements barely visible in the fading light. Then he crossed his arms over his chest, closed his eyes, and said, "Coirpre ban cellach. Ruarc!" At the last word, he opened his eyes and pointed at the pile of sticks he had worked over for so long. At once, the wood was covered with flame which flared for several seconds before settling down to a fire of useful proportions.

"Was the last word the spellword?" asked Endrew.

"Yes, 'ruarc'."

Endrew nodded and settled the word into his mind.

"That could be very handy," he said.

"It takes training to use spells of that rank," began Kineth, then he stopped. "I am sorry, young lord. I often forget how so many of our ways come easily to you without practice."

"All but a few spells are beyond me, and perhaps this one is also," said Endrew. "At the least it is one more bit of the ancient tongue I can learn, even if I cannot yet work the spell."

"No matter," said Briduen. "What counts is that we have our fire. I would not have minded a cold meal, but the thought of spending the night here in the darkness would have driven me mad."

"Oh," said Kineth, "I suspect it would take a good deal more strain than that to alter your faculties. Now, you two sit back against that rock and enjoy the fire while I prepare our supper."

Endrew walked to where the priest indicated, then unbuckled the sword of King Alrick and sat with his back against a large rock. Briduen sat beside him and they chatted about nothing for several moments, then fell to silent staring into the depth of the leaping flames as if the fire held secrets they could discover by looking hard enough.

Kineth fanned the smoke from his eyes and fussed over the food, then announced, "It should be ready in moments. Are you both hungry?"

"Hungry?" echoed Briduen. "After this day's ride, I shall eat with my father's appetite."

At the mention of Alrick Endrew turned to his wife, slipping his hand around hers. "Have you recovered from the pain of his death?"

"No," she said, an angry edge to her voice. "By the gods, I hope I never do."

"What is known about his death?"

"It was poison, as we then guessed," she said without turning, "though how it got into his wine cup, none can say."

"You cannot believe—"

"That you or any of your countrymen had

anything to do with it? No. From practically the beginning of your stay here you had countless opportunities to do such a deed, as did many of your fellows, in less public circumstances. Everyone but Gartnait allows as much." She turned to face him at last. "Besides, that does not take into account how you and my father felt about each other. No, husband, I am quite satisfied on that matter."

"Then who?"

"Gartnait made only the briefest inquiry, but seemed settled on his first conclusion about you. I thought perhaps he had been guilty himself, so great are his hatred and jealousy of you. I thought he so feared my father's love for you–" She paused to gather herself, "but I think such a deed is too foul for even he."

"We shall one day know the truth," said Endrew.

"I know we will," she answered, "and with that truth will come revenge."

"Perhaps," said Endrew, "though revenge is often hardest on the one who gains it."

She smiled at him, one half of her face in the harsh light of the fire and the other in blackness. "That is the sort of thing I would have expected you to say. It is what my father would have said. That is why I wanted you to have his sword."

Endrew let go of her hand and reached beside him to draw the blade from its sheath. "I loved him more than I would have believed I could love a king of Glender. He was a great man," he said, turning the sword so the flames reflected off its bright length and flickered before his eyes. "And this is a great weapon."

"May you use it to do great deeds."

The clank of metal against metal caught their attention, but the sound was nothing more than

Kineth banging spoon against platter. "The food is ready," he announced, handing the first plate to Briduen.

Endrew lay Alrick's sword across his lap and reached out to take his own plate from the priest. "Thank you, Kineth. You take good care of us."

"It is my pleasure to do so," he said, sitting down with his own plate in his hands. "Now, let us bless the meal."

Kineth closed his eyes and spoke the ancient blessing, the words coming easily to his lips from long habit. Endrew looked down as the priest spoke and found his gaze held by the light of the fire still reflected in the king's sword. The entire length of steel danced with tiny flames that seemed to grow brighter as Kineth spoke, flames that danced in front of Endrew's eyes and cast a spell that held him motionless.

"Endrew," came a small voice from inside the reflected fires. "Endrew," echoed other voices, fainter and more distant. "Endrew, congall aed cenn magair," they said in the ancient tongue.

Endrew could not move as he listened to what he knew to be the voices of the gods themselves, voices he had longed to hear while in his cell. He had prayed to hear them answer him then and had thought himself lacking when they did not do so. Their silence had fueled first his doubts, then his faith. Now the gods held him and spoke to him from within the light of the sword blade.

Then the camp exploded with a roar as a pale, hairy form leapt flailing among them. Briduen and Kineth rose to meet the attack, but their action went unnoticed by Endrew as he sat rapt, stared into the flames, and listened to the voices of the gods.

18

His eyes saw only the flickering light that danced along the sword's length and his ears heard no other sound than the gods' voices. He heard them grope for the words he would know and he struggled to answer them in the ancient language of worship.

"What do you wish of me?" he asked, haltingly, in the half-familiar sounds of that tongue.

"Only a great and mighty deed," answered a voice.

"What is the deed?"

"To heal," came another god voice, "heal the land."

"Heal that which was broken apart," echoed another voice, more lush and resonant even than Kineth's.

"But how?"

The gods spoke incomprehensibly for a moment using words he did not understand. "You will know," said a voice at last. "You will know when it is time to act."

"But—"

"Remember the spellword 'cellach'," ordered the deepest of the god voices. "Cellach."

"Remember it," echoed the others.

"Cellach," Endrew repeated, the first syllable hissing quietly from between his teeth and the second stopping hard in the back of his throat. "Cellach," he said again to weld the sounds firmly into his mind.

"Cellach," said one of the gods again. "Use the word to heal."

"I will. I promise it."

Then suddenly the flaming lights that seemed to come from the sword blinked out and the voice that screamed was Briduen's, calling his name.

Endrew lifted his head as if from a trance and saw his wife between himself and the fire. She waved a flaming brand in front of her as she retreated from a creature that advanced with slow and easy confidence.

"Endrew," she screamed again. The great beast lifted its arms as if to reach for her. Endrew saw the white fur which covered its body hanging longer from those arms, swaying like the sleeves of a lady's court gown as it moved forward. Briduen swung the burning stick at the creature and he heard it roar in pain and saw it bat her weapon aside. Then the creature stumbled as if something had struck it heavily from behind and Endrew rose to his feet to face it.

He raised the sword over his head and made ready to strike, then he hesitated as he saw Kineth clinging to the creature's back, throwing one arm around the beast's throat as if to choke the life from it. Blood from one or more wounds poured down the priest's face in dark red streaks, but his eyes shone huge and white in the firelight.

"Kineth, let go," he shouted, but before the priest could react, the creature's long arms reached over its head, grabbed the nuisance that clung to its back, and tossed the man away as if he were no more than a doll.

Endrew heard Briduen scream out the priest's name from behind him, and before the sound had escaped her lips the sword slashed down at the white-coated beast. He caught it on its left shoulder and a spurt of blood spattered its pale coat. He looked slightly up into the creature's face. Its pale lips parted, revealing large canine teeth as it roared in pain and anger, then flailed at Endrew with its claw-tipped hands.

The knight managed to duck the blows, then landed another of his own to the creature's rib cage. Again the great beast lashed out, but this time it caught Endrew and sent him reeling. The young lord landed in a heap, his head just missing a stone that might have rendered him unconscious, then he rolled to avoid the lunge of the creature's pursuit.

Over and over he rolled, trying to make those long arms miss as they rained down blow after blow. Then he found his footing and rose, narrowly ducking a swing of a huge fist that sailed so close to his head he could hear it. He stepped back to plant his feet, caught the creature's torso with another cut of his great sword, then flew backward as the beast knocked him to the ground with a blow that sent the air rushing from his body. He lodged against a boulder and had nowhere to roll as the creature threw itself upon him. All he could do was raise the tip of the sword and hope.

The beast's face hovered close to his own for a moment, its almost human eyes wide with pain and surprise. Then it rose, tearing the sword hilt from Endrew's grasp. It stood over him, the great blade piercing its trunk. Then, never taking its eyes from Endrew's, it put both hands on the hilt and slowly drew the sword from its body.

It loomed over him as he lay helpless there, then it lifted the king's sword high overhead with both hands and its mouth opened wide. A great scream broke from the creature's throat as it started the blade on its downward course, but Endrew struck first with the only weapon left to him. He pointed to the beast's fur-lined face and shouted Kineth's spellword. "Ruarc!"

Immediately, the entire area crackled with magic power and a great ball of flame erupted all around the creature's head. Endrew rolled to one side as the sword crashed down and the beast's hands shot to its face. A terrifying roar, louder than any that had preceded it, issued from its throat as Endrew scurried after the fallen weapon. He picked it up from the ground where it had landed, climbed upon a rock that brought his height to that of the creature, took aim, then sent the monstrous head flying from its shoulders with a single blow.

He stood, panting from the brief intensity of the battle, then turned and shouted, "Briduen!"

"Here," she answered from among the rocks, and he hurried to her side.

"Are you harmed?" he asked crouching beside her.

"No, but Kineth—" she said, gesturing to the groaning priest she knelt by. "Why— why did you not rise?"

"The gods," he said. "The gods spoke to me from the light reflected in your father's sword."

Kineth coughed and opened his eyes slightly. "Truly?" he asked. "The gods spoke to you?"

"They did," said Endrew, "but think not on such things now. What are your wounds?"

"They are many and great," rasped the priest. "The gods, what did they say?"

"They told me to heal the land," said Endrew as his hands probed Kineth's body for damage. He felt crushed ribs, an arm broken in several places, and he guessed a cracked skull hid beneath the bloody scalp. Even worse, from the way Kineth lay twisted, he feared the priest's spine might be broken. "Now be quiet, I must try to tend these wounds first."

"Forget that," said Kineth, choking as he said it, "did they speak of anything with words you did not know?"

"Many things," said Endrew, prodding the priest's lower limbs for feeling, "but they gave me a spellword. 'Cellach.'"

"This is a great wonder," said Kineth. "The gods speak only to the highest priests of the way."

"Hush," said Briduen. "You must let Endrew heal you, even as he healed himself."

"No, let me speak. You need to know what this means."

"Tell me later."

"There may be no later," said the priest. "Healing is the highest art of all. You cured yourself in the circle of stones because of the power of that place. There is nothing you can do for me here." Kineth's eyes snapped shut as the pain of a racking cough flashed across his face. "Now, listen," he insisted, "You need to understand all that has happened. There is no one word for 'cellach' in our language. It means to lift up that which was allowed to fall."

"That makes no sense," said Briduen.

"Quiet, now," said Endrew, placing his hands on the priest's shattered chest. He closed his eyes and made prayer to the gods. He lacked the spellword but he had healed himself without one. Forget the power of the upright stones. Please, he thought, please do not let our great and good friend die now. He has so much to do yet, so many ways he wishes to serve you—

Then the sound of Briduen's quickly drawn breath stopped his prayer and he looked down into the unmoving eyes of the priest's face. He stared at the rigid body for a moment, then lifted his head and shouted, "Why? You let me live. Why not him?"

He stared off into the mute darkness until the sense of helpless rage bled away. "I am sorry," he nearly whispered.

"You did what you were able," said Briduen, softly placing her hand on his arm.

Endrew shook his head. "I could have learned more; I could have known the word with the power of healing."

"Kineth said the spell was beyond you."

"I could have risen to meet the beast as it attacked. Kineth was not a man of arms to do battle with such a creature."

"You were held by the gods."

"And for what? I gained a spellword. Our friend died that I might have a single word."

"He died trying to protect us both. Perhaps that word will prove worth his sacrifice."

"How?"

"We cannot know," she said. "All we can know for certain is that the gods took that moment to give you a mission of healing and a tool with which to do it."

"One word?"

"Yes," she said. "Somehow that word will allow you to heal the land."

Endrew rose, still looking down at the priest's body. "I do not even know what that means. How can a land need healing? And what land?"

"You will answer these questions when it is time."

"That is what the gods said."

"Think no more on it for now. We need to give Kineth an honorable burial and dispose of that wretched thing," she said, pointing to the headless corpse that lay white among the rocks.

They gathered stones and built a pile around and over the body of their friend to keep the birds and scavenging animals from him. Then they struggled with the creature, each of them holding it by a wrist, until they dragged it a distance from their fire.

"One of the batu men?" asked Endrew.

"Yes," said Briduen, puffing with the work. "We shall not see another."

"Good," he gasped. The weeks of enforced inactivity had weakened him until the events of this day had nearly exhausted his ability to continue. "How can you be sure, though?"

"Kineth said they are solitary creatures. It is unlikely that two would occupy the same territory."

"He also said it was unlikely we would see this one," said Endrew, allowing the long arm he held to fall to the ground.

"Then let us hope he did not err twice."

They walked back to the fire and Endrew slumped to the ground, staring into the fire for a moment, then at the burial mound of their friend.

"You are exhausted," said Briduen. "Sit, while I–" She paused to look at the scattered remains of their meal strewn around the area. "Well, I suppose I will be able to put something together."

Endrew lifted his head and looked at her helpless face, its features– now perfect in his eyes– frozen in an expression of helplessness. "You have not the first clue as to preparing food, have you?"

"I have seen it done."

Endrew smiled. Before she left Chaussey, his

sister's culinary skills were also limited to the ordering about of servants. "Here, let me," he said gently. "My father and I often cooked for ourselves when we hunted alone."

"But you are so tired."

"It will give me something to do, else I shall fall asleep where I sit."

She watched as he cooked, muttering about her own uselessness. After eating they sat next to each other and leaned back against a large rock. Endrew's eyes fluttered shut time after time, then Briduen scooted away from the rock so she would not fall asleep and he felt her force his head into her lap.

"Wake me," he said, and with those words he dropped into the first rest which passed untroubled by nightmares that he had known in weeks.

After a time, he felt her shake his shoulder gently and heard her speak his name. His eyes flew open, and just for a moment he feared he was back in the blackness of the cell. "Is something wrong?"

"Are you able to watch for a while?" she asked. "I do not think I can stay awake any longer."

"Of course," he said, rising to his feet.

They passed the night taking turns at watch in that manner and neither greeted the dawn truly rested. They breakfasted, though, and made their final farewells to Kineth's grave. Then they saddled the horses and rode down the steep slopes that took them closer to Glender's western shore, leading the priest's mount behind them.

Briduen had no more idea than Endrew what course to follow, so they gave the horses their head and trusted to luck as the beasts plodded ever westward. They stopped to rest less on this downhill part of the trip and even urged their mounts to greater haste when they slowed too much. Then, well into the afternoon, they rounded a bend in the trail and saw below them a tiny village nestled in a protected cove.

"You see?" said Briduen, "the gods are truly with us."

"They must be, or we would have never met."

Briduen turned in her saddle to smile at him. "You make me happy."

"It is all I wish to do," he said simply, then they rode down toward the village.

Steep roofs of wooden plank and shingle topped every building, and small fishing skiffs barely large enough for one or two men littered the stony beach. At a small pier, though, bobbed several larger, open boats and one good sized ship.

"Why would such a vessel be moored in a place like this?" asked Briduen.

"Who cares?" answered Endrew. "Perhaps it is available for passage."

Briduen stared at the ship with a furrowed brow. "Perhaps."

They rode down a narrow dirt path carved out of the trees and brush by frequent usage, then stopped before entering the village. Briduen peered intently at the town and Endrew leaned forward in the saddle to look at her.

"Is something amiss?'

She shook her head slowly from side to side. "I am not sure," she said. "That ship– I simply cannot think of a reason why a ship such as that should be here and not at Cinioch."

"Perhaps we–" he began.

"–should snoop about before riding in there, asking to trade horses and coins for passage?" She finished for him.

Endrew chuckled. "Kineth was right."

The village held Briduen's gaze for a moment, then she turned as if she had only half heard. "Right?"

"About marriage. For the rest of my days I shall have someone to do my thinking for me."

Briduen smiled. "When we are safe in Chaussey, you may do all the thinking for both of us."

Endrew leaned over and kissed her on the forehead. "Some of it, anyway."

They led the horses far enough off the path so they would not be easily noticed and tethered them there. Then Briduen lifted the hood of her cloak to cover as much of her face as possible and they walked into the little town.

The path quickly became a lane, then with a slight turn, widened to become the main street. Timber buildings lined the road on one side with the shore on the other. They walked with a studied pace designed to suggest they had business to perform but were not in so great a hurry to do so as to draw attention. All they managed to accomplish was to have the head of every person they passed turn to stare at them.

"This is not what I had hoped," muttered Briduen.

"This is a tiny village," answered Endrew. "They would know if a strange bird flew overhead, much less recognize us as outsi—"

His sentence broke off as she grabbed him firmly by the sleeve and drew him off the street and into the doorway of a shop.

"What is it?" he asked as they stood with their backs to the street, looking at a collection of fish that stared back at them with unblinking eyes and gaping mouths.

She lifted a fish by the tail and held it dangling for a moment while the shopkeeper looked at them with an expression that mirrored those of his wares. She stole a glance back over her shoulder, then asked the vendor, "This is a bit too fresh. Do you have anything smoked?"

The man silently nodded, then turned. She dropped the fish she held and said, "Just ahead, by the pier, I thought I saw a soldier's uniform."

"A coincidence," said Endrew. "No one could have arrived here before us."

"I know, but there must be more to it than that. There is no reason soldiers should be here at all."

"Like the ship."

"Exactly."

The shopkeeper returned, holding a rack of dried fish. "You will find this good," he said.

Briduen smiled at him from within the fold of her hood. "We wish to take a ship up to the north of Glender. How much smoked fish will we need for such a trip?"

The man made a face designed to indicate mental calculations, glanced at the couple to gauge the amount he might tack on for their inexperience, then waved his hand across the rack. "This much?" he chanced.

"Give us a little more," said Briduen, "in case of unfavorable winds. Oh, and do you have something to carry it in?"

"Of course," said the vendor and he turned to put the fish into a bag of heavy cloth with drawstrings. "Here," he said, handing her the bag, "is there anything else?"

"No," she said. "How much do you need in payment?"

The fishmonger made small helpless hand gestures. "Five royal silvers?"

"Good enough," said Briduen, taking the coins from her pouch.

"Thank you," said the man, bowing his head repeatedly. "Thank you, young lady."

Briduen half turned to go, then stopped. "Oh, by the way. I thought I saw a soldier up the street a bit. Is it tax time already?"

"No, thank the skies above," said the vendor. "The soldiers are here with that ship at the dock. It just came back in today."

"What a relief," said Briduen.

She walked back into the street, and Endrew reached out to grasp her elbow. "You paid three times what that fish was worth."

"And learning we had not somehow been pursued was worth three times more the amount."

Endrew snorted. "Was the information so reliable? For five pieces of silver, that fellow would have told you that pigs have wings and fly to the moon nightly. And you should have asked him from whence the ship returned."

"The only thing that bothers me," she continued, paying no attention to him, "is that we do not know who is on the ship. Now, that is what I should have asked."

"So back to your fishy friend, then. Perhaps he—"

Again she grabbed his sleeve, only this time she did so with even greater urgency. The two of them crowded into a narrow space between two buildings and froze there. Then Briduen peeped back out into the street.

"What?" whispered Endrew.

"I do not believe it," she answered. "Ministers Cailwyn Cyniod and Rhodri Owain are on that dock. They would recognize me in an instant. You also, I suspect, even with your beard."

"Bad luck to have them here."

"More than mere bad luck," she said. "They left the castle only four or five days ago. They must have come here, sailed out, then come directly back."

"The negotiations with Wollaire?"

"No, Gartnait put an end to them. Now, what kind of mission could they perform in so short a time?"

"We may never know."

Briduen drew back into the gap between buildings, looking straight ahead with a scowl on her face. "At any rate, they prevent our leaving for the moment."

Endrew looked over her head and let his gaze wander to the shore. "Perhaps not," he said.

"What are you thinking?"

"What would be so suspicious to their eyes," he asked, "if two fishermen walked to the shore, climbed into one of those small boats, and sailed out into the channel?"

"One of those tiny things? We shall drown before we exit the cove. And who will sail the boat?"

"I will."

"You?"

"Yes. Now, march straight down to the shore. You see that one boat, the one with its sail wrapped around that pole?"

"What of the horses?"

"Leave them as payment for the boat's theft. The villagers will sort it all out later. Do you have your flask with you?"

"Yes."

"Good. Between the water we carry and the smoked fish you purchased, we should be able to reach Wollaire."

"What are you doing?" she asked as he lifted his cloak and fumbled with his sword belt.

"Fishermen do not generally carry blades like this out to sea." He tucked the weapon under one arm, then lowered the cloak to cover it. "Does that look passable?"

"From a distance, I suppose."

"That should do. Now, let us go."

"The ministers may simply leave straight away. At the least, can we not wait for darkness?"

"Every minute we wait increases the odds that someone will stumble onto us."

Briduen sighed and the two of them stepped back into the street and walked slowly toward the little boat Endrew had selected. No voice sounded an alarm, no one challenged them to halt, and in seconds they reached the skiff.

"It leaks," said Briduen.

"They all leak," said Endrew, pointing to boats on either side. "We shall use that cup on the floorboards to scoop out the water. Get in."

"I hope you know what you are about," she said as she stepped into the boat and steadied herself against its rails.

"We shall see," he said, pushing it away from shore and taking several steps into the shallow water before he climbed in. "Get up there in the ... in the ... in the front," he said, waving his hand to direct her to the bow. He sat on the board that ran from side to side near the stern, grasped the tiller handle for a second, then looked up at the mast.

A thin rope ran from the furled sail up through a fitting, then back down the mast to where it was lashed off on a cleat. Endrew loosened the line and pulled the sail as high as it was able. "Lateen rig," he said, "just like the Racer's Pride." Then he reached to where the main sheet dangled and pulled in until the sail filled with the light breeze from the south.

"There," he said, as he put one hand back on the tiller. Then the smile faded from his lips as his movement of the handle had absolutely no effect on the boat's direction.

"Endrew," said Briduen, "why are we going sideways?"

"I am not sure."

An edge of panic rose in her voice. "Do something quickly," she said. "We are drifting toward the pier."

Endrew looked up and saw distant faces, including those of the Glender ministers, turn from their conversation to look out at this sight of a boat so ill managed.

19

Endrew frantically scanned every feature of the boat, then glanced up at the dock. No one on board the Racer's Pride had explained how vessels maintain headway, and for one moment he had visions of sailing the little skiff right up onto the pier and across the ministers' feet. Then he spotted the centerboard sticking up from its well. It looked out of place, somehow, and he shoved the thing down with a snap. Almost at once, the boat stopped skidding along sideways and began to make for the mouth of the cove.

"What are they doing," asked Endrew. He did not dare turn around for fear of arousing more suspicion.

"They are looking away," said Briduen. "You have managed it. No, wait," she added after a pause, "Caelwin Cyniod has left Rhodri Owain and is walking to the end of the pier."

"Does he recognize us?"

"I think not," she answered. "He is merely standing there with his hands on his hips, that is all."

"Yet he suspects something, I know it."

"His suspicions matter little. Once we are out of this harbor, such a small boat will be easily hidden on so great a sea. If he does not act swiftly—"

"What?" asked Endrew as she stopped.

"He is turning back to Rhodri Owain. They are speaking." She paused for long moments, then every muscle seemed to relax. "They are turning away. There will be no pursuit from that quarter."

Endrew breathed a sigh of relief and said, "Thank the gods." Then he adjusted the sail and tiller to clear the sand bar that enclosed the cove, and took them out into the open channel.

Immediately, the wind seemed to increase and the boat heeled sharply to one side. Endrew instinctively shifted his weight to the opposite rail and said, "Pay it no mind. The boat is supposed to sail thus."

"Tipped over so the water pours in?" asked Briduen. She gripped the sides so hard that her knuckles whitened.

'We are in no such danger," he said, flashing what he hoped was a calming smile in her direction. A bit of spray came in over the bow as they plowed through the choppy seas, though, adding to the water already in the bilge. "Here, make yourself busy," he said, "and throw some of this water overboard. It will help take your mind off everything else."

"Oh, yes," she said, "having a boat sink out from under me always takes my mind off my problems."

"Nobody is going to drown, I promise you."

She threw a cup of sea water over the side, then looked up at him. "I know."

Endrew marked what he thought to be a southwesterly heading and steered the tiny craft out to ever deeper water. Briduen managed to get the bilge dry enough so she only had to go back to bailing for a few minutes in every hour. By the time the sun fell toward the horizon, they were well away from

Glender.

"We have succeeded," she said, looking back the way they'd come.

"Succeeded? I have dragged you from your homeland and abandoned my friends to cruel captivity there. Where is the success in that?"

"I have no reason to stay there now," she said. "My father is dead and my husband is here."

"You have a royal title and a brother."

"The title means nothing to me, and as for Gartnait ... well, he was always a cold lad and he grew more cold and distant as he matured. I fear he will make the people of Glender long even more for my father. And as for abandoning your companions, you need lose no time worrying on that account. Gartnait was planning to kill you, I am sure of it. I think he was only letting you stay in that cell until a holiday came along and he could make a spectacle of your execution. How would your countrymen's lot be improved if you were dead, rather than escaped?"

Endrew shrugged, then looked up at the sail and made a slight adjustment for a shift in the wind. "Still, it seems cowardly to flee to the comfort of my home, while my fellow dukes languish in Glender."

"You can help them more from a position of freedom. You can work to raise their ransom and bring them home to join you."

Endrew took one last look at the sun as it dropped out of sight behind the distant irregularity he knew to be the low hills of central Wollaire. "One thought bothers me on that account."

"What is it?"

"Now that your father is dead and Gartnait is king, will he honor the terms of the original ransom?"

"Oh," she said after a moment. "I had not thought of that."

"You may be sure," said Endrew, "that he has."

They sat in the boat, watching darkness grow all around them. Their world was silent except for the beat of waves against the bow and the gentle hiss of trailing foam as they continued heading toward the opposite shore.

No sooner did Caelwin Cyniod and Rhodri Owain return to Talorcan than they discovered the whole city in an uproar about the disappearance of Endrew and Briduen, by magic it was widely said. Gartnait's temper was reported to be as foul as anyone had ever seen it, and the two ministers vowed to keep out of his way until he calmed.

"I knew it," said Cyniod, when the pair was safe within his suite at the keep, "I knew there was something peculiar about those two in the boat." He dropped into a high-backed armchair and slumped down in irritation.

"Oh, come now," said his fellow, "you cannot be sure that it was they you saw. What are the odds that we would have blundered into them at the very moment they made their escape from our shores?"

"Odds? Do not speak to me of odds. What are the odds of our survival if Endrew and the princess somehow figure out what we have been about and communicate it to Gartnait? As happy as the boy is to be king, I doubt he would take our poisoning his father as a personal favor."

Rhodri Owain leaned forward and placed a finger to his companion's lips. "Hush, friend, else your words stray too far from your mouth." The minister of trade stood and straightened his robes. "Besides, the problem is really someone else's."

"What do you mean?" asked Cyniod.

"If Endrew and Briduen somehow piece together our alliance with the ministers of Wollaire, why, the young duke will make straight for Foshay like a bee to honey. After all, who sent him and his friends into captivity?"

Cyniod sat up straight and pondered that for a moment with the side of one finger to his chin. "Yes," he said at last, "you are correct. Foshay and Pyer would be the first ones with a problem. We would be next though, do not forget that."

"But since Foshay would be first in Endrew's line of attack, do you not suppose that our Wollairian counterparts could be persuaded to take steps to eliminate the young couple before they can cause any of us difficulties?"

"But how? Endrew proved impossible to kill before. Remember the fiasco with Lord Wierenn?"

"That is not for us to worry ourselves about. The problem of how to do it is not ours, but Foshay's."

Cyniod leaned back with a smile. "He was handy enough with his poison when we were the ones to wield it. Let us now see how eager he is to use it on one of his own people."

"I will enjoy watching that pompous ass dance to our tune for a change."

"Send a message. We shall meet Foshay and Pyer again as soon as it can be managed."

"At once," said Rhodri Owain, pouring two cups of wine from the bottle that sat near him. Then he handed one glass to Caelwin Cyniod and raised his own in a toast. "To our good friends in Wollaire. May their actions be swift."

Cyniod raised the cup to his lips. "And sure."

The channel between lands opened wider as it flowed north from the narrow passage between

Kauley and Domnall Ua Cnoba, and it took Endrew all that night, the following day, and the better part of a third to reach Wollaire in the small boat. By then, Briduen was able to steer and trim the sails for herself while Endrew napped, and both of them were thirsty and more than a little tired of smoked fish.

They beached the open craft and abandoned it without a backward glance, then trudged up toward the dunes that crowned the shore. They walked through tall eel grass and climbed a great mound of sand so Endrew could get his bearings.

"Can you tell where we are?" asked Briduen.

"Not with certainty," he replied. "Somewhere near Baretton, or down the coast from it, perhaps."

"And Chaussey lies beyond? We could have sailed straight across."

"And been another day or two in that boat? No, thank you all the same, I should sooner walk this last portion of the journey."

"Then let us begin it."

Endrew reasoned that if they struck inland, they stood a good chance of missing any town, so they held to the shore, walking near the very waves where the hard packed sand made their going easier. In no more than a few hundred paces they came to the outlet of a small stream and filled their flasks with fresh water, then they walked for the remainder of the afternoon, following the coast as it meandered toward the northwest.

"Shall we stop for the night?" asked Endrew when the sun fell low in the sky.

Briduen shook her head. "I nearly froze in those nights on the water. Without a fire, I see no reason to spend another night in the open."

"We may not have a choice. Besides, it will be

dark soon."

"We will be able to see. A beach is different from a forest in that there is nothing to steal the light from above."

"Very well then, we continue for now."

They walked for several hours after total darkness, then stopped to rest on a drift log that sat up the beach, half buried in the sand.

"Are you tired?" asked Endrew.

"Exhausted," she answered, "but able to go on a bit yet."

Endrew kissed his wife on the cheek. "You princesses are a hardier breed than I would have imagined."

"This one is."

"Your father's influence, no doubt."

"My mother died when I was little. I have only the faintest memories of her, but I do remember that she always wanted me to act the perfect little lady. My father, on the other hand, had wanted a second son. When she died, he set out to converting me."

"I am happy to report he failed utterly."

"I am not so certain. I still feel more comfortable in a saddle than at a royal fete."

"That makes you no less a lady."

"Or at the least, I hope, one able to bear difficulty without too much whining and complaint."

"Complain all you like. You have had cause."

Briduen rose to her feet. "Complaint accomplishes nothing, but takes air from the body which could be put to better use in action. Come, let us walk on a while yet."

"Very well, another hour or so. But then we must sleep, regardless of where we are."

Briduen sighed in the dark. "Agreed."

They continued up the coast along the damp

sand, stumbling over the occasional dark stones that dotted the shore. They splashed across a wide stream that cut a path only inches deep through the tidal sands to add its waters to the sea, then rounded a headland and saw the twinkle of a few lights ahead.

"A town?" asked Briduen.

"It is too small to be Baretton. A fishing village, perhaps."

"Shelter, at any rate. Come."

She took him by the hand and they hurried up the shore toward the few flickering points of brightness that told of people. They found a village of huts nestled in a cove much like the one they had sailed from. The larger buildings, shops perhaps, all sat dark and blank against the night sky.

"No inn," said Endrew, as the barking of a dog announced their presence.

"Then choose one of these huts where a torch glows. Surely someone will shelter us."

Endrew led Briduen to a low daub and wattle structure and knocked on the board assembly that passed for a door, "Go away," came a man's voice from within.

"We are travelers in search of comfort for the night," Endrew shouted back.

"Then travel on," returned the voice, "you will find no comfort here."

"But I am Duke Endrew of Chaussey."

"And I am King Giarley," came the reply, and a woman's voice within laughed at the claim.

"My wife is with me," called Endrew.

"Then shame on you for taking her upon the road so ill prepared."

Endrew turned to Briduen. "Do you have a gold coin you can spare in that purse of yours?"

"For a chance at a night's lodging, of course," she said, handing one to him.

"Here," said Endrew, shoving the coin through the boards of the door far enough so it would show on the other side. "See this? We can pay."

He heard movement within and pulled the coin back. Then the sound of a drawbar being raised preceded the opening of the door. A man of middle age held a lantern up and looked out at the couple.

"Just the two of you?"

They nodded.

"Let me see the coin."

Endrew handed it to the man, who bit it, then turned it in the light to examine it. "This is from Glender," he said.

"We have just come from there. I told you I am Endrew of Chaussey. I was held prisoner in Glender until my wife helped me to escape."

The man eyed them both suspiciously, then looked back at the coin and turned it over several times in his fingers. At last he seemed to arrive at the conclusion that whatever the land of the coin's origin, gold was, after all, gold. He stepped aside and gestured with his head that they should come in.

Their corner of the hut was hardly commodious but it provided some small amount of warmth from the night air. The following day found them on the road again with a clearer picture of where they were, and before nightfall the towers of Baretton Keep rose ahead of them.

Duke Piren of Baretton was as ambivalent about their arrival as he was said to be about nearly everything else. Out of respect for a fellow noble he acted the part of the gentleman, though, and saw that Endrew and Briduen were given fresh clothing, decent food, and a mounted escort to Chaussey. He also provided them with a private chamber for as long as they wished it so they might rest from their adventures. This room saw their first true night together as a wedded couple.

They both approached the tall canopied bed with a certain nervous mixture of fear and eagerness. Endrew looked down into Briduen's eyes, the perfect lights of her soul that he had once thought too close together, then shyly stroked her cheek with the back of his hand.

"So," said Briduen, closing her eyes and nuzzling against his hand, "it seems this moment has finally come."

"It seems."

"Margid told me years ago that this would either be a thing of great joy or unforgivable sadness, depending on the man I married." She looked up into his face and smiled. "I think she feared father might force me to wed someone against my will."

"He told me he knew better."

"That proves his wisdom and having married you proves mine. Come to bed, husband."

She took his hand and he paused only to snuff out the oil lamp that sat nearby.

They stayed at Baretton one full day more, during which they spent the majority of their time in their chamber, then the couple rode toward Chaussey with Piren's escort. The road was a wide and easily followed path that skirted the coastal hills and by the morning of the second day, Endrew began to recognize landmarks. Soon after that, he found himself riding through the tiny villages that made up his province and each town sent up a riot of rejoicing as he was recognized.

By late morning of the second day, the party broke out of a patch of forest and Endrew set his eyes again on the fields and orchards that surrounded Chaussey. The town and keep sat comfortably beside the river that wound its way slowly through the broad valley. It was all he could do to keep from spurring his horse toward the city walls at a full gallop.

"It is lovely," said Briduen, "the fairest city in all the world."

"I had hoped you would find this place as beautiful as I know my people will find you."

Endrew led them up to the main gate where a guard in uniform stepped forward and challenged the group to halt.

The soldier banged the butt of his spear against the ground and stamped his foot smartly at the same time. "Your business, please?" he asked, then the man broke from his crisp, military bearing and leaned forward. "Duke Endrew, is that you, sir?"

"Indeed it is, soldier. I am home, and my wife with me."

"A wife— Well, if that does not— Well, here now, do not waste your precious time standing here talking to likes of me. Go on in." The guard bowed repeatedly, then hurried over to where his companions sat nearby and pointed to the riders.

Endrew led Briduen and their escort up the streets toward the keep, but word of their arrival raced ahead and every lane was clogged with people of all classes shouting their good wishes and shoving each other for a chance to be closest to the duke as he passed. Endrew waved to the crowd and called as many by name as he was able. Finally, the horses pushed their way to the outer gate tower of the castle and Endrew saw a familiar figure standing in the opening with his feet apart and his hands on his hips.

The figure lifted a hand and two lines of soldiers rushed out to form a human barricade to hold the crowd back.

Endrew threw one leg over the horse's back and dropped to the ground, nearly running to the man. "Bentlan, I–" Somehow, other words failed him and he found himself staring dumbly into the officer's face.

"Welcome home, my lord. I hope you shall find everything as you left it."

"Since I left it in your keeping, I expected nothing less."

Bentlan bowed his head at the compliment, then Endrew threw his arms around the shoulders of the soldier. For a moment, Bentlan seemed startled by this expression of familiarity, then he lifted his hands to clasp the young duke and they stood thus for several moments while the crowd cheered even louder than before.

"Ah, my manners," said Endrew, at last. "Come meet my wife."

"Wife?" said Bentlan. "How did you manage to secure a wife in all of this?"

"A long story which I shall tell you later. Here," he said, raising his hand to help her to the ground. "This is my wife, the Princess Briduen of Glender."

"The daughter of the king? Gracious, my lord, when you do a thing, you manage to do it up proper."

"More even than you might guess. Now, will you have one of your men see to these horses? Oh, and be sure that our fine friends from Baretton are well fed before they return home."

Bentlan bowed. "It shall be done. Uh, and there is one other thing."

"What is that?"

"Everyone shall be wanting to know when the grand ball and feast will be held in honor of your return. What shall I instruct the steward?"

"Oh, give us a week, at least. Two would he better."

"Two it is, my lord."

They managed two weeks and a day of privacy to set up housekeeping and settle into something that resembled a domestic routine, keeping their worship of the gods to themselves for the time being. Predictably, Briduen's Glender origins prompted a wide range of mutterings but each day found more people won over to her side. The servants were persuaded first when they found she always made requests of them instead of orders. Various officials were impressed by her unique blend of practical optimism. All Bentlan needed to know was that the princess had freed Endrew and helped arrange his escape. In the end, everyone saw how happy the young duke was with her, and that was enough to settle the issue.

On the night of the festival Briduen and Endrew entered the great hall hand in hand. Applause broke out as the guests saw them, Endrew wearing a brocade jacket with his ducal seal draped around his neck and the flowing sleeves of Briduen's gown making her look like a bird about to rise in flight. They strode about the floor, greeting everyone, while musicians played from their balcony at one end of the room and whole hogs roasted on a spit over the fire that burned in the room's center. Smoke rose in a white column and disappeared among the timbered arches high overhead.

At last, everyone sat down to the feast and the hall was loud with laughter and frequent shouts of good wishes to the duke and his bride. Then servants cleared away the plates while others filled the wine cups and the musicians struck up a livelier tune.

"I know that song," said Briduen. "I used to dance to it as a girl."

"Then you must again, my lady," said a merchant who sat at her left.

"Yes, Endrew, come," she said, rising from her chair. "Dance with me."

"Oh, Briduen," he said, "You have seen me dance. It is not my greatest skill."

"Oh, posh. Then you, sir," she said, turning back to the merchant. "Will you grant me this dance?"

"With honor and pleasure, my lady," he said, "assuming your permission, sire?"

Endrew smiled. "You do me a great favor."

The merchant rose to take her hand, though the pace of the music challenged both his girth and the size of the meal just consumed. Endrew smiled as he watched the two of them whirl about the floor. Her head flew back when they spun and her mouth opened wide with laughter as her feet tapped out the rhythms of the dance. The whole hall seemed alive with movement, but Endrew saw only Briduen.

"She is a treasure," said a voice beside him.

"Oh, Bentlan. Yes, that she is. Please, sit with me while I watch."

The two men drank as they observed the dancers. Endrew drained his cup, and at once a servant leaned over his shoulder to fill it.

"I am glad to have you back, my lord," said the officer, "and to see you so happy."

"I gained two great happinesses during my captivity," said Endrew.

"Oh? And what is the other?"

"Someday I shall tell you," said the duke.

"Someday soon, I hope, I shall share what I found in Glender with all the people of Wollaire."

The dance ended and Briduen and her partner leaned against the table, gasping. "Come, husband, you must dance the next one," she said. "No excuses now."

"Yes, my lord," added Bentlan, "favor us all with your grace."

"But—"

"Oh, please, my lord," said the merchant. "She has quite exhausted me." He reached across the table to lift his cup. "Oh, blast," he said, "empty."

"Here," said Endrew, shoving his own goblet toward the thirsty man, "take mine. I see I have no chance at avoiding this display of my own ineptitude."

"It is only fair," said the merchant, pausing to empty the cup as Endrew rose and walked to join Briduen. "Every man must dance with his own wife at least once in a given evening."

"I suppose," said Endrew and he reluctantly let Briduen lead him through the steps of the dance that followed.

People cheered as they saw the duke and his wife dancing together and Endrew forced a smile onto his face, though for the most part he would have preferred battle with a cadwegan to this. Then, as the music built toward the climax of the tune, Endrew stopped spinning as he noticed the merchant clutch at his throat. For a moment, he had a vision of Alrick teetering at the wedding celebration, then the merchant's eyes rolled back in his head and he fell.

Endrew left Briduen and rushed to the fallen man. Bentlan hopped over the table and joined the duke. Endrew listened at the man's chest, then said, "Dead."

Bentlan's face clouded over, as if a death on the

premises was a failure on his part, then he reached for the cup that sat on the table's edge. He sniffed at it for a second, then ran his finger around the inside of the rim.

"Poison?" asked Endrew.

"I think so, sire," answered the officer. "And this was your cup. That wine was meant for you."

20

Bentlan ordered the body removed and the room cleared. The guests left, more or less silently, looking back over their shoulders at Endrew and Briduen as they went, their brightly colored garments in stark contrast to the ashen complexion that had suddenly been visited upon the assembly.

The captain waited until they were all gone, then posted guards outside the great doors and turned to face Endrew and the princess. "My lord," he began, "what—"

The duke, still stunned by this repetition of events, raised a hand to silence him. "Come," he said, "this is all too much to take in at a moment. Sit with us as we try to sort things out."

Bentlan walked to where the couple sat alone at a long table designed for twenty. He bowed and drew up a stool on the opposite side. All three sat in silence for a time, then he said, "My lord, what do you wish done?"

Endrew shook his head. "I am not sure."

"Well, something must be done," Briduen said. "Someone tried to kill you."

"And you as well, perhaps, my lady," said the captain.

"Me?"

Bentlan nodded. "It is the custom at weddings

in Wollaire for a husband and bride to drink from the same cup after a toast to their happiness is made. Perhaps someone in this crowd waited only for the dance to end before making such a toast."

"But this was not a wedding," she said.

"You were married in your own land, my lady. The people of Chaussey viewed tonight as your wedding celebration. Surely someone would have called for you to drink as I have described and none would have thought it strange."

"Then we are no safer here than we were in Glender. If such an attempt was made on us once, another will surely follow."

"Do not fear on that count, my lady. My men will stand guard over the two of you during day as well as night. I will have your food tasted before it is served. You will take your meals in the privacy of your own chambers to avoid—"

"No." said Endrew, rising to his feet. "I have known the dungeon of Talorcan Keep. I will not live like a prisoner in my own land."

Briduen reached up to take his hand. "But someone wishes you dead."

"That is part of ruling. My father told me there is always someone who wishes a duke dead."

"Not your people," she said. "I have seen the love they bear for you since the first village we passed through upon entering your province. Bentlan has told me how you worked beside them so all your people could survive that first winter after the war began. No, love, there is none among this province who could wish you the slightest ill."

"Then who?"

"I am not sure, but these attempts must—"

"Attempts?" asked Bentlan. "Someone has tried

before?"

"Yes, in Glender. Endrew was shot through the chest with an arrow while hunting."

"Can you be sure it was not an accident?"

"Endrew said he saw a figure draw and shoot at him, though he could not tell who it was."

"And then your father was poisoned?" asked Bentlan.

Briduen nodded. "His wine," she said, "much like tonight."

Bentlan sat a moment in silence, and the scar on his face turned a brilliant red as he focused his angry attention on the attempts at Endrew's life. "Now I see it," he said at last.

"See what?" she asked.

"You have both been in great danger and will continue to be so. Someone wishes you dead; someone with the power to reach as easily into one warring land as the other."

"But who?" asked Briduen. "Could my brother—" Her voice trailed off as she pondered a villainy she would have hoped beyond Gartnait.

"Unlikely," said Bentlan. "Men such as Prince—" He paused a moment to correct his mistake with a slight bow. "I am sorry, I mean to say men like King Gartnait appear more direct than to rid themselves of enemies by such roundabout means. No, I suspect that certain ministers of both lands might be involved."

Briduen's jaw dropped in shock. "Bentlan, you suggest a conspiracy."

"I do indeed," he said. "The events you have endured could only have been done at the bidding of men who operate with power in both Wollaire and Glender. There is no single man who wields such might, but a group of high officials from both lands could manage it."

"But why?" she asked.

"Ah," said the captain, "there you have me. What would motivate such men as already have the affairs of nations in their control?"

Endrew, who had stood silently through all this, slapped his hand on the table, making the others jump at the sudden noise. "Money," he said.

"My lord?"

"You ask what could motivate such men? Well, that is the simple answer. These base men are moved by the basest possible motive, money."

"But ministers are well paid and live like royalty," said Briduen, "at least they do in Glender."

"Here also," added Bentlan.

Endrew shook his head. "When a man is sufficiently greedy, no amount of payment is enough. No, think of it. When did these attacks begin?"

"With your wounding, but–"

"That is not what I mean," he said. "This trouble started after I convinced your father to lower the barriers of trade between our two lands. He instructed your ministers of trade and negotiation–" Endrew snapped his fingers as the names escaped him.

"Caelwin Cyniod and Rhodri Owain," offered Briduen.

"Yes, those two. King Alrick had them enter talks with their counterparts in Wollaire."

"Pyer and Foshay," said Bentlan. "Of course, they must all have been lining their own pockets with a share of the tariff money for years. If what you guess is true, the last thing they would want is free trade. Why, the discord of war must have made them delirious."

"That could explain what Cyniod and Owain were doing in that fishing village instead of the port of Cinioch," said Briduen. "They must have just returned from a secret meeting abroad."

"Or at sea," suggested Endrew.

Bentlan snarled as if he had a murder in mind. "I knew there was something about that snake-faced Foshay that—"

"Enough," said Endrew. "You have wanted an excuse to behead Foshay since he summoned the dukes to exile."

"Is that not reason enough?"

"No," said Endrew, "nor is this." He sat again and looked into the faces of his wife and old friend. "We have no proof that will allow us to act. Nothing bears evidence of our suspicions. No oath, no document, nothing."

"Then what are we to do?" asked Briduen. "Must we wait until they succeed in killing us before proof is at hand?"

"No, we shall leave Chaussey and go into hiding for a time while I gather the power to do something about this."

"Hiding?" said Bentlan. "There is nowhere you two could be truly safe. Besides, who will manage the province?"

Endrew reached across the table to put his hand on the captain's shoulder. "You will, my friend, along with the council. You will handle things as ably as you did while I was in Glender."

"But Bentlan is right," said Briduen. "Where could we go that we would not be discovered?"

Endrew stared off into an imagined distance, picturing an island with twisted trees enshrouded in ghostly mists while waves crashed against rocky shores. Far away, Domnall Ua Cnoba waited: a place of ancient name and long forgotten worship. Perhaps those who followed the way, or even the gods themselves, also waited.

"I know of one place," said the duke. "Somehow, I think we will be safe there."

"Where?" asked Bentlan.

"I am sorry, my friend, I cannot risk the saying of its name, even to you. Now, do not look so hurt, for I would put both of our lives in your hands a thousand times over. But do you not see that if the name were overheard we should be done for?"

Bentlan nodded. "Yes, I see that." He glanced around the room and imagined unseen ears, then nodded again. "Yes, I do see that." He paused a moment, then lifted his head. "But how will you journey without being followed?"

"Our journey will begin by boat."

"But upon their return, the sailors could tell–"

"There will be no sailors. We shall tend the boat ourselves."

"The two of you?"

"Did you think we had a boatload of helpful little sailors to carry us from Glender to here?"

"Well, I had supposed–"

Endrew smiled at the captain's embarrassment. "You supposed wrong. The two of us managed the feat quite nicely."

"Well," said Bentlan, regaining his composure, "you send some people off for a stay in foreign places and they come back married to beautiful princesses and with their heads all full of the oddest conceits. Next you will tell me you can perform miracles."

"No," said Endrew, "not yet."

Bentlan heard the seriousness behind the words and paused to ponder it. "My lord?" he said at last.

"No," said Endrew. "No more talk now, for we leave this very night."

"Tonight?" said Briduen.

"Yes." Endrew rose from his seat and looked into Bentlan's eyes. "We go now to gather clothes better suited to our journey. You must go to the river and search out a boat small enough for we two to manage but large enough to bear the open sea. Provision the boat with food and water for a week, no, two would be better. Wake a greengrocer if you must, but be sure the food is fresh and untainted."

"It shall be done within the hour."

"Good. Come to our room when all is ready, then we will be off."

The three parted for a time but soon Bentlan's knock came to announce his return. Endrew opened the door and the two of them, now dressed in heavy woolens, stepped out into the hall. Each had a bow slung across a shoulder and a quiver of arrows tucked beneath their cloak. The sword of King Alrick hung at Endrew's hip.

"Is all prepared?" he asked.

"My men guard the boat and its contents."

"Good, then have these brought with us."

Bentlan pointed to the clothes lashed into bundles with leather thongs and three guards handed their spears to companions and stepped to get them. "Very well," said the captain with a formal bow, "to the river, though you look better dressed for a hunt or a raid than a boat ride."

They walked out of the keep and through the city's quiet streets until they came to the main gate. Then, before reaching the bridge, they turned and walked down to the dock wall that kept the river in its bank on the town side. Boats of all sizes were tied against the current, but Bentlan led the party on until they came to a knot of guards standing under the light of a single torch.

"There, my lord," said Bentlan pointing down to an open boat half again the size of the one they had escaped Glender in. "It is not much to look at, but it seems to be dry and seaworthy."

"That is all we ask," said Endrew.

The duke helped Briduen climb into the craft, then he followed.

"Be careful, my lord," said Bentlan. "Autumn is on us and the sea can be—"

"Fear not, good friend," said Endrew. "We shall be safe enough on the water."

"When will you get word to me?"

"When we are both ready and able. It may be months, or even longer. Now, cast off the line."

Bentlan gestured for one of the guards to slip the rope from the cleat that held it. The man coiled the rope and tossed it into the boat which Endrew then pushed out into the current with an oar.

"But winter is coming," Bentlan called out over the water, "how will you survive?"

"By our wits, old friend, and by the grace of the gods. Now, goodbye for a time. Watch over my lands."

"I will," called the captain. He waved for a moment, hoping that his gesture could be seen in the torch light but he was not sure. The boat and its passengers were already lost to the night. "I will," he said again, then he lowered his hand.

He stood staring after them for several moments until one of the soldiers said, "Begging your pardon, Captain, what are our orders?"

"Orders? Oh, send the men back to the barracks. They have done well." Then he turned to look again at the river while the soldiers started toward the city gate. "By the grace of the gods?" he muttered to himself. "Has he also come to know the way?"

Endrew sat in the boat's middle, pulling at the oars that did little more than hold the craft straight as it glided over eddies that seemed to want to spin the vessel across the river's surface.

"The wind is at our back," said Briduen from the stern, her hand on the tiller, "should we raise the sail?"

"I think not," said Endrew. "Not until it grows light, at least."

"Sensible," she said. "There is nothing to be gained by running into something at night."

"Besides, this is not a lateen rig. I have not the slightest idea what to do with that second sail in the front. Perhaps I can make sense of it in the light."

Endrew felt her playful smirk in the darkness. "Oooh," she said, "now we have it. You feared to tell Bentlan he had found you a vessel with which you were unfamiliar."

"Well—"

"Oh, excuse me. I forget that you are a warrior and fear nothing."

"I—"

"Not 'fear' then, a mere oversight, perhaps."

"Briduen—"

"Forgive me, husband, we have spent so much of our married life in boats—"

"Come here," Endrew said in the same voice that moved troops to battle.

"But, the tiller."

"Forget the tiller. Come here."

She let go of the handle and slid toward the

boat's center where he reached out a hand, placed it behind her head, and drew her close for a long and gentle kiss.

"Will you always reward my teasing thus?" she asked when their lips parted.

"It was the only way I could think to silence you."

She knelt before him and reached up to touch his cheeks with the palms of her hands. "Endrew, what will become of us?"

"We shall be fine. The gods will see to it."

"Then you have no fears for the future?"

"My only fear is that you will come to regret leaving all you had for this life of flight and uncertainty with me."

Briduen drew in a sharp breath. "Love, where you are, that is my life."

Endrew let the boat float freely as he threw both arms around his wife. "And not another woman in the world could bear your loss and these hardships with your spirit."

"Then it is good that we found each other. Do you suppose the gods managed it?"

Endrew thought a moment. "I cannot imagine why the gods should take such an interest in the doings of mortals."

"But if they did, does that not mean that they intend happiness for us eventually?"

"I suppose it does."

"Then let us hold fast to that thought, that the gods have arranged everything so we might someday live in peace and happiness."

They spent the remainder of the night drifting with the current, taking turns napping while the other held the oars. Eventually, though, the sky lightened and Endrew crawled into the bow as Briduen rowed. He hoisted the main sail and let it run out to one side so they might progress faster than the river moved them. With the one sail up, the boat handled much like the lateen he had grown used to and he soon sat comfortably in the stern with the tiller resting beneath his arm while Briduen lay near him with her head in his lap.

"But what is the other sail for?" she wondered.

"I cannot be certain, but there are two ropes running back from it instead of one."

"Perhaps the lines are supposed to run on either side of the mast?"

"Probably so," said Endrew, "though it looks like if we were to raise the sail now it would be blocked from the wind by the main sail."

"It must be meant for when the wind is at our side," offered Briduen,

"Then we shall use it soon enough when we reach the open water, for we shall have to sail well out into the gulf that separates our lands before tacking back and forth down to Domnall Ua Cnoba."

"How long will this take?"

"Days in so small a boat, perhaps even a week or more."

Briduen sighed. "I cannot imagine anyone with whom I should rather spend the time."

The journey lasted nine days in all. The river soon delivered them into the sea and they fell off on an easterly heading. After turning to the south, Briduen first discovered that the boat did indeed move faster while pointed into the wind when the foresail was raised and pulled fairly close to the main. Soon, they got into the routine of loosening the jib line from the cleat that held it and letting the sail flap as they came about from one heading to another, then pulling the opposite line taut for the new angle of the wind. By the time the island of Domnall Ua Cnoba grew close, they considered themselves skilled at handling the boat's rigging.

"It seems a frightening place," said Briduen as they glided past twisted trees that lifted skeletal branches in silhouette against the sky.

"Auell told me that it was a place of ancient magics, feared by all who pass it. What better place to hide?"

Briduen turned to catch his eye and smile, but there was something in her expression that said she remained unconvinced.

Endrew piloted the boat along the northern shore of the island, growing closer to the rocks until at last the wind left their sails and the limp cloth slapped noisily above them as the boat rocked in the swells. "I think I see a beach between those outcroppings there," he said.

"Yes," she called over the noise of the waves, "but there is no way we can sail in. The island blocks the wind."

"Then lower them. I can row us this last part."

Endrew slipped into the seat and placed the oars in the oarlocks as Briduen loosened the lines that held the sails aloft and tugged them down into bundles in the boat's bow. Endrew glanced once over his shoulder and drew the vessel toward shore. Briduen cautiously moved past him into the stern and took the tiller.

"You pull," she said, "I can steer."

"Very well, but only for an hour or two. After that, you row."

She pursed her lips to indicate she knew as well as he did that they would stand on solid ground in mere minutes, then turned her attention to missing rocks that hissed with foam as the sea swirled around them. "Close now," she called at last, "one more pull ... and another." Then the sound of round stones passing beneath the boat's keel said they had landed and Endrew pulled the oars aboard the craft and stepped out into the water.

"Is it cold?" asked Briduen.

"My father always told me that if I found the water warm I should look around for which of my companions was smiling most broadly."

"Oh, you," she said, walking to the vessel's bow, then took his hand and stepped onto the rocky shore.

Together they pulled the vessel as high on the beach as the two of them were able, though fully half of it still sat in water.

"Do you think a passing ship could see us here?" she asked.

"It is not impossible. Auell sailed the Racer's Pride quite close to shore. But do not worry, after we empty the boat we should be able to haul it out of sight."

"Then let us get to work," she said, glancing around at the island's bleak scenery. "As much as this place makes me nervous, I fear nothing more than detection now."

The two of them set about taking the bundles from the vessel and carrying them up to where low shrubs and waving grasses could provide cover. Endrew found that the mast could be lifted from its place and they removed the rigging to accomplish this. The seat and tiller came away and soon nothing remained but the boat's hull.

"Alright, then," said Endrew. "Are you feeling strong?"

"Mighty."

"Oh, yes, I can see the power just dripping from your tiny frame."

Briduen whacked him on the shoulder. "Save your breath for lifting," she said. "Now pull."

The two of them grunted as they heaved the boat up toward the cover provided by the plants that grew above the beach. Every pull brought them panting to rest for a moment, then another effort followed. In this manner, they slowly moved the boat up the shore.

From within the shelter of taller plants and trees that stood further back from the water's edge, eyes watched the couple work. No word was spoken as the eyes gazed in silent wonder, but the watchers noted every movement, spotted every gesture, studied every nuance of communication that passed unheard between the strangers.

And behind and to one side of the group that watched from the safety of the trees, another set of eyes pondered the scene. "Damned island," a voice muttered too softly to be heard more than inches away. "This place is getting too crowded for my tastes." The eyes flicked back and forth between the couple on the beach and the group that watched from hiding. Then Endrew stood to flex his back and twisted so his face could be seen. The bearer of the eyes nearly snarled in recognition. "Of all people in the world," the voice whispered. "Him."

21

Endrew and Briduen groaned with effort as they dragged the boat the last few feet into the brush above the high-water mark, then stopped to catch their breath. Then they pivoted the craft so its bottom faced the water and propped it up on one side to provide shelter. More exhausted from the voyage than the strain of moving the boat, they both dropped to the ground for a moment's rest. Then they rose to fetch the supplies they had left on the beach and ferried them up to the campsite. Soon, the pebbled shore was clear of any sign they had been there except for slight depressions that showed where their feet had sunk in among the millions of small stones.

Endrew cut shrubs and lashed them to the boat's bottom to camouflage the craft while Briduen gathered fallen wood. Together they kindled a fire and watched breathlessly as tiny embers swelled and grew until warming flames gradually rose before them. Briduen extended her palms toward the fire.

"Wonderful," she said, with a satisfied sigh. "So many days on the water had me frozen clear through and out the other side. But will the smoke show?"

"Not in this fog." Endrew scanned the desolate surroundings, half lost in the mists which draped everything. "Perhaps coming here was not so clever an idea, after all."

"Nonsense," said Briduen. "We have set our feet upon but the tiniest portion of this island. We have safe shelter for the time being and perhaps we shall find caves or hidden valleys safe from winter winds once we have explored a bit."

"You are right, of course," he said, leaning to kiss the top of her head. "And we must begin searching this place in earnest to find what food it may supply."

Briduen placed a hand on her stomach. "I admit to growing unenthusiastic about what Bentlan sent with us. Do you think there will be game here?"

"Probably. The island sits so close to Glender that some animals must have made the crossing."

"Could animals have survived after the land sank?"

Endrew scratched his head. "If such a thing truly happened, I suppose they could." He glanced at the rocky shore, then turned his attention to the craggy hilltop that crowned the island, trying to picture it as the peak of a mountain range, but found it difficult to imagine so cataclysmic an alteration to the world.

"Well, if there are animals here," said Briduen, "they are safe enough from me for the time being."

"I know what you mean," said Endrew. "If the grandest stag in the forest walked between us right now, I should lack the energy to draw a bowstring."

Briduen and Endrew sat motionless and stared into the flames for a long time, then gradually shifted their positions until they leaned against one another beneath the shelter of the upturned boat. Finally, after several hours had passed, their hunger overcame their exhaustion and they set to preparing a meal from among the supplies Bentlan had provided. For just the slightest moment they paused and crossed their hands over their chests to speak the ancient words of blessing. Then they ate and made ready to retire, still unaware of the eyes that continued to watch them from cover.

In the morning, they woke to the unfamiliar sounds of birds flitting through the branches. Briduen yawned and stretched one arm to her side, then rolled to face Endrew and smiled sleepily.

"I had forgotten how pleasant the morning can be," she said. "How long were we at sea?"

Endrew rubbed his eyes. "Long enough to know I slept better under this boat than I ever could in it."

In no hurry to be anywhere in particular, they rose and breakfasted, pausing to ask blessing for the meal and give thanks for the first good night's rest since leaving Wollaire. Then without discussion they agreed the need to explore outweighed all others.

"Shall we walk around the island's shore?" asked Briduen.

Endrew shook his head. "We do not know how long a trek that might be. Besides, walking on the beach shingle is too difficult with all those blasted little rocks. No, let us climb to the highest point this place offers. That way we may gauge the size of the island and might also stumble across signs of game."

They pointed themselves inland and hiked for a bit more than two hours, sometimes through tall grass and hip-deep shrubs that caught at their clothing and other times up steep slopes that looked like the very heart rock of the world clad only in the thinnest skin of brown and yellow lichen. The trees grew fewer and more grotesquely twisted as they climbed.

"There," said Endrew, pointing ahead, "that looks to be the highest place."

Briduen raised her head to look at the barren spot he indicated. "I can see just fine from here. Besides, the fog—"

Endrew reached back to take her hand. "The fog this morning is barely a mist, and a broken one at that. We shall be able to see everything."

The princess rolled her eyes and blew out a forced breath, but followed him as he resumed their course. At last they saw that they neared the crest, and though backward glances and their imaginations had readied them for spectacular sights, neither was prepared for what greeted them as they took the last few steps.

Hand in hand, they stood in total silent shock for a time, then Briduen shook her head. "Do my eyes lie?" she asked.

"Only if mine share the deceit."

They remained transfixed, motionless except for their hair which whipped about their faces in the wind that blew straight in from the sea. Atop the peak stood a circle of tall stones, a virtual duplicate of those in Glender, and within the stones rested a clean, perfectly manicured carpet of lush, green moss.

"How can it be so fresh," asked Briduen, "when the rest of this peak is starved for water? Why, there is not enough soil atop this rock to get your hands dirty."

"It is the power of the gods," said Endrew.

"Then let us give thanks for finding this place."

Together they walked into the circle and turned to face each other.

"Make the prayer for both of us," Endrew said to his wife, "there are still so many things I do not know how to say."

Briduen nodded, then they both closed their

eyes and crossed their arms as she spoke the words of blessing and thanks, asking that the gods who had guided them safely to this place of wonder continue to ward them in the days of their chosen exile ahead. Endrew listened as the ancient words rolled off her tongue, lulled by the calming sound of her speech. She paused for a moment and he marked how smooth her voice was when contrasted with the staccato crackle in his ears as the sea wind rushed by. Then the words began again, but this time in a new voice.

Their eyes popped open and they saw themselves surrounded by a group of men. Each was heavily bundled against the chilling breeze and swirling lines of color marked every face. Endrew's hand rushed to the hilt of Alrick's sword.

"Nayatt," said one of the men, raising a hand as if to stop the young lord's action by sheer force of will. The man slowly reached up with his other hand and pushed back his hood to reveal a bald head colored and decorated like their faces. Then he spoke again and the other men raised their hands, palms upward to demonstrate that no one in the group held a weapon.

"Who are you?" asked Endrew, in the language of the gods.

The bald man answered, but his words were swift.

"What did he say?" Endrew whispered to Briduen, convinced he'd missed something.

"He said they are those who remain."

"Hmmm, I heard correctly, but it makes no sense in either language. Those who remain from what?"

Briduen grabbed his arm. "From ancient times. These must be the followers of the gods, descended from those who worshiped here when both our lands were one."

She turned back to the bald man and asked in the worship tongue, "And do you follow the way?"

At that, the man said, "Ayann," and nodded in the affirmative. Then he crossed his arms over his chest and broke into a chortling, gap-toothed smile which the others in the group soon echoed.

Something in the expression bothered Endrew and he gazed intently into the man's eyes for the first time. He was startled to see in them no sign of that spark which reveals intelligence. He looked from face to face and found every countenance equally devoid of light.

"They are all simple," he said quietly.

"My love?"

"Have you never looked into the face of one without wits. The expression is the same as this."

"But why? Why should all these people be fools?"

"The laws in both our lands prohibit incest and intermarriage for fear of such progeny. If these people truly are descended from those who worshiped here when the land fell, is it any wonder that they would be thus after so many generations alone on this island?"

"Then it is a miracle of the gods that they survived at all."

"Indeed," said Endrew, "but it spoils a part of my plan."

"And that is?"

"I had hoped this place might hold followers of the way who could teach me more about the gods. I have spell words I do not know uses for. The gods have told me I must heal the land, but they have not given me the means to do so." He turned to look back into the bald man's still-smiling face. "How can I be instructed by that?" he asked, waving a hand in the man's direction. "We might as well be in the company of as many children."

The bald man cocked his head and knitted his brow with confusion. Then the smile returned and he clapped his hands. At this signal, the group of men began to descend, heading for the far end of the island. The man turned toward Endrew and Briduen and made tiny gestures with just the tips of his fingers that they should follow.

"We might as well," said the princess. "By now they must have the best campsite the island offers."

Endrew's frustration showed through his words. "I would not wager large sums on it," he mumbled.

They followed the men until the sun was high in the sky. Then a whiff of smoke drifting through the trees told of a nearby fire and soon they stood among more than a hundred followers of the way in a tiny village of wood and stone huts. People of all ages chattered rapidly in the ancient tongue while a few expressed themselves not in words, but in tiny bird-like chirps.

"Not a full mind in the lot," said Endrew, shaking his head.

"Oh, husband, do not be so harsh," said Briduen as many of the women grasped her hands. "These people are friendly and may help us survive in this lonely place."

"I suppose."

She gently freed herself from the hug of one especially large woman and placed a soft hand on Endrew's arm. "I know you are disappointed, love, but try to make the best of things. I have never met anyone so foolish that I could not learn something from them."

"Even such as these?"

"And are you so much better than these?" asked a voice from off to one side.

They both turned to look at where a man leaned against the side of a stone dwelling, his arms folded defiantly and an insolent expression on his face. In his eyes rested the lively spark missing in the others'.

"Are you of this place?" asked Briduen.

"Only for the last year or so," said the man.

"Then who are you and how did you come to be here?" asked Endrew,

"My name is Taran," said the man, "and how I came to be here is no more your business than how you came to be here is mine."

"And do you follow the way," asked Briduen, "as these others do?"

"You mean all that prayer to the gods and such?" Taran paused to scan the village, then shook his head. "Not yet," he said at last, "though you never know. They may make a convert out of me some day." With that, the man stood and walked away without the least gesture or bow.

"Odd fellow," said Endrew. "A Glender, by his voice."

"Well, we shall have ample time to get to know him," observed Briduen. "He seems in no greater hurry to go anywhere than we are."

The bald man with the painted face came over, smiling and chattering, and tugged at Endrew's sleeve. He led them to the door of a hut and indicated that it was theirs for as long as they wished.

"Thank you," said Briduen in the language of the gods, "but all our belongings are with a boat at the other end of the island."

The man waved away the objection with a giggle and pointed to the path by which they had entered the village. A half dozen people walked toward them carrying everything Endrew and Briduen had brought from Wollaire.

"Thank you," said the princess, taking the man's hand in hers. "Oh, Endrew, is it not wonderful to have such friends?"

One side of Endrew's mouth curled up in a bemused smile. "I suppose we should be grateful they did not drag the boat all this distance,"

The bald man let loose another flurry of words. Endrew caught only a part of them, but he understood enough to know that his thoughts were partially prophetic. More of these people were bringing the boat by way of the shore, and the craft would soon rest among those of the villagers in a nearby cove.

"Thank you," said Endrew, with a smile. "Thank you for taking such good care of us."

The man bowed several times and crossed his arms in acceptance of their gratitude, then he walked away. Within minutes of their arrival, the novelty of being strangers had worn off and Endrew and Briduen found themselves standing alone.

They moved their few possessions into the little hut, then Endrew stood in the doorway and shook his head.

"What is it?" asked Briduen.

"How could these people survive in this state for so many generations?"

"Only by the grace and power of the gods."

"But Kineth said the power of the gods had faded as fewer people believed."

"But here, everyone believes. Perhaps the power of the gods is greater in this one place because of their faith. Could that not be?" she asked. "Could not their faith fuel the power and that power insure their survival?"

"A circle that feeds upon itself," mused Endrew. "It seems logical, but too simple."

Briduen shrugged, lacking any other explanation and Endrew turned to look out again at the village and its inhabitants. Somewhere in the back of his mind the tiniest spark of an idea began to form, but it hid just beyond clarity and words for the time being.

They passed several days among the followers of the way, finding the people cheerful, willing to help, and anxious to share whatever they possessed. Endrew and Briduen contributed what remained of their food to the general supply and the villagers delighted in the change of menu. Several times Endrew joined men as they ventured out in search of birds and rabbits and his marksmanship with the bow won him great, giggling acclaim. Twice he went with them to fish, but though he was able to manage their little sailing boats he lacked even the slightest notion how to handle a net. His awkwardness in this area caused the men to laugh until tears ran down their cheeks and smeared the swirls of paint there.

As the days passed into weeks, they both found they looked increasingly forward to those times when the entire village gathered in open worship. Their prayers in Wollaire had been private and even Glender had offered only the secret nights of devotion in the forest. But this place was unlike the others. Different men of the village, their faces always painted with whorls of bold color, took turns leading services. Endrew marveled as each of them, so ill equipped otherwise, spoke eloquently of the gods with the words of ancient tradition and custom.

Taran always stood alone and to one side as the people met in these assemblies. Endrew watched but never saw the least hint of contempt in the man's expression and he wondered at why Taran should attend so faithfully without being a follower of the way.

One day Endrew approached the shore of the cove and found Taran sitting on a log, tossing pebbles into the water. Quietly, he walked over and sat near the man. "Have they converted you yet?" he asked.

"Not yet," said Taran, with a shrug. "Probably never will."

"Too bad," said Endrew. "There is much comfort in following the way."

Taran tossed a stone in a high arc into the water so that it landed with a loud "ploop." They both watched as small circular waves radiated out from where the stone struck the water's surface. "You see that?" asked Taran. "You see?"

"See what?" asked Endrew. "The splash?"

"All of it. The rock hit the water because I threw it. It splashed because it hit water. Things happen for reasons."

"Yes, but I do not see—"

"Reasons," said Taran. "All I want is reasons. These reasons I can understand, but other things are beyond me."

"There are things we cannot know," said Endrew.

"Then why can I not be at peace in knowing which things I cannot know," said Taran, his voice rising in pitch and intensity. His hands let the remaining pebbles fall to the ground and he drew in a long breath. "When first we met, you asked how I came to be here. Well, I was a soldier of Glender. Summer before last we fought in Wollaire and that campaign ended with a battle that filled a valley. You cannot believe what it was like."

Endrew's mind shot back to the vale and for a second he saw his father's banner fall before the Glender charge. "I think I can," he said, almost in a hush.

"Men all around me on both sides were hacked to bits before my eyes. There was no reason. Some who had escaped the summer's battles without a scratch were struck down by illnesses. No reason. Good men died, bad men lived. No reason. They herded all of us aboard ships to return home with the idea of going back the next year and the next and the next. No reason," he nearly shouted.

"What did you—"

"I never reached Glender. As we passed near this island, I slid over the side of the ship and dropped into the water. It was late in the day and light was growing dim. No one saw me go."

"But the water is so cold. How did you survive?"

Taran smiled. "Ah, for that there is a reason. Somehow I managed to swim toward shore, though it was dark when I arrived. I remember crawling up onto the beach but being nearly stiff from the cold and unable to move further. I would have surely died during the night."

"But the people of this place found you?"

Taran nodded. "And brought me to their village and treated me as if I was one of their own." Then he paused and chuckled. "And for that there is surely no reason. By the skies above, I have given them none."

"These people need no reason," said Endrew. "They act not by intellect, but by pure faith in the gods. They are—"

He stopped suddenly and froze with his eyes on the water. Bits of light and darkness rose, merged, and scattered where the water met the shore and Endrew found his hands on either side of his head, holding it tight lest the swirling notions within cause it to explode. At last the idea that had lurked without form in his mind for so long had come together.

"What is it?" asked Taran. "Are you ill?"

"I know what I am supposed to do," said Endrew.

"Do?"

"Yes, do." Endrew rose, his feet almost dancing with excitement. "Come," he said, "we must go tell Briduen."

"Tell her what?"

"That I was a fool when I said these people could teach me nothing. They— and you— have shown me the path that I must follow."

"I do not understand."

"Faith. Pure, blind faith. That is what is required to work miracles, not spells or lore."

"I still do not—"

"Come, come," said Endrew, reaching to lift Taran to his feet. "If I am able to do what the gods have commanded me, neither you nor I nor any other soldier of our lands will ever fight again. Will you help me?"

"If it will help to bring peace."

"Can you sail one of these people's boats?"

Taran glanced past where the islanders' boats softly rose and fell in the cove, out toward the waves that crashed in from the open sea. "Sail? No."

"Never mind," said Endrew, tugging the man toward the village. "You can learn. We have much to do and part of it involves messages to be delivered."

22

Endrew handed Taran one of the sealed letters, then helped him push the little fishing boat out into the water.

"Now, remember," he called out as Taran raised the sail and began his journey to Cinioch in Glender, "enter the port by night and leave again as soon as the message is delivered."

"I have no intention of being held there," Taran called back over his shoulder. "Drowning is my main concern." The craft shuddered from side to side as he tried to find a balanced position.

The villagers waved and chortled while Endrew stood with his arm around Briduen's shoulder. Together they watched in silence as the man sailed past the rocks that bordered the cove.

"Will he be safe?" asked the princess when Taran was out of sight.

"He should be. He knows how to manage the boat and I told him to stay in the lee of the islands for shelter. The trip there will take him no time at all but his return course puts him straight into the wind. No, I would be surprised to see him back by tomorrow night."

"And when will you return?"

Endrew looked at the sky and gauged the clouds as they slipped overhead. "I shall have the easier time of it with the wind at my side both ways. Tomorrow afternoon, I should think."

"Be careful, love."

Endrew held her close for long moments then bent to kiss her lips. "No other thought occurred to me." Then he turned and stepped back into the water and shoved the boat toward the cove's mouth. He waded out until the chilling wetness rose above his knees, then he pulled himself up into the craft. Ignoring the smaller foresail, he raised the main and set a course along the island's west shore and thence to Kauley in Wollaire.

The journey was lonely without Briduen present and he passed much of the time in prayer, hoping to gather strength for what might come. As he had assumed, the wind held favorable for the first leg of the trip and by dusk he spotted what had to be the beacon which burned at the entrance to Kauley harbor. He pointed the boat to the left so he could beach it south of town and sneak in on foot to deliver the letter and escape.

He watched from the trees and waited until the lights at most windows flickered out for the last time, then he crept nearer. Pressing his back to the wall of a building, he edged toward the street, then peered around the corner to see who yet stirred. Two guards in uniform sat on crates near the landward end of the main pier while a third stood a few paces away. More may have been posted up the street, but no sound nor sight gave away their presence, so Endrew made one last prayer, stepped from cover, and walked toward the soldiers.

"Who goes there?" called one of the men as he approached.

"No one important," said Endrew.

The guard who had stood apart raised his lantern. "Hold there and identify yourself."

Endrew halted twenty feet from the men, then turned his attention to the pair at the crates. "I ask your forgiveness," he said.

"For what," asked a soldier.

"Ainmuire menn boruma," he said, raising his arms and bringing them across his chest. "Maelgar."

The air crackled with the sudden release of the power word and the two men sagged limply to the ground. The third man stared slack-jawed at his fallen comrades, then slowly turned toward Endrew. His wide eyes seemed even more fearful in the reflected light of the lantern.

"Are they dead?"

"Merely asleep," said Endrew. "Now, listen carefully and you will end this night without further incident. I have a message that must reach King Giarley at once."

"Then you are late in its delivery," said the guard. "The king slipped from his horse while riding to the hunt. He is buried nearly a month now."

Endrew stepped back a pace at the shock of this news. "Then who rules the land?"

"The ministers, I suppose," said the man. "Most of the dukes are prisoners in Glender and the king had no children."

Endrew paused a moment, then looked back to the soldier. "Then this letter must go straight way to Foshay, the minister of negotiation, at the capital. Will you do this for me."

The guard nodded. "Without fail."

"Good. Now, what time are you relieved?"

"Not until dawn."

"And does anyone check on you during your watch?"

"No." His glance stole to the fallen duo. "Are you going to do that to me?"

Endrew smiled, hoping to calm the man. "I cannot be followed tonight. You do understand."

"Not a word until morning. I promise. Why, may I rot if I so much as clear my throat loudly."

"And I can guarantee your promise will be kept." Then the spell word again leapt from his lips and the soldier dropped to the ground. Endrew bent near all three to hear their deep and even breathing, then said "Ainmuire menn boruma, I ask your forgiveness." Then he rose and walked away from the dock and back into the shadows of the forest that edged the town.

He slept for a bit, then pushed the boat back into the water and pointed toward Domnall Ua Cnoba. The wind had shifted a bit more from the east than he would have liked and he was forced to tack to the north several times. By evening, though, he reached the south end of the island, then turned the boat into the cove. To his surprise both Briduen and Taran waved to him from shore.

"You managed your journey quickly," he called to the man.

"Your fine instruction, no doubt."

"More likely the gods watched over you."

"Perhaps." Taran waded into the water and helped Endrew beach the boat. "Did all go well?"

"Fine, and you?"

"We have only to wait for the dark of the moon to know if they will come."

"They will," said Endrew, splashing ashore. "Gartnait will be crawling the walls for a chance to get his hands on me." He walked to where Briduen waited and took her in his arms for long, silent moments. At last he stood back and said, "King Giarley is dead."

"How?"

"A hunting accident, it is said, though I have my doubts."

"Surely you do not suspect your lords Foshay and Pyer of killing your king."

"They are as capable as Owain and Cyniod were of poisoning your father. But whether they managed it or not matters little, there will be other problems."

"The question of succession?" she said.

"Yes. Your brother may now press his claim against all of Wollaire, not just one province."

"The war will grow even wider," said Briduen. "You must stop it."

"That is exactly what I intend to do in little more than a fortnight."

Endrew spent the next two weeks in constant prayer and meditation, only pausing to eat when Briduen insisted he must do so lest he lose strength. At last he ceased his meditations and devoted his energy to worrying whether he had timed matters correctly. He had tried to give himself enough time for messages to reach their destinations but not so much that the ministers of both lands had the chance to conspire. He hoped that Foshay's ambition and Gartnait's desire to see him once again in irons would drive the plan forward. Until the morning after the night of the new moon, he could not be sure, but as dawn rose and he looked down from the stone-ringed circle he could see a ship anchored just off either shore of the island with more bobbing in the distance.

"Damn them all," he said. "The letters specifically said to sail without troops."

"Oh, husband, you were not so naive as to think they would follow that instruction."

Endrew scowled. "No, I suppose not, but I had hoped. I do not wish to see a battle break out." He turned his attention back to the water and could just make out several tiny dots, as what must be small boats made their way to shore from the ships. "Are the villagers in place to greet and escort our guests."

"They are," said Taran. "From the look of things, I would say the emissaries of Glender and Wollaire should reach the summit here at about the same time."

"Mael bel donnchad," said the bald man, pointing toward first one of the ships and then the other. "Ab uatu."

"Yes," said Briduen, "big boats," and she placed a hand on his arm.

"Look to the south," said Taran. "Line squalls."

The others turned to see the grey line of darkness rolling toward them from the sea.

"I fear we shall be a bit weather beaten before this day is out," said Briduen.

"Aye," said Taran, "it is a cold rain that rides so harsh a wind this time of year."

Endrew said nothing, but only closed his eyes and dropped to his knees to make final preparation while the others watched over him. His thoughts were of the gods and only of the gods as he prayed that he was ready for what lay ahead. An hour passed, and then another, but he finally heard the sound of chanting as two bands of villagers led the strangers closer. At last his ears told him they had arrived.

Voices erupted with surprise and anger as each group reached the crest and beheld the other. Gartnait's voice boomed above the others, though, and he called out, "What is the meaning of this? Briduen, I see you standing there behind those two men. Where is Endrew? I was told he would be here."

"We were told the same," said Foshay.

"And you were both told correctly," said Endrew. He whispered one final, quiet word of prayer, then lifted his head and opened his eyes. Before him stood the men he'd summoned, but just beyond them waited twenty or more soldiers from each land, every one of them armed with crossbows and eyeing the opposition suspiciously.

"Lord Endrew?" asked Caelwin Cyniod.

Endrew rose and drew back the hood of his robe, letting his tawny hair whip around his lined and painted face. The wind wailed and the first large, splashing raindrops struck the back of his head. "Yes," he said, "and I want to thank you all for accepting my invitation."

"Invitation, pah," spat Gartnait, raising a hand over his eyes to shield them. "You know why I have come."

"I do, but you might be surprised to find that the ministers of my own land have come on the same errand."

Gartnait wrinkled his brow. "The same—"

"Lords Pyer and Foshay of Wollaire, and your own lords Cyniod and Owain have more in common than their offices, Gartnait. At the very least they are largely responsible for the war between our lands. At the most, they are guilty of the death of your father and possibly King Giarley as well.

"We had nothing to do with Giarley," shouted Pyer.

"It is a lie," called Owain.

"The man is mad," said Foshay. "Why, look at him. Is this the semblance of a duke of Wollaire or that of a mad hermit?"

"I would be the first to admit my mind does not

work as yours does," said Endrew, "and for that I shall always be grateful. Furthermore, I discovered a great truth while in Glender, and I want to share it with you. It is something I once would have thought mad if I had heard it from the lips of another."

"And that is?"

"The gods live."

The men from both lands reacted to his statement with indulgent laughter. "You brought us to stand out in the rain to hear this? Why, everyone knows the gods have been dead since before memory," said Gartnait.

"Dead to the mind of man, perhaps," said Endrew, "but live, they do."

"And how do you know this great truth?" asked Foshay.

"Because they have spoken to me. They have charged me with the task of healing the land."

"Land," said Gartnait, "what land?"

"Our land. That which we now call Glender and Wollaire was once one and at peace. Now it is divided and troubled. It must be made one again and have the gods restored to it. I will do this with the sword of King Alrick Nectu and the power of the gods."

Foshay gasped. "You dare speak of uniting—"

"That sword," called Gartnait. "It should be mine."

"Ridiculous," said Rhodri Owain.

"Impossible," cried Pyer. "The barriers to trade—"

"It shall be one land," shouted Gartnait, "but I shall be king."

"Gartnait," called Endrew, above the din, "do you not see what has happened here? Is your anger such that you cannot recognize how these ministers

Returning of the Way

have kept the lands apart for their own profit? When I persuaded your father to lower tariffs, they had him poisoned. Then they tried to kill me in my own home after I escaped. Gentlemen," he said, looking from one minister to another, "stop me if I have left out any part of the tale."

"Lunatic raving," said Caelwin Cyniod. "I could never do what this boy has said."

"Nor I," said Foshay. "Why, he accuses me of trying to harm one of my own countrymen. I am incapable of such a thing."

"You lie," came a gruff voice from among the villagers who stood behind him, then a sudden movement and a flash of steel ended with a knife between Foshay's ribs. The minister's cry of pain was muffled by a sudden clap of thunder.

"Showann!" cried Endrew.

"Yes," said the duke in his familiar, gravel rumble as he rose with the still dripping dagger in his hand. "You thought I was dead, eh? Well, I said I would have my revenge, and I have."

"How did you—"

"Manage the escape? I rode the river for a bit, then changed course and made my way over the southern mountains. I persuaded a fisherman to sail me home, but the fellow grew troublesome and he... fell overboard. The current carried me here and I have hidden from these dullards ever since." He waved his arm to indicate the villagers. "You cannot imagine my joy at the sight of these traitors. Now, I have one more chore to perform."

"Save me," called Pyer as Showann wheeled to face him with the knife.

"And did you truly kill my father?" screamed Gartnait at his own ministers. The sudden fire of a distant lightning flash glinted off his sword as he raised it overhead and stepped toward Rhodri Owain, but Caelwin Cyniod lunged forward with a knife and caught the young king in the chest. Another thunderclap rocked the mountaintop.

    Briduen's scream pierced the loud rumble as the blade struck her brother, and the soldiers of both sides gave in to their nervousness as the hilltop rang with the twang of crossbow strings.

    "Stop them," shouted Briduen. "You must make them stop."

    Endrew raised the sword in both hands, hoping that his faith was as complete as that of the simple folk of this island, hoping that he had understood the gods' meaning. The spell word he had received from them had cost Kineth his life in the fight with the batu man. Only now would he know whether that life had been given in vain and whether his faith was equal to the task.

    "Cadell ap maelor!" he shouted in final supplication, then he added the spell word, "Cellach!" and drove the sword downward with as much force as he was able to muster.

    A sudden flash of lightning and simultaneous thunder froze every figure but Endrew for a time. The lightning danced in his hands and a surge of power greater than any he had previously known snapped all around him as he felt the sword slice through the moss of the circle and then into the very rock beneath. Deeper and deeper it penetrated until it stopped just short of the hilt. Then the thunder's rumble possessed the very mountaintop which shook and roared as the sky had. All thought of fighting ceased as everyone present dropped to the ground and held on, lest they be thrown down the slope.

    The spell word "cellach," Kineth had said,

meant "to raise that which was let fall." Now Endrew lifted his sight from the sword hilt and looked out to where the ships bobbed in the high and sudden waves. Slowly, ever so slowly, the shore line spread outward from Domnall Ua Cnoba until it reached the vessels and left them leaning to one side on dry land. The squall line passed northward, and with it the division between land and water. In shrieking bursts, the mountain continued upward and the sea fled further and further into the distance. At last, after many long, terror-filled minutes the rumbling ceased. The darkest clouds were now far to the north, leaving only a gentle, misty rainfall on the peak.

Everyone rose in awed silence to scan the horizon, and Endrew also stood to see this rebuilt world he had helped to make. The south end of the island now claimed another half mile of land, but the greater difference lay to the north. As far as the eye could see, no water remained to separate Glender from Wollaire. Domnall Ua Cnoba was no longer an obscure speck in the midst of the sea, but once again the tallest peak of a southern range.

Briduen moved first, rushing to where her brother lay. "Oh, Gartnait," she said, rolling him over. Blood covered his side where Cyniod's knife had struck and a stray crossbow bolt protruded from his body.

"Forgive me," he said, then his eyes closed forever.

Endrew felt unsteady on his feet, but he lurched forward to join his wife. "Let me help him," he said, bending to crouch beside the body.

"It is too late," she said, "he is gone." Then together they rose.

Every person present stood as if rooted to the spot and shifted their gaze between Endrew and the sword embedded in the mountaintop. Slowly, those with weapons dropped them and every head was soon bowed.

Endrew spoke quietly as the only other sound present was the gentle hiss of lightly falling rain and he felt neither the strength nor need to raise his voice. "I meant what I said. The gods still live and they commanded me to unite and heal the land. I have shown you their power. Do any now doubt it?"

He paused, but heard no reply. "Then go back to your homes and tell what you have seen. Never again will the people of Glender and Wollaire raise a hand against one another in anger." Then he turned and gestured to where the hilt of Alrick's sword protruded from the moss. "And let this sword stay embedded where it is as a sign of the power of the gods, that people of both lands may journey here to see the proof of what you tell them."

"As you will it," came a chorus of quiet voices.

"Now, go," said Endrew. "And take with you the bodies of those who have fallen, so they may be buried according to custom near their homes."

Slowly, the cluster of people broke up and scattered down both sides of the mountain until only three remained.

"Well," said Taran, "you do have a flair for the dramatic."

Endrew wanted to reply but felt drained from casting the spell. "At times," was all he could muster.

"Are you injured?" asked Briduen, seeing how he fought for balance.

"Only a bit dizzy," said Endrew. "Remember when Kineth warned that spells are sometimes hardest on those who cast them?"

"I do," said Briduen, then her attention turned

to the people who trudged down the mountain. "You know you will have to deal with the ministers."

Endrew nodded wearily. "I suppose."

"And the people will want you for king now, of both lands. You are the only one with titles in both Glender and Wollaire."

"I suppose you are right," said Endrew, "though I wish it were not so."

"You would turn down a throne?" asked Taran.

"Gladly," said Endrew. "A throne is just another kind of prison, one where you are bound not by bars but custom and ceremony."

"Endrew," said Taran, "you just raised land from beneath the sea. You can create your own custom and ceremony to suit your whim. Who would dare stand before your power?"

"The power is not mine, but the gods'."

"But you wield it."

"And that is precisely the problem. A man with that much power is in danger of taking that power too seriously."

"But you are not like other men," said Briduen, "and you have the gods to help guide you."

"Why, man," said Taran, "you can have anything you wish."

Endrew turned to look at him. "Having the gods to guide me, as she said, is everything I wish." Then he turned to look at Briduen. "Well, almost everything. Having you beside me is the rest."

She looked up into his eyes and smiled, then took the sleeve of her robe and wiped the paint from one of his rain-streaked cheeks. His hand reached up, held hers for a moment, then he drew her close and held her body tight against his.

At last they stepped apart. "I fear we have a great many things to do," said Endrew.

"Then we may as well be started," said Briduen. "Come."

"You will have to steady me," said Endrew.

Briduen took hold of his arm with one hand and reached the other around his waist. "Of course, love."

The three of them walked down a trail toward the lowlands, and Taran had to listen to Endrew and Briduen discuss the relative merits of whether they would make their home in Chaussey, build a new city in the freshly raised lands that now united the two former enemies, occupy Talorcan or the capital of Wollaire. Neither of them wished to offend the other and they both refused to state a firm preference.

At last, Briduen looked back over her shoulder to where their companion walked. "Where do you think we should best live?" she asked.

Taran, by then long tired of the discussion, rolled his eyes. "Only the gods know," he said.

Endrew looked back to where the man walked. So, he thought, the returning of the way had truly begun. A thin, weary smile crossed his lips for that was all the victory he needed, to keep on.

Credits

"sword image" credit: TheStockLair/shutterstock.com

back cover image credit: iStock.com/Diana Hirsch

Acknowledgment

To my Publisher, who insisted on taking this out of a drawer.

About the Author

Steve Tarry (a softie who still gets weepy at happy endings despite the cynicism of the present age) lives in Tacoma where he reads, writes, plays pickleball, occasionally acts and directs, and tends his house and yard.

He says he first got the idea for this book from reading about a real-life minor character from the Hundred-Years War. "All I had to add," he says, "was a bit of magic, long-absent gods, a couple of monsters, a fondness for small sailboats, and a pack of unscrupulous villains."

Also by the Author

Watch for the forthcoming "The Accidental Hero" series, when Ice House Press releases the first of four volumes, "Playing in Time."

It too manages a lot of magic, actual deities, monsters, villains, ravishing beauties, and a laugh or two on just about every other page.

Sorry, no sailboats.

Printed by Libri Plureos GmbH in Hamburg, Germany